Maybe Moonglow wasn't such a horrible place after all.

How could it be, when she found herself suddenly so happy here?

"What are you grinning at?" Dan was staring at her, his head tilted quizzically to one side.

"Was I?" She sipped her lemonade, using the glass to hide the smile she couldn't suppress. You'd have thought she was in Manhattan, about to dine on rack of lamb with a gorgeous investment broker, rather than in Moonglow and about to eat hot dogs with an itinerant handyman.

No. Not just a handyman. Dan. In some strange way, she felt as if she'd known him forever.

It wasn't like her at all to become so mesmerized, so infatuated, by a man so quickly. Use your head. Slow down, she told herself. Stop, for heaven's sake.

Only, Molly wasn't listening. At least, not to her head.

Dear Reader,

The excitement continues in Intimate Moments. First of all, this month brings the emotional and exciting conclusion of A YEAR OF LOVING DANGEROUSLY. In *Familiar Stranger,* Sharon Sala presents the final confrontation with the archvillain known as Simon—and you'll finally find out who he really is. You'll also be there as Jonah revisits the woman he's never forgotten and decides it's finally time to make some important changes in his life.

Also this month, welcome back Candace Camp to the Intimate Moments lineup. Formerly known as Kristin James, this multitalented author offers a *Hard-Headed Texan* who lives in A LITTLE TOWN IN TEXAS, which will enthrall readers everywhere. Paula Detmer Riggs returns with *Daddy with a Badge,* another installment in her popular MATERNITY ROW miniseries—and next month she's back with *Born a Hero,* the lead book in our new Intimate Moments continuity, FIRSTBORN SONS. Complete the month with *Moonglow, Texas,* by Mary McBride, Linda Castillo's *Cops and...Lovers?* and new author Susan Vaughan's debut book, *Dangerous Attraction.*

By the way, don't forget to check out our Silhouette Makes You a Star contest on the back of every book.

We hope to see you next month, too, when not only will FIRSTBORN SONS be making its bow, but we'll also be bringing you a brand-new TALL, DARK AND DANGEROUS title from award-winning Suzanne Brockmann. For now...enjoy!

Leslie J. Wainger
Executive Senior Editor

Please address questions and book requests to:
Silhouette Reader Service
U.S.: 3010 Walden Ave., P.O. Box 1325, Buffalo, NY 14269
Canadian: P.O. Box 609, Fort Erie, Ont. L2A 5X3

Moonglow, Texas
MARY McBRIDE

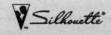

INTIMATE MOMENTS™

Published by Silhouette Books

America's Publisher of Contemporary Romance

For Anna Greve Sadler—
Oh, Annie! If we only knew then what we know now.

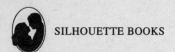 SILHOUETTE BOOKS

ISBN 0-373-27154-9

MOONGLOW, TEXAS

Copyright © 2001 by Mary Myers

Printed in U.S.A.

MARY McBRIDE

When it comes to writing romance, historical or contemporary, Mary McBride is a natural. What else would anyone expect from someone whose parents met on a blind date on Valentine's Day, and who met her own husband—whose middle name just happens to be Valentine!—on February 14, as well?

She lives in St. Louis, Missouri, with her husband and two sons. Mary loves to hear from readers. You can write to her c/o P.O. Box 411202, St. Louis, MO 63141, or contact her online at www.eHarlequin.com.

Prologue

"Are you *sure* you're a deputy U.S. marshal, Shackelford?"

Tom Keifer, a deputy marshal himself, just one week out of basic training in Georgia, had begun to think he'd taken a wrong turn off Highway T, or that maybe there were two Dan Shackelfords in this backwater county in South Texas. The man standing before him right now didn't look like any government agent he'd ever seen.

Knowing Dan Shackelford was on extended medical leave, Keifer had somehow expected to find him in a dim back bedroom of a shady little convalescent home, where the injured deputy would be sitting in a wheelchair reading—a serious, thin and rather pale man in leather slippers and pressed pajamas.

That hadn't been the case.

The address Keifer was given turned out to be a defunct trailer park, and Shackelford looked like a bum, wearing ripped jeans and last week's whiskers and lean-

ing one arm on the door frame of his dented trailer
while his free hand curved around the long brown neck
of a bottle of beer. Lunch, no doubt, Keifer thought with
some disgust. Judging from the roadmaps of his eyes,
he'd probably had the same thing for breakfast.

The young deputy eased a finger under his tight,
damp, button-down collar even as he viewed the man's
sleeveless T-shirt with pure disdain.

"Daniel L. Shackelford?" he asked again irritably,
actually hoping this derelict would tell him he had the
wrong man and point him down the road to the home
of a competent, clean-shaven deputy. "Can you confirm
your mother's maiden name?"

"Liggett." He raised the beer bottle, took a long wet
swig, then aimed a deliberate, almost affable belch in
Keifer's direction. "Do you want to see my badge and
my secret decoder ring, Junior?"

The young man took a half step back, not bothering
to disguise his disapproval. He had the right man, much
to his disappointment. "I don't think that will be necessary."

"Great." Shackelford grinned sloppily and leaned a
little farther out the door. "Then how 'bout a beer?"

"WITSEC's been compromised," Keifer blurted out.

"What?"

"I said WITSEC's been compromised," he repeated.
"You know. Witness Security?"

"I know what the hell it is." Shackelford's expression hovered somewhere between a bleary-eyed *Who
gives a rip?* and a grim-lipped *Go on. Tell me more.*

"Unidentified hackers broke into the system over the
weekend. There's no telling who or what they were
looking for, if anything, and no way to know if they
found it. But the Marshals Service has put nearly seven

thousand people under protection since the seventies, and they're all in jeopardy now.''

The man in the doorway let out a low whistle, blinked inscrutably, then took another long pull from his bottle.

''So, headquarters is bringing in every available deputy,'' Keifer continued, ''in addition to postponing vacations and retirements, and they're terminating all medical and personal leaves as of today.'' He stiffened his shoulders. ''Yours included.''

Shackelford hissed an expletive.

''Here.'' Keifer shoved a manila envelope through the opening of the trailer's screen door. ''All the information you need is in there.''

Having performed his assignment, the young deputy was eager to leave, to get away from this obvious loser and get on with his own future heroics in the line of duty. He had only contempt for a burned-out, washed-up rummy like Shackelford. The guy had probably never been any good at the job, anyway.

''Any questions?''

''Just one,'' Shackelford drawled.

''Yes?''

''Did you say yes, you did want a beer, or no, you didn't?''

Dan yanked open the lopsided venetian blinds on the trailer's window. Sunlight strafed the cluttered interior and fell across the letter he had pulled from the manila envelope. The United States Marshals Service emblem was embossed so thick it almost cast a shadow on the page. So did the name on the letterhead. Robert Hayes, regional director. The message below it was handwritten. A familiar scrawl.

Our files are screwed, amigo. Got you a low-priority witness (see attached) living in seized property in Moonglow. Easy duty. She doesn't even have to know why you're there. The quieter we keep this, the better, if you catch my drift. Just hang around her awhile, then get your bad self back to the real world.

Bobby

P.S. Didn't you used to live in Moonglow?

Chapter 1

Molly Hansen had been in Witness Security for nearly a year, but she still woke up every morning as Kathryn Claiborn and had to remind herself that she didn't exist anymore.

This morning was no exception, except what woke her wasn't her alarm clock, but rather the clattering of trash cans and a jolt to the side of her house that nearly pitched her out of bed. While she scrambled for her robe, she scrolled through a mental checklist of natural disasters, eliminating each one as soon as it came to mind.

An earthquake didn't happen on just one side of a house. It couldn't have been a landslide or a mud slide because this part of Texas was so dry and flat that things didn't slide; they just sat still and baked. It wasn't a thunderstorm because the sun was shining. That left only a rampaging bull or a five-hundred-pound armadillo.

Or, now that she was peering out the window into the driveway, a big Airstream trailer about to crash into the side of her house. Again. She grabbed for the windowsill just as the trailer hit. This time the impact brought the curtain rod crashing down on her head.

"You idiot," she screamed, battling her way out of yards of gathered fabric. "Jerk!" Molly stomped over the fallen drapes, down the hall to the kitchen, and out the back door where the big aluminum behemoth was apparently making a third run at her defenseless little residence.

She reached for the nearest weapon, which turned out to be a hoe, and swung it with all her might at the blundering vehicle, half expecting the hoe to clang on impact like an enormous bell, but instead there was a sickening *thunk* as the gardening tool sank deep into the metal skin. It worked, though. The trailer stopped, and none too soon, mere inches from the house.

Molly was trying to extract the blade of the hoe when a man stalked down the driveway, yelling at her.

"What the hell were you trying to do?"

"I was trying," she huffed, still tugging at the hoe, "to keep you from ruining my house, you idiot."

He stopped a few feet away from her, turned toward the little clapboard bungalow with its warped shutters and peeling paint, studied it a moment, and then said, "Hell, lady. In case you haven't noticed, somebody's already ruined it."

The grin that followed didn't prompt one from Molly. She was hardly amused. She thought if she could wrest the blade of the hoe from the trailer, she'd like to sink it into this good ol' boy's skull. That would wipe the stupid smirk right off his handsome face.

"Jerk," she muttered, glaring at the hoe again and twisting its handle to no avail.

"Here." A tan, muscled forearm slid against hers and his fingers curved around the handle just beneath her grip. "Let go."

"I will not."

"Let the hell go." He gave her a shot with his hip that sent Molly careening sideways, then using only one hand, he popped the hoe from the back of the trailer as if it were no more than a butter knife and tossed the implement away.

"That's some dent," he mused, crossing his arms and contemplating the damage.

"Well, it matches the rest of them." Molly snatched up the hoe and held it like a shotgun. "Now, I'll thank you to get this junkyard special out of my driveway."

He turned to look at her, his green eyes lazily taking her in from head to toe. "You're Molly Hansen."

It wasn't a question, really. Just a flat statement. But Molly found herself nodding, anyway, as she once again reminded herself that she wasn't Kathryn Claiborn. At the same time a little kernel of suspicion was forming in her brain. After all, she was Molly Hansen and in Witness Security because her life was in danger. Kathryn's, anyway. "And you are?"

"Dan Shackelford. I've been hired to make repairs on your ruined house, Miss Hansen," he drawled. "Where do you want me to start?"

He seemed to be studying the roofline now with the same degree of intensity that he had studied her a moment before.

"I don't want you to start," Molly said, then increased not only the volume but the adamance. "Do you hear me?"

"Half those shingles look rotten. I'll bet this place leaks like a son of a gun."

It did, but that was none of his damned business. The house, as Molly understood it, had been seized from a Honduran drug dealer who only used it to establish a permanent address. The government owned the house. Molly just paid nominal rent, mailed to a post office box in Houston.

"Who sent you?" she demanded. "Who hired you?"

He sauntered to the wall, reached out to flick some paint chips from a board. "When's the last time this was painted?" he asked over his shoulder.

"How should I know?"

"Been here long?"

"No. Only about…"

Molly's mouth snapped shut. When she entered the program, they had warned her not to answer even the most innocent of questions. Be skeptical, they had said, especially of strangers too eager to strike up a conversation. If you have any suspicions, don't hesitate to call.

"I need to make a phone call," she said, clutching the trusty hoe and locking the back door once she was safely inside.

"So, what you're saying then, Deputy, is that I don't have to worry about this Shackelford character? That he really was hired to make repairs?"

Molly was whispering into the phone, her lips practically brushing the mouthpiece. She'd been peeking out the kitchen window at the character in question, but at some point he'd disappeared around the back of the house.

The U.S. marshal on the other end of the line once

again confirmed that Dan Shackelford was working in their employ.

"Well, that's a relief," she said. "Thank you, Deputy. Oh, and tell Uncle Sam thanks for fixing up my house."

She put the receiver back in its cradle and let out a long, audible sigh before peering out the window again. The trailer was still hulking diagonally in the drive, but she didn't see hide nor hair of its owner.

"You need a new lock on the front door."

The sudden voice behind her had Molly reaching for the hoe again as she whirled around. "How did you get in here?"

"You need a new lock on the front door." His gaze cut away from her face to take in the rest of the room. "What a pit."

Molly was less frightened than irritated. "Well, it's my pit."

Except it wasn't, and she was sorely tempted to tell him that her little stone cottage in upstate New York might someday be on the National Register of Historic Places, and that her kitchen—her sweet, cozy kitchen with its big brick fireplace—had already been featured in *Early American Homes* and *Hearth and Home*. Only that had been Kathryn Claiborn's house, and Kathryn was, for all intents and purposes, dead.

Molly looked around at the ancient metal cabinets, the faded red Formica countertop and the scarred linoleum floor. The appliances had probably been manufactured when Roosevelt was president. Not FDR, but Theodore. *My God, calling this place a pit was flattering it.*

"I've been too busy to decorate," she said lamely.

"Uh-huh." He was leaning over the sink, jiggling the rusty lock on the window while looking into the back-yard.

While Shackelford scrutinized the landscape, Molly scrutinized him. He was about six-two, lean as a greyhound, probably in his mid-thirties, and he needed a haircut desperately, not to mention a shave. New jeans, too. The ones he wore were faded to a soft sky blue, replete with fringed rips. Her gaze traveled down his long, muscular legs in search of the obligatory hand-tooled boots worn by every self-respecting male in Moonglow, only to discover a pair of flip-flops instead. Flip-flops! Oh, well. They went with the ratty Hawaiian shirt, she supposed, and the sunglasses that hung from a thick cord around his neck.

He didn't look dangerous. He didn't even look competent! But the marshal's office had said he was okay.

"Mind if I park my trailer under that live oak back there?" he asked.

"Fine. As long as you don't drive through the house to get there."

Molly glanced at the clock above the refrigerator. "Oh, God. I'm going to be late for work."

"Well, you just go on," he said. "Don't worry about me. I expect to have all new locks and dead bolts installed by the time you get home."

"Home?"

"From work."

"But I work *here.*"

"Oh." He looked confused for a moment, then shrugged. "Then I guess I'll just have to do my best to stay out of your way, Ms. Hansen."

"Well, I certainly hope so, Mr. Shackelford."

Dan slid behind the wheel of his black BMW, then glared in the rearview mirror at the Airstream looming there. He swore roughly. He used to be able to thread any vehicle through the eye of a needle at ninety miles an hour in the dark of night. Now he couldn't maneuver a goddamned trailer into a cement driveway in broad daylight.

Little wonder Bobby had assigned him the lowest of low-priority witnesses. Kathryn Claiborn's terrorists, the Red Millennium, had all but blown their own heads off in labs in the U.S. and Beirut and Ireland this past year. As far as U.S. Intelligence knew, there was nobody left for the woman to identify, but they kept her in WITSEC, anyway, just in case. It was easier to put someone into the program than to get them out.

The worst thing that was going to happen to her during this computer crisis had already happened when Dan backed his trailer into her house. And the worst thing that was going to happen to him was discovering once and for all that he was washed-up.

He turned the key in the ignition. Well, hell. He could always make a halfway decent living on the demolition derby circuit. And maybe, if he was really, really lucky, he'd be demolished in the process.

This time he shifted into Drive, easing the ancient Airstream out onto Second Street, then circled the block until he found access through a narrow vacant lot into Molly Hansen's backyard. After half an hour he had the trailer unhitched, his lawn chair unfolded in the shade of the live oak, and a warm beer in his hand.

It was only nine-thirty, but he felt as if he'd already put in a full day's work trying to ignore Molly Hansen's long blond curls and the dangerous curves of her body. He hadn't been with a woman since…

Damn. He'd promised not to think about that. His

nightmares were bad enough. How many times could you watch your partner die because of something you'd done or failed to do or simply overlooked? How long could you try to dream it different, only to have it all turn out the same? The answer, after nearly five months, was indefinitely. He took a long pull from the bottle and let the warm lager slide down his throat. Unless, of course, you overmedicated yourself into besotted oblivion, which was still his favorite place to be.

Not Moonglow, that was for sure. He'd never expected to come back here, to come full circle. Bad boy leaves town. Bad man comes back. Dan closed his eyes. Hell, it seemed there had been nothing in between.

Molly showered, dressed, put on her makeup, took her morning coffee into her tiny back bedroom office as she did every day, then proceeded to spend more time at the window watching Dan Shackelford *not* working than she spent working herself.

Trust the government to hire a good-looking bum who didn't know a hammer from a Heineken, she thought, glad it wasn't her money that was paying him to sit around swigging beer all morning.

For a moment, while she was showering, she'd actually gotten a little excited about the prospect of fixing up this falling-down house. Not that she'd ever really like it, no matter the improvements, but maybe she'd hate it a little less. Now it looked as if any repairs would be accomplished in an alcoholic haze. Her house would probably look worse, not better, once Dan Shackelford was done with it.

All of a sudden Molly wanted to cry, but she wouldn't let herself. If she started, even so much as a sniffle, there was no telling if she'd ever stop.

"I hate my life," she muttered, settling once more in front of her computer screen and forcing herself to focus on sentence after sentence, paragraph after paragraph of the most unrelentingly boring and ungrammatical prose in the history of English composition.

When she'd applied for the position of English instructor at the online university, it seemed the perfect choice for her new persona. It didn't pay much, but her need for privacy and safety was greater than her need for money. There was nothing to spend it on in Moonglow, anyway. She'd approached the job with her typical determination to succeed, but the challenge of correcting her invisible students' errors in spelling and grammar had quickly dissipated when she found herself correcting the same mistakes over and over and over again.

"I hate *your* life, Molly Hansen," she muttered at the screen. "I hate your cutesy-poo name, too. And I hate your bleached-blond hair. I hate everything about you, including that bum who's set up residence in your backyard."

It had all gone wrong so fast that she'd barely had time to comprehend it before she had been whisked into WITSEC. Kathryn Claiborn's life, the one she had struggled so long and hard to achieve, had literally blown up in her face.

She'd been crossing the campus of venerable Van Dyne College, where she was director of financial affairs in addition to being associate professor of business, taking her usual shortcut through the basement of the Chemistry Department on her way to the Administration Building, when her world had exploded. One minute she was waving a cheerful hello to Dr. Ian Yates and the pale, white-haired fellow by his side, and the next she was waking up in a hospital with bandages on her face and half a dozen federal agents *in* her face.

Nothing had been the same after that. Kathryn Claiborn had died, giving birth to Molly Hansen. Kathryn Claiborn had been so frightened at the thought of having her throat cut by the white-haired terrorist whom only she could identify that she had willingly abandoned her job, her home, her fiancé, even her very self in order to insure her survival.

"Way to go, Kathryn," Molly said with a sigh.

There was no way she was going to be able to concentrate on slipshod essays this morning, so she turned off her computer, then went to the window to see if her handyman was still swilling beer. If he was, it wasn't where he'd been swilling it earlier. His ratty lawn chair was empty.

Molly glanced at her watch. She had a one o'clock appointment for a root touch-up. Maybe, since it was Tuesday and hardly anybody in Moonglow got her hair done this early in the week, Raylene could fit her in a little bit early.

Raylene Earl wasn't exactly a friend. Unable to disclose anything about her life prior to her arrival in Moonglow, Molly wasn't in a position to make friends. Of course, that didn't keep the hairdresser from talking her head off.

Raylene's hair was pink this week.

"Well, I dunno," she was saying. "They call it Sunset, so naturally I was expecting something on the gold side. You know, the way the sun sets here in Moonglow. I'm getting used to it now, but lemme tell you, it played hell with my Passionate Pink lipstick and nail polish. I'm wearing Strawberry Frappé now." She waved a hand under Molly's nose. "What do you think, hon?"

"I like it," Molly replied, her typical three words in exchange for Raylene's hundred.

"Yeah? I dunno. I think it looks like I stuck my fingers in a jam jar or something." She pursed her lips, studying them in the mirror over the top of Molly's head. "Buddy says why worry when they kiss just the same, but then what can you expect from a man who wears his skivvies inside out half the time and swears it doesn't matter?"

"Does it matter?" Molly got in her three words while Raylene dragged in a breath through her strawberry-frappéed lips.

"Of course it matters. Good Lord, Molly, would you want somebody reading your waist size every time you bent over?"

Molly laughed. "I guess not."

"Not that you're not a tiny little thing, even if you do persist in wearing clothes that don't show off your choicest parts. They're having a sale at Minden's this week. Thirty percent off everything, if you're in the mood for a little change."

"Oh, no thanks."

What Raylene didn't know was that Molly had already undergone a change of huge proportions. Kathryn had left behind a closet full of conservative suits and dark, understated shoes. There was no need to replace them. Nobody here wore suits except the banker and the undertaker, and those outfits tended toward odd colors and western cuts. In laid-back Moonglow, most people thought glen plaid was somebody's name.

Ordering online, Molly had slowly filled her closet with soft skirts, tunics, a few khaki shorts and slacks.

It had taken her a while to get the colors right. Kathryn, with her dark hair, light blue eyes and fair skin, was a Winter, who looked best in blacks and whites and true reds. Blond Molly, on the other hand, couldn't handle Kathryn's colors. She had no idea what season Molly had turned into, but, to her dismay, she now looked best in shades she'd always detested. Washed-out blues, sherbet hues. So, in addition to hating her life, she hated her clothes.

"Oh, I know what I meant to ask you the minute you came in," Raylene said as she dabbed more bleach preparation on Molly's roots. "What's the deal with the trailer? You got relatives visiting from up north?"

"No. Not relatives. A handyman is doing some repairs on my house. He's from around here, I guess. At least, that's what I assumed."

"Oh, yeah? What's his name?"

"Shackelford."

Raylene's hands dropped to Molly's shoulders. "Not Danny Shackelford!"

"Well. Dan."

"Oh, my Lord!" Raylene whooped. "Oh, my dear sweet Lord."

In the mirror Molly saw a woman she hadn't yet met come through the door. The hairdresser saw her, too, and immediately called out, "JoEllen, you're not gonna believe who's back. Not in a million, jillion years."

"Who?" JoEllen didn't look all that interested until Raylene told her the handyman's name, but once she heard it, she was whooping, too. "Danny Shackelford. If that's not a blast from the past, I don't know what is. How long's he been gone, Raylene? Fourteen, fifteen years?"

"More like nineteen," Raylene said over her shoulder. "He took off right after old Miss Hannah passed away, and that's been close to twenty years." She met Molly's eyes in the mirror. "How's he look? You'll break my heart if you tell me he's got a potbelly and a receding hairline."

"He looks fine," Molly said, lifting her shoulders in a little shrug beneath her plastic cape.

"Fine! Oh, honey, you can do better than that. Now, what is it? Fine as in you wouldn't kick him out of bed? Or fine as in you'd sell your soul to the devil to get him there?"

JoEllen, the newcomer, chuckled while she poured a cup of coffee. "If memory serves, that wouldn't be all that hard to do, Raylene."

"He was pretty wild, I take it," Molly said, suddenly not all that comfortable with the thought of Dan Shackelford roaming like some feral beast through her house.

"Wild?" Raylene exclaimed. "Well, let me put it this way. If Moonglow had had a zoo, Danny Shackelford would have been the main attraction. Right, JoEllen?"

The two women drifted off to other topics then, with Molly putting in her occasional three words while her thoughts strayed repeatedly to the man lazing under the live oak in her backyard. A sleepy lion on some distant savanna, waiting for a slower, weaker creature to appear.

Dan was putting in the last screw on the new brass lock of the double-hung window in the living room so he had a perfect view of Molly Hansen walking along Second Street on her way back from town.

Her stride was long with her feet turned out slightly, like a ballet dancer. Her skirt swung softly around her shapely calves with each step. What idiot at WITSEC had thought a woman like that would be invisible in a town like Moonglow? She stood out like a diamond in a pile of wood chips.

"God bless it!"

The screwdriver slipped and gouged a chunk out of his thumb. A little reminder from the gods that he was here to do a job, not ogle a pretty blonde from a window. Then, a second later, as if to really drive home their point, the deities pinched the flesh of his thigh between the entrance and exit scars.

"Yeah. Okay. Okay," Dan muttered, grimacing as he finished tightening the screw on the lock. "I get the message."

He tossed the screwdriver into the paint-stained toolbox he'd bought early that morning from Harley Cates after it had occurred to him that a handyman couldn't very well show up without the tools of his trade.

Harley had recognized him right off the bat, which had been more than a bit disconcerting, considering he hadn't seen the old codger in nearly twenty years.

Dan had dug around in Harley's barn for a while, deflecting the old man's questions as best he could.

"How much do you want for this old toolbox, Harley?" he'd asked him.

"I'd ask twenty from a stranger, Danny, but since you're Miss Hannah's boy and all, I'll take fifteen."

Dan had opened his wallet, relieved to see that he had the fifteen bucks.

"You back to stay, son?" Harley asked, folding the fives and sliding them into his back pocket.

"No, I'm just passing through."

"Don't let much grass grow under you, huh? Shackelfords are like that. All but Miss Hannah, God rest her soul.''

Dan looked out the window again now. Molly Hansen was pulling a little grocery cart behind her. He could almost hear Miss Hannah saying, ''Don't stand there like you've put down roots, boy. Where's your manners? Go give that little girl a hand.''

''Thanks, anyway. I can manage.''

''Aw, come on, Molly. I've got a bad enough reputation in this town already. What'll people say if they see me strolling empty-handed while you're lugging that cart?''

Molly cocked her head. Her handyman was wearing his sunglasses, so she couldn't see his eyes, but judging from his grin, she sensed they were twinkling. ''I just got an earful of that reputation of yours, Shackelford, down at the beauty shop.''

''Oh, yeah? You mean somebody in Moonglow actually remembers me?''

''Sounded to me as if your name is prominently featured in the local Hall of Fame,'' she said. ''Or was that the Hall of Shame?''

The wattage of his grin diminished a bit. ''Well, don't believe everything you hear. Especially in a beauty shop.''

Molly's right arm brushed his, and she deliberately maneuvered her shopping cart a few inches to the left, putting more distance between them.

''Who's still talking about me after all these years?'' he asked.

''Raylene Earl.''

''Oh. Damn.''

He whipped off his glasses and came to a complete standstill on the sidewalk.

"Raylene Ford? Then I guess she must've married Buddy Earl. I'll be damned. Is she still…?" His open palms came up in a descriptive fashion.

Ordinarily such a blatantly sexist gesture would have made Molly angry, but knowing the pride Raylene took in her generous endowments, she found herself laughing instead. "She remembers you pretty vividly, too."

"We had our moments," he said, repositioning the dark shades on the bridge of his nose, cutting off her view of his deep green eyes.

"I'll bet you did."

They were both quiet, caught up in their own thoughts, the rest of the way to the house. Molly couldn't help but notice that Dan wore a goofy little half grin that she suspected had something to do with Raylene. For some strange reason, she found herself envying the hairdresser for that. Heaven knows, nobody had such fondly amusing memories of Kathryn Claiborn. Not even her fiancé.

She had stopped at the post office after she left Raylene's, and picked up another letter from Ethan Ambrose, her longtime fiancé. He knew she was under the protection of WITSEC, but he didn't know where. All of his letters to her from New York were filtered through Washington and Houston before they ever arrived in Moonglow. Molly picked them up each week, read them and put them in a desk drawer. For some reason she couldn't begin to understand, she hadn't written Ethan back. She just didn't know what to say. She just didn't feel like his Kathryn anymore.

They had reached the end of the driveway and were

at the back door when Dan reached into the pocket of his palm-tree-studded shirt.

"Your new keys," he said.

"Thanks." Molly was wondering if she should invite him in for a glass of lemonade or something. She chided herself for not picking up a six-pack at the store.

"Guess I'll knock off for today," Dan said, already heading for the rear of the house. "See you tomorrow."

"See you," Molly said, fitting the shiny key into the shiny new lock, thinking of course he didn't want to spend any time with her after his work was done. Who did she think she was, anyway? Raylene?

Dan stabbed a fork in the steak and flipped it, taking a moment to appreciate the fine parallel burn marks from the grill. It was the first time in a long time he wasn't drinking his dinner with a bag of pretzels on the side. Smoke from the fire filtered up through the leaves of the live oak. Too bad there wasn't a nice little breeze to blow it toward the house, he thought. Who could resist a steak on the grill?

Don't, he cautioned himself. Easy as this job is, you can't afford the distraction. You screw this up and it's so long, Dan. When you were good, you were very, very good. When you went off the rails, you were gone.

He heard the screen door in back squeak open. He wouldn't fix that, he thought. It was as good as any alarm.

What it signaled now was Molly, coming around the corner and sauntering barefoot across the lawn while the sunset tinted her hair a reddish gold.

"Smells good," she said.

"Doesn't it, though?" He jabbed at the steak with the fork. "Just about done, too."

"Mmm."

Her deep-throated murmur was so sensual, Dan nearly stabbed himself with the damn fork. He took a swallow of his beer to cool himself off. "There's plenty here. Want to join me?"

"Oh, I… Well, I just made a Greek salad."

He thought that was more of a yes than a no, but he didn't want to press his luck. "They're selling feta cheese in Moonglow? What is this world coming to?"

She laughed softly. "Would you like some?"

"Bring her on out," he said.

By the time Molly was back with her big wooden salad bowl and—smart girl that she was—two steak knives, Dan had unfolded a second lawn chair, put half of the steak on each of two paper plates and popped open another bottle of beer. He opened one more when she said that sounded good.

"This is nice," she said, digging into her steak. "I mean, it's nice not having to eat alone."

"Amen to that."

For a minute, just on the edge of sundown, sharing a good meal with a pretty woman, Dan was nearly feeling human again. And then the big Crown Victoria cruiser with the Moonglow Sheriff's Department insignia on the door swung into Molly's driveway.

It figured, Dan thought. You couldn't come home without a homecoming party.

Molly didn't like the set of Sheriff Gil Watson's thick jaw as he lumbered across the lawn, or the half-dare, half-smirk tilt of his lips. The man took his job way too seriously in her opinion. Moonglow wasn't exactly the South Bronx.

Watson aimed a little nudge of his cap in her direction, mouthed a curt "Howdy, ma'am," then stuck out one of his huge, hammy hands toward Dan.

"Heard you were back, Danny," he said. "It's been a while."

"Gil," Dan said. "Looks like you took over your old man's business."

Done shaking hands, the sheriff hooked his thumbs through his big black gun belt. "Dad retired five years ago. Just seemed natural then, me taking up where he left off. Folks were used to saying Sheriff Watson."

"Hell, I know I was. Your daddy picked me up by the scruff of the neck and threw my butt in jail more times than I like to remember."

There was a brittle edge to Dan's laughter that was apparently lost on the lawman, but not on Molly. She swore she could feel static electricity coming from the handyman. It almost made the hair stand up on her arms.

The sheriff lifted a hand to run it across his jawline. "Been in town long?"

"Just got in today."

"Doing some repair work on Miss Hansen's house?"

"Yep." Dan shifted his weight and took a long pull from his beer.

"Is that what you've been doing all these years?" Watson asked, shifting his considerable weight, too, and somehow looking down at Dan even though the two were roughly the same height. "Working as a handyman?"

"More or less."

"In Texas?"

"Pretty much."

"Plenty of work, I'd expect."

"Enough."

Molly could almost smell the testosterone. The evening air reeked of it. It was definitely time for a bit of feminine sweet talk.

"We were just having some dinner, Sheriff. Steak and Greek salad. Would you care to join us?"

Watson touched the brim of his hat again. "Oh, no, ma'am. I've got evening rounds to make. I just stopped by to say hi to Danny here." He took a step back, adjusting his gun belt over his ample gut. "I'll be going now. Nice seeing you, Miss Hansen. Danny, you, too. You keep your nose clean, you hear?"

My God. In all of her thirty-one years, Molly had never actually heard somebody seethe, but that was precisely what Dan Shackelford was doing at the moment. He was hot enough to cook a steak on. She could almost hear his temper crackle, so it surprised her when his voice emerged fairly level and calm.

"See you around, Gil."

It was only after the cruiser had pulled out of the driveway and moved on down the street that Dan swore harshly and tossed his paper plate with all its contents into the glowing coals of the grill.

"I lost my appetite," he said.

"Don't mind him, Dan," Molly said. "Big fish. Little pond. You know. Watson just likes to make waves. And there's no shame in being a handyman. God knows we need more of those than self-important lawmen."

He just looked at her then for the longest while, shaking his head kind of sadly, before he said, "Good night, Molly. I'll see you in the morning."

Then he disappeared into his trailer.

Chapter 2

The next morning Molly kept to her usual routine of waking early and getting to her desk by eight o'clock. The regular hours helped keep a sense of normalcy in her disrupted life. And that life promised to be even more disrupted now that Dan was going to be there, measuring, hammering, generally getting in her way, not to mention taking up more of her thoughts than she wanted to admit.

By nine o'clock, she had read and graded six essays entitled "My Favorite Season," with summer the hands-down winner, in spite of the fact that she had spent half the time looking out the window for signs of life under the live oak.

By ten o'clock, she was worried in addition to being ticked off. Just when was all this measuring and hammering and getting in her way supposed to begin? She wasn't running a trailer park or a campground, for heaven's sake, and she certainly wasn't running a retirement home for handymen, although that looked to be the case.

She poured a mug of coffee, then trudged across the yard and pounded on the Airstream's door. She stood there, tapping her foot for what seemed like half an hour before the door finally swung open.

"You look terrible," she said, offering the first words that came to mind when she saw the rumpled hair, the red eyes like flags at half-mast, the stained T-shirt and the ratty boxer shorts with their wrinkled happy faces.

"Is that coffee?"

Molly looked down at the mug she had almost forgotten was in her hand. "Coffee? Oh, yes. It is."

"Is it for me?"

"Oh. Sure. Here." She pressed it into Dan's not-so-steady hand, then watched him swallow at least half of it before she asked, "What time were you planning to start work? I've made a list."

He winced. "A list?"

"Things that really need to be done." She reached into the pocket of her skirt and withdrew the piece of paper she had scribbled on earlier. "The showerhead in the bathroom needs to be replaced. And the sink drips in there, too. You already know about the roof leaking, right?"

He nodded as he sipped the coffee.

"The wallpaper is peeling in the bedroom, too, but I wasn't sure if you were just supposed to make structural repairs or—"

"Just give me the list."

"You probably can't read my writing. Number three looks like *kitchen flower* but it's really *floor*. There's a spot near the pantry where—"

"Just give me the goddamned list," he barked, nearly

ripping it out of her hand, then slapping the empty mug in her open palm while Molly stood there blinking.

"I'm sorry," he said immediately.

"You should be," she snapped. "I was only trying to help."

"I got up on the wrong side of the bed, that's all."

Molly snorted. "Yeah. The underside."

"Okay. Look, give me a couple minutes to get cleaned up and then we'll go over this list of yours and work up some kind of a plan. How does that sound?"

"All right, I guess. Fine."

"Fine."

"Fine," Dan snarled into the mirror mounted over the Airstream's minuscule bathroom sink where he'd just narrowly escaped slashing his carotid artery while he shaved. "Fine and dandy."

Posing as a handyman had seemed like a good idea at the time, considering that his official presence was supposed to be kept under wraps. The Marshals Service couldn't afford to create panic in several thousand witnesses, not to mention the agency's devout wish to avoid bad publicity. But after installing the window and door locks, Dan realized he'd reached the limit of his do-it-yourself expertise. For somebody who could break down and reassemble just about any weapon ever made, he was at a loss when it came to domestic nuts and bolts. Molly was a smart woman. She'd have his number—zero!—before he could hammer a single nail.

She was a sweet woman, too. God bless her for trying to step between him and that no-neck, ham-handed Gil Watson last night, and then attempting to bolster his wounded handyman ego as if she weren't some hotshot East Coast financial whiz. If she was miserable here in the armpit of Texas, she was much too gracious to let it show.

He'd been miserable here, but not because he'd been leading some secret, lesser life. He'd been miserable because he had to spend every waking minute proving himself to a couple hundred people to whom the name Shackelford was synonymous with white trash. Catching a last glimpse of his face in the mirror, Dan wasn't at all sure they weren't right.

He knocked on Molly's back door and mumbled another apology when she finally let him in.

"I thought I'd run down to Cooley's Hardware and pick up some of the things on your list," he said, digging the paper out of his shirt pocket.

"Let me get my handbag and drag a quick brush through my hair."

Dan started to tell her she didn't need to come along, but as he watched the sway of her backside and the soft swing of her hair on her shoulders, he changed his mind. He didn't even try to convince himself it was because his job was to protect her from unseen terrorists. Hell. As if he even could.

"I'm ready." She was back, all blue-eyed and smiley, with a floppy straw hat on her head and a big straw bag hooked over one shoulder.

Dan slid his dark glasses in place, pushed his headache to the back of his brain, and said, "Okay. Let's go."

Molly had only been in Cooley's Hardware on Main Street once. Her brain became so overloaded from the narrow aisles with their crammed shelves that she'd left without purchasing what she'd gone there to get. She felt the same today, on the verge of short-circuiting as she wandered along behind Dan who was pitching odds and ends into a shopping cart.

"This place hasn't changed a bit," he said, reaching over her head for something on a shelf. "Almost feels as if I never left. Scary." He feigned a shiver, then lobbed whatever he'd retrieved into the cart.

"How long ago did you leave?" Molly asked, continuing to trail along behind him.

"Nearly twenty years. Hell, a lifetime."

"Hmm. That young man working at the cash register probably wasn't even born then. Just think. In the time you've been gone, an entire generation has been born, graduated from high school, probably even gotten married and started families of their own."

Dan must have stopped the cart suddenly because Molly walked right into him, her breath whooshing out in an audible *oof.*

"Are you trying to make me feel old, Molly?" he asked irritably. "Trying to push me into some kind of midlife, male-menopausal crisis? 'Cause if you are, I can tell you right now you're doing a bang-up job."

"No. I wasn't. For heaven's sake, I was only…"

But before Molly got another word out, a shrill, very familiar voice called out, "Well, bless my stars and all the planets, if it isn't Danny Shackelford."

Raylene Earl was sidling toward them, wearing a pair of the tightest jeans Molly had ever seen, and an orange-and-white striped tank top that did amazing things to her chest. Her breasts sort of preceded her down the narrow aisle, then smushed into Dan when Raylene nearly hugged the life out of him.

"Danny. My Lord," she exclaimed, stepping back on her spike-heeled sandals. "You haven't changed one little bit. Not one teensy-weensy bit."

"Neither have you, Raylene." His grin wobbled somewhere between downright embarrassment and outright lust.

The hairdresser rolled her eyes in Molly's direction. "Did you hear that, hon? What a sweet thing to say. But then you always did have a silver tongue, Danny. My Lord. I can't believe you're back. Molly said so, but it just didn't seem to sink in until I laid my very own eyes on you five seconds ago."

Dan just stood there, seemingly as hard-pressed for the proper response as Molly was. But that didn't bother a single pink hair on Raylene's head.

"Look at you," she said, threading her Strawberry Frappé fingertips through Dan's hair. "You always did tend toward that scruffy look, didn't you? You have Molly bring you down to my shop and I'll give you a trim. I do Buddy's hair and he likes it well enough. Both my boys, too. 'Course, it's free so they can't really complain."

"So, you and Buddy got married," Dan said.

"Only 'cause you upped and disappeared." Raylene giggled and gave a brisk wave of her hand. "I'm kidding. I knew I'd be Mrs. Buddy Earl from the time I was in kindergarten. It just took me till I was nineteen to really settle in to the idea."

"Is he still the best mechanic in Moonglow?"

"You bet your buns he is. The best in the whole county. He's got his own garage now and even works weekends on the NASCAR circuit."

Raylene dragged in a breath and crossed her arms, a nearly impossible feat in Molly's humble opinion. She shook her pink head in wonderment. "Danny Shackelford. My Lord. So, what've you been up to all these years?"

"Oh, nothing. This and that. You know."

If his answer struck Molly as vague bordering on obscurity, it seemed to make complete sense to Raylene.

"This and that," she echoed, flinging a long-lashed wink toward Molly. "Probably a little more of this than of that, if I know you. Molly, this man is the world's greatest kisser. I'm telling you that right now. The best bar none."

"Jeez, Raylene," Dan muttered, donning his glasses again and turning up the collar of his shirt as if he wanted to disappear inside it.

"Well, honey, I'd be proud of that, if I were you. I don't care what your other talents turned out to be. In the smooching department, you were El Numero Uno. Probably still are, too." She cocked her head. "Is he, Molly? Come on. 'Fess up now."

"Rrraaaylene." Molly dragged the woman's name out to at least four childish syllables.

"Okay. All right. I'm nosy. I admit it. I..."

A deep male voice on the store's intercom cut her off as it boomed across the aisles, "Raylene, we got that hinge you were looking for up here at the counter."

"Well, I'd best collect that and get it home while Buddy's still in the mood to fix my kitchen cabinet. Now, you come into the shop for that trim, Danny. Molly, you bring him in, you hear me? See y'all later."

"I feel like I've been picked up and put down by a tornado," Dan said with a beleaguered sigh. "Let's get out of here before she comes back."

Molly laughed. "Raylene's got a good heart."

"I wonder how the hell I ever even managed to kiss a pair of lips that move ninety miles an hour."

"Well, I guess you used to be faster," she said, "in the olden days." Molly grinned in the face of Dan's

dark glare, then chuckled to herself as she again followed along behind him.

"Will that be all for you, sir?" the young man at the
counter asked.

"That should do it," Dan said, hoping his credit card
still had a little play in it after he'd been on medical
leave at reduced pay for so many months.

"Oh, wait," Molly said, suddenly appearing with a
roll of wallpaper. "We need this, too."

"That's just a sample roll," the clerk said. "I'll have
to call in back for the real stuff. How many rolls do
you want?"

Dan could feel himself breaking out in a thin, cold
sweat.

"Did you measure?" Molly asked.

"The bedroom? Nah. Didn't need to. I just eyeballed
it." He leaned casually on the big, ancient counter, trying to speed-read the label on the paper roll and trans-
late centimeters into square feet. This morning's headache sprang back, full blown. "Gimme twenty rolls,"
he told the clerk.

"That's a lot of paper," the young man said. "You
want a couple buckets of glue to go with that?"

"Sure," Dan said, pulling his sunglasses down his
nose and glowering menacingly over the rims. "And
gimme the good stuff. Not that kindergarten paste you
people are always trying to hustle. You hear?"

The young man swallowed hard. "Yes, sir."

It took two trips to haul everything out to his car,
and when Dan came out of Cooley's door the second
time, with his arms loaded with wallpaper rolls as heavy
as cordwood, he wasn't exactly astonished to see Gil

Watson's big, shiny black boot up on the BMW's front bumper.

"This is a thirty-minute parking zone, Danny. 'Fraid I'm gonna have to write you a ticket."

"That isn't fair," Molly called out.

"Sign's right there." Gil pointed his pen. "Nice Beamer, Danny. You got the registration slip?"

As a matter of fact, he did, but despite the Texas plates, the car was registered in D.C. and there was no way Dan was going to show it to Gil or anybody else in town. "It's back at the trailer. Someplace. Hell, I don't know."

"But the car's yours, right?"

Molly scraped her hat off and slapped it against her thigh. "Well, of all the…"

Dan batted her with a roll of wallpaper to hush her up. "Yeah, it's mine," he said, opening the trunk, dumping the rolls inside, then slamming it closed. "I saved all my pocket change for a decade, Gil. Worth every damned penny, too."

"Just checking." The sheriff ripped a pink copy of the ticket out of his book. "Here. You can pay this any time in the next sixty days down at the city clerk's office. I'm sure Anita will be right tickled to see you."

Dan jammed the ticket in his pocket, glaring at Gil's big backside as he lumbered down the sidewalk. "Fascist," he muttered just under his breath.

Nearby, Molly looked as if she were about to take a bite out of her straw hat. "I'm going to write a letter to the *Moonglow Weekly Press* about this," she said. "It's just not right."

"It's personal, Molly."

"I know," she sputtered. "That's what I mean."

"Well, I appreciate your wanting to fight my battles

for me, but it really isn't necessary.'' He grabbed her hat and plopped it on her head, then opened the passenger side door. ''Get in, Rocky. I want to show you someplace special.''

''Where?''

''Just get in.''

Although she'd lived in Moonglow for nearly a year, Molly had never been east of First Street. In fact, she'd just assumed that the town didn't exist beyond First, and when Dan's car went flying over railroad tracks, she was even more surprised. She never knew they were there.

''This must be the proverbial other side of the tracks,'' she said with a little laugh.

''Not proverbial, Molly, darlin'.'' Dan turned the wheel and the car slid to a halt in a rock-strewn, weed-overgrown driveway. ''This is the *actual* other side.''

The dilapidated house by the side of the driveway made Molly's little bungalow look like a palace in comparison. Here the windows that weren't boarded up were jaggedly broken. The front porch appeared out of synch with the rest of the house, canting east while everything else canted west. A daylily was growing right up through the porch boards.

''Is this where you lived?'' she asked.

''Yeah.'' Dan slipped his glasses off, then wrenched his gaze from the house to her. ''How'd you know?''

Molly shrugged. ''I can't think of any other reason to come here unless heartstrings were pulling you back.''

''Heartstrings,'' he said. ''Sometimes I think that was all that held this old place together.''

"Do you want to get out and have a closer look?" Molly asked, her hand already on the door handle.

Dan shook his head. "Too many snakes."

Molly thought he might as well have said too many memories from the way his mouth twisted down at the corners and the way his knuckles turned white as he gripped the steering wheel. "Tell me," she said softly. "About the heartstrings."

"My mother ran off when I was two," he said, his eyes locked on the ramshackle house. "And after that, my father dragged me around from one oil well to another in Texas and Oklahoma. By the time he died, I was twelve years old and I hadn't lived any one place for more than two or three months. Then I came here, to live with Miss Hannah."

"Your aunt?"

He shook his head. "My grandma. Born a Shackelford and died one, and never did bother to get married in spite of my daddy coming along." He laughed softly. "She said she couldn't live with a man for more than a couple of weeks without wanting to blow his head off with a shotgun, so she figured she was better off living alone than going to prison."

"I know the feeling," Molly murmured. "So, you were twelve when you came to live with her?"

"Twelve going on twenty-one. But she managed to knock a little sense and a few manners into my head."

"I'll bet this place was all shiny and spit-polished back then," Molly said as she watched an armadillo scuttle around a rear corner of the derelict dwelling. She was wishing she could have seen the place back in its prime. Wishing especially she could have seen the boy who was twelve going on twenty-one.

"The county would never give Miss Hannah a proper

address," he said, still staring through the windshield. "That was the bane of her existence. So she made up her own. Thirteen twenty-eight Mockingbird Road." He laughed. "She wouldn't accept mail any other way."

"Stubborn," Molly said.

"Oh, yeah."

"And poetic."

Dan's eyes drifted closed a moment. When he opened them, the green light there was hard as an emerald. "Miss Hannah died when I was seventeen. I walked out that door and I never came back."

"Until now." *Thank heaven,* she almost added, wondering where that thought had come from.

"Yeah. Until now."

He reached forward to twist the key in the ignition. "Let's get out of here."

What a stupid thing to do, Dan thought as he wrenched the cap from a beer bottle and slung himself into the lawn chair. Piling bittersweet memories on bad ones wasn't all that bright, and taking Molly out to Miss Hannah's place was just about the dumbest thing he'd ever done.

What did she care? Kathryn Claiborn had enough of her own bad and bittersweet memories to contend with. She didn't need to be saddled with any of his, that was for damn sure.

When they'd gotten back to Molly's house, and while she was whistling and sorting out their purchases in a back room, Dan had picked up the phone in the kitchen and put in a call to Houston.

"Bobby, I can't do this."

"Sure you can, amigo. Hell, just consider it a paid vacation. We have no reason to believe the Claiborn woman is in any jeopardy. Far as we know, there's not a single member of the Red Millennium who hasn't blown himself up.''

''Bobby...''

''You have to do it, Dan.'' Robert Hayes's voice lost its southern affability and took on a bureaucratic chill. ''Everybody else is working double, even triple shifts. You hear me? I've already gone to the wall for you, son, but I'm not putting on a blindfold and smoking a final cigarette on your behalf. You got that? If you don't do this, you're done. There won't be anything more I can do.''

Dan twisted the cap off another beer now, thinking it would be easier if he just ran an IV into his arm. Eliminate the middleman, so to speak. The way he was going to be eliminated soon.

Against regulations, Bobby had shown him his psychological workup a few weeks after he got out of the hospital.

The bullet that Deputy Marshal Shackelford took meant nothing to him. It was the bullet that killed his female partner that shattered his confidence. In my considered opinion, without long-term counseling, which Deputy Shackelford dismisses as ''voodoo drivel,'' he may never regain his former level of confidence, thus making him entirely unsuitable for the duties he is asked to perform.

''Long-term counseling, my ass,'' Dan muttered. You either did a job or you didn't. You withstood the heat or you left the kitchen. If you said you lived at Thirteen Twenty-eight Mockingbird Road, then by God all your mail better be addressed as such or you'd slap it back in the mailman's bag.

He was glad Miss Hannah couldn't see him now.

* * *

Molly ate her spaghetti dinner at the kitchen counter, keeping an eye out the window as she slurped up the long strings of pasta. She'd called out to Dan earlier against her better judgment.

"Hey! How about some spaghetti for dinner?"

He'd saluted her with his bottle and called back, "No, thanks."

Somehow, after their visit to town and Miss Hannah's house, the day had just frittered away. Molly hadn't gone back to work. God knows Dan hadn't even started. He'd opened a roll of wallpaper, stared at it thoughtfully, then rolled it back up and gone outside to his lawn chair where he'd been ever since.

But despite his handyman shortcomings she liked him. Really liked him. Maybe she was drawn to his loneliness because of her own. Still, he didn't seem to have the least bit of interest in her. He hadn't asked her a single question about herself. Not "Where are you from?" or "What do you do?" or even a silly "What's a nice girl like you doing in a hellhole like this?"

It shouldn't have surprised her. She wasn't a very interesting person now, and probably hadn't been even when she'd had a life. The most interesting thing that had ever happened to her was getting blown up by a terrorist's experimental bomb, and that was something she could only discuss when and if she ever got to court, which seemed very unlikely now that the Red Millennium was considered dead as a doornail.

Whoever said that blondes have more fun, she thought dismally, was way off the mark. Dan, on the other hand, seemed to be having fun, swilling beer while slung out in his shady chair. Maybe she'd do that, too. After all, it was her backyard.

She scraped what was left of her spaghetti into the trash can, pulled out the plastic sack and hauled it to the big metal can out back.

"Nice evening," she called out, getting only a nod in reply.

Maybe blondes had more fun because they were persistent, she thought. Like Raylene. She stood a little straighter, throwing her shoulders back, making the most of her 34Bs, then sauntered toward the trailer.

"Pretty sunset," she said. It wasn't exactly an opening Raylene would have used, but she couldn't quite imagine herself saying, "My Lord, Danny. Don't you look cute out here all by your lonesome? Want some company?"

Molly cleared her throat. "Want some company?"

At some point, he had changed into a pair of khaki shorts, and when he shifted in his chair, resting an ankle on a knee, she couldn't help but notice the muscles of his thigh and the long cords of his calves. A little stitch deep inside her pulled tight.

"I'm off the clock, Molly."

"You're in my backyard, Dan."

His mouth slid into a grin as he tipped his bottle her way as if to say *touché*. That little stitch inside her tweaked again.

"Got an extra beer?" she asked.

He jerked his thumb in the direction of a cooler. "Help yourself."

She extracted a cold bottle, twisted off the cap and took a long drink. "That's good," she said, folding her legs and lowering herself to the ground beside his chair. "I keep forgetting how much I enjoy an occasional beer. Salud." She reached up to tap her bottle against his.

Dan promptly switched his beer to the other, more

distant hand, sighing at the same time and recrossing his legs.

"How'd you get the scar?" Molly asked.

"What?"

"Right there." She touched her finger to the gnarled tissue on his thigh. "How'd you get it?"

"Staple gun."

Molly blinked. "What?"

"A staple gun. I was putting down a carpet and I stapled myself to the damned floor."

She laughed. "I don't believe you."

"Okay."

"How *did* you get it? Really."

"I'd tell you," he said, "but then I'd have to kill you."

"Right." Molly took another sip of the cold beer. Be persistent, she told herself. What would Raylene do now? "I've got a scar in just about the same place. Wanna see it?"

"No."

She was already edging up her hemline to disclose the spot where shrapnel from the Chemistry Building basement had supposedly penetrated her leg. The final consensus was that it was a fragment of a Bunsen burner. "Right there. See."

His gaze drifted almost lazily from her ankle to her thigh, idled there a moment, then turned away. "Nice," he murmured.

Good God. Her leg felt warmer somehow just from his gaze. Imagine if he touched her.

"Don't you even want to know how I got it?"

"Nope."

"Aren't you even the least bit curious?"

This time his sigh was closer to a growl. "Molly, I'm

sitting out here trying to medicate myself into a few hours' sleep. I'm not in the mood to play Twenty Questions about damaged body parts. Okay?''

''Sorry.'' She pushed up from the ground, then furiously whacked twigs and grass clippings from the back of her skirt. Hot tears were stinging her eyes so she didn't see Dan rise from his chair, but he must have, because the next thing she knew, she was wrapped in his arms and his lips were close to her ear.

''You don't want this, Molly,'' he whispered roughly. ''Trust me on this.''

''I wasn't...''

''Yes, you were.'' His embrace tightened painfully around her ribs as his hot breath nearly seared her ear. ''Now leave me the hell alone.''

When he practically pushed her away, Molly was hard-pressed to keep her balance. And even though she could hardly see for the tears in her eyes, even though she wanted to run, she and her bruised ego walked slowly toward the house and slammed the door behind her.

Sometime during the night, somewhere between the low trill of the crickets and the high whine of the locusts, Dan thought he heard the insistent ringing of a phone through the open trailer window.

He wrenched up on an elbow, eyed the clock and listened to the sound of Molly's voice floating through the air.

Who the hell was calling her at three in the morning?

He dropped back on the air mattress, scowling, and let darkness wash over him again.

Molly was slamming around the kitchen the next morning, opening drawers for no reason, slamming them shut again, cursing the slow-brewing coffeemaker, crashing a mug down so hard on the countertop that it broke in her hand. She didn't even hear the back door squeak open.

"Morning, sunshine." Dan dropped his toolbox on the kitchen table. "If you've got another cup, I could use some coffee."

She ripped the pot from beneath the brew basket, sloshed the dark liquid into a mug and slapped it down on the table. "There you go."

"Molly, about last night…"

She held up a hand. "I don't want to discuss it, Dan. Please. Let's just pretend it didn't happen."

"Fine with me." He took a tentative sip from the steaming mug. "Who called you last night?"

"What?" She could feel her eyes widen perceptibly. How did he know?

"I heard your phone ringing around three. Who called?"

"Nobody."

"Somebody," he countered, eyeing her over the rim of the mug.

"It was a wrong number."

"Do you always chat with strangers in the middle of the night?"

"The guy was very contrite," she said. "He apologized. At length."

Molly couldn't tell if he believed her or not. Those green eyes could be so cool and inscrutable sometimes. What business was it of his, anyway, that her phone had rung last night at three, or that a man's raspy voice had asked for Kathryn?

"You seem a little edgy this morning," he said, slinging a hip on the table. "Anything wrong?"

"Wrong?" she croaked. "What could possibly be wrong? I make a blatant play for every man who comes to do work on my house. Sometimes they respond. Sometimes they don't." She lifted her shoulders in an exaggerated shrug. "No big deal."

Just like the phone call, she told herself. It was no big deal. She probably only imagined that the caller had asked for Kathryn. It made sense. She always dreamed about her old self, and her dream had simply carried over to the caller's question. The guy had probably asked for Carolyn or Marilyn or somebody. Not Kathryn. It had nothing to do with the terrorists. Anyway, the Marshals Service would have alerted her if anybody was snooping around. They had told her that.

She glared at Dan. "Are you here to work or not?"

He drained the mug and put it down on the table. "Have hammer, will travel, darlin'. Wire Dan. Moonglow."

Dan was up on the roof with a mouthful of nails when Molly came out the door wearing her floppy hat, with her straw bag hooked over her shoulder. She lifted a hand to shade her eyes when she called up to him. "I'm going into town. Need anything?"

He spat out the nails. "Hang on. I'll go with you."

"Oh, that's okay. I won't be gone long. You just keep on keeping on." She gave him a sprightly little wave and started down the driveway.

Dan muttered a curse, shoved the hammer through his belt loop and started a controlled slide down the pitch of the roof toward the ladder. He realized immediately that loose and rotten shingles precluded any notion of control, and the next thing he knew he was hang-

ing on to the guttering for dear life while his legs flailed
in empty space.

Okay. Damn. He loosened one hand and reached for
the ladder, only to send it sliding down the sidewall to
hit the ground with a distinct thud.

"Molly," he yelled.

"I'm right here, Ace." Her voice drifted up from
below, accompanied by something close to a chuckle.
A fairly nasty one.

"You wanna pick up that ladder for me?"

"This ladder?"

"Aw, come on, Molly. I really don't want to break
my neck." As soon as the words left his mouth, the
guttering gave a horrible groan and began to buckle.
"Molly, get the goddamned ladder. Now."

"I'm getting it." There was panic in her voice now
rather than amusement. "Here. Let me just…"

"Dammit. Never mind."

Dan tried, not all that successfully, to launch himself
away from Molly and the useless ladder as he and ten
feet of metal guttering came crashing down.

"The last time I saw you, Danny, I think my dad was
treating you for a broken nose." Dr. Richard Pettigrew
Jr. shoved the X ray into a slot on the light box and
studied the black-and-white picture that emerged.
"Well, you're lucky this time. It's not broken."

"Lucky me." Dan looked at his throbbing ankle.
Bullets didn't hurt half as much, he thought.

"I'll just wrap it," Rich Pettigrew said, "lend you a
pair of crutches and let you go. You'll have to stay off
of it for a few days, though. Keep it iced and elevated
as much as possible. And stay away from roofs."

Molly flew out of her chair in the waiting room as soon as he angled the crutches through the door.

"Is it broken?" she asked.

"Sprained," he answered through clenched teeth.

"Oh, that's good. Well, I don't mean it's *good*. I meant sprained is a lot better than broken."

"I know what you meant."

She was fluttering around him like a gnat.

"Look out. You're gonna make me trip over the damned crutches now."

She stepped back, hands on hips, her chin thrust up into his face. "Are you implying that I made you fall from the roof?"

Dan hobbled past her. "You just could have been a mite quicker with that ladder, is all," he grumbled.

He could hear her muttering all the way to the parking lot, mostly about handymen with a pretty snide emphasis on the *handy*.

"What are you stopping here for?" he asked when Molly pulled into a parking space on Main Street.

"I'll just be a minute." She reached around his crutches for her handbag in the back seat.

Dan looked out the window. This stretch of Main Street didn't have a single store. It was mostly offices, real estate, insurance and—hello!—the telephone company.

"You need to pay your phone bill?" he asked innocently.

"Yes. That's right. It'll just take me a second."

Dan watched her disappear through the door. "People in WITSEC pay their bills through the regional offices, babe. But you don't know I know that. Who called you last night, Molly? Who?"

Chapter 3

"Here, Hopalong. Take these." Molly jammed two capsules into his left hand and a glass of water into his right. "And don't look at me like I'm trying to poison you. They're pain pills."

"Shackelfords are suspicious by nature," Dan said, tossing back the capsules while casting another bleak look at his throbbing ice-packed ankle on Molly's footstool.

She hadn't said much after their stop at the phone company. She was being a good little witness, keeping her own counsel. He guessed that she'd run into a bureaucratic brick wall trying to find out where that phone call had come from.

"Hand me those crutches, will you?"

"Why?"

"Because I need to go out to the trailer and get something, that's why."

"I'll go," she said. "What do you want? A beer?"

Dan felt a shameful anger rip through him. It wasn't even noon, for God's sake, and she figured he was ready for a bender. What he wanted from the trailer was his gun. He leaned sideways and snagged the crutches himself.

Just as he managed to get them comfortably under his arms, the phone rang. Molly jumped as if she'd just put her foot down on a hot coal, then simply stood there, staring at the ringing hunk of plastic.

"Are you going to get that?" Dan asked.

"I wasn't expecting a call," she said nervously, stepping back to put a little more distance between herself and whoever was on the other end of the line. She had every reason to fear the terrorists of the Red Millennium. Did she know that most or all of them were dead?

Dan made a mental note to pick up a caller ID box just as soon as he could get into town. It surprised him that she didn't already have one, actually. But then maybe the powers that be in the service *had* told her and assured her that she was safe.

"Do you want me to answer it?" he asked on the seventh ring.

"No. That's all right. I'll get it." She approached the phone as if it were a rattlesnake. "It's probably a wrong number, anyway. Nobody ever calls me."

Somebody, baby, Dan thought as he watched her pick up the receiver and whisper a tentative hello. Her whole body relaxed then and she turned to him, smiling.

"It's Raylene."

"Good. Give her my love," he said, gripping the crutches and stabbing his way toward his temporary home.

Inside the trailer he figured that the only way to get his Glock secretly into the house was to put it in a gym bag. As long as he was doing that, he tossed in his toothbrush, too. It wasn't such a bad idea, spending a night or two close enough to Molly to do her some good if it came to that. It wouldn't. But what the hell? Being close to Molly had an appeal all by itself.

"Raylene wanted us to join her and Buddy tonight at the Sit and Sip," she said when he reentered the living room. "I told her we couldn't because of your ankle."

"Good move."

"She said…well, wait a minute." Molly stood up, slung out a hip and expanded her chest about three inches. "Take care of that poor baby, hon. You hear? We'll all go two-stepping some other time. Danny used to do a pretty hot two-step. My Lord." Molly's Texas twang dissolved into giggles.

"Believe it or not, I did used to do a pretty hot two-step," he said, trying to juggle the gym bag and the crutches. "Don't let my current situation fool you."

"Oh, it doesn't," Molly said. "What's the bag for, Handy Andy?"

"I'm going to sleep in here for a couple nights, if you don't mind. That way, when I wake, screaming in pain, you won't have so far to run."

He was prepared for one of her sharp little barbs, but instead she gave him a look of such sweet sympathy, such warm concern, all of it tinged with such innocent, ineffable longing, that if he hadn't been on crutches, he might very well have fallen to his knees and begged her to marry him right here, right now.

"You can sleep in my bed," she said, sending his entire nervous system into a momentary frenzy before she added, "I don't mind sleeping on the couch."

"I don't want to put you out, Molly."

"You're not. I'm really happy for the company." She gave a little shrug. "I probably shouldn't say so, it makes me sound like such a jerk, but I really don't have any friends here."

"Why not?" Dan could have kicked himself. He knew why not. A secret past and an unknown future, that's why. Plus the service had probably given her that song and dance about not trusting anybody. She probably shouldn't have trusted *him*.

"Maybe I'm shy." She tried to laugh. "Socially challenged, I guess."

"I can fix that," he said.

"You can?"

"Sure. Pick up that phone and call Raylene. Tell her we'll meet them at the Sit and Sip at eight o'clock tonight."

"But what about your ankle?"

"Well, it could just be a blessing in disguise, you know." He winked. "This way I can just sit and sip, and I won't have to two-step with Raylene."

Dan could still drive since it was his left foot that was injured, and the black BMW pulled into the gravel lot of the Sit and Sip in a magnificent cloud of sunset-colored dust.

Molly had taken pains to dress properly for the honky-tonk, even knowing that whatever she wore would pale in comparison with Raylene's outfit. Dan told her she looked nice when she slid into the passenger seat, but when his eyes lit on Raylene in her spandex bottom and sequined top, he seemed to be registering more than merely "nice" on his compliment meter. On a scale of one to ten, Raylene was a 36DD. My Lord, Molly thought.

"Well, there you are," the hairdresser exclaimed. "We thought you'd never get here, didn't we, Buddy? You remember Danny Shackelford, don't you? And this is my friend, Molly Hansen."

While Dan and Buddy shook hands, Molly just stood there, slightly thunderstruck by Raylene's use of the word *friend*. Did the outgoing, invincible hairdresser actually think of her that way? She longed to believe it was true, more than just Raylene being Raylene. She needed a friend now, more than ever before.

There was a band on the stage, playing at full country tilt, and no sooner had they all sat down than Raylene was dragging Buddy onto the dance floor.

"You ought to be thanking your lucky stars you sprained that ankle, Danny," she called back gaily over her sequined shoulder, "or else I'd be dancing your feet right down to the bone."

"You see," Dan said, his lips close to Molly's ear. "I told you it was a blessing."

When the waitress came to take their order, it was no surprise that she, too, remembered Dan and had her own little bit of Shackelford lore to relate. With the music so loud, it was almost impossible to hear, and Molly only picked up scattered words such as *motorcycle* and *keg* and, last but not least, *sheriff*.

It did surprise her, though, when Dan ordered a club soda with a twist of lemon. She decided he was simply being cautious after taking those pain pills. It was probably a good idea.

An hour later, after both Raylene and Buddy had given her lessons in two-stepping, Molly felt like a sweaty mess as she followed Raylene into the ladies' room.

"My Lord," the hairdresser exclaimed when she

looked into the mirror. "I think my hair's turned two shades darker. You think all that cigarette smoke could do that, Molly? Turn a person's hair from pink to purple?"

"It's probably just the lighting in here," Molly said, digging in her handbag for her lipstick and coming up with a roll of mints. "Raylene, could I borrow a little bit of that Strawberry Frappé of yours?"

Even as Molly asked, Raylene was applying it liberally. She answered with her lips pressed to her teeth. "Aw, honey, I don't know why you'd even bother. I've been watching you and Danny. If ever I've seen kissing on a man's mind, it's on his. You'd only get strawberry all over that cute Hawaiian shirt of his."

"Kissing?"

"Yeah. You know. That's when two people put their lips together and start talking without any words." She rolled her eyes. "Kissing, Molly. My Lord. How long has it been, girl?"

"A long time," Molly admitted.

"I guess so if you can't see what I'm seeing." Raylene blotted her lips, then added another layer of color. "You take my word for it. Your dry spell has come to a screeching halt, honey." She closed one dark-lashed eye in a wink. "Tonight's the night, if you know what I mean."

Oh, God. No, she didn't know exactly what Raylene meant, and Molly did a panicky search for feet in the nearby stalls in the hope that the whole town didn't know what Raylene meant, either. Luckily, no feet were visible.

"For pity's sake, Raylene," she said, trying to sound worldly and offhand. "The man's got a sprained ankle."

Raylene wound her lipstick back in its plastic tube, then snapped the cap on with authority. "Molly, I hope you never meet a man who lets a little sprained ankle keep him down. And I hope you catch my drift." She gave herself a final, critical once-over in the mirror, seemed pleased with what she saw, then linked her arm through Molly's. "Well. You ready for another dancing lesson?"

"I hope you don't believe half of these stories people are telling about me," Dan said on their way home from the Sit and Sip.

"They're not true?"

"Well, if you halve the quantity of the booze, and double the times Miss Hannah slapped me up the side of my head, then, yeah, they're basically true."

"Speaking of drinks," she said, "how was the club soda?"

"Like creek water. But I didn't know what was in those pills you made me swallow, so I didn't want to take any chances."

What he meant was he didn't know if her mysterious caller might emerge from the shadows around the dance floor and two-step Molly into oblivion. Sobriety was a necessary evil at the moment.

"You should probably take another one before you go to bed," she said. "How's the ankle?"

"Tolerable."

Actually, it hurt like hell and the rest of him wasn't all that comfortable, either, after an evening of watching Molly out on the dance floor, mentally undoing the buttons on her blouse and imagining his fingers running over the hidden scar halfway up her leg.

It isn't going to happen, pal, Dan kept telling himself.

You read her file. What about the fiancé she left languishing in New York? Once she settles in to her new identity, she'll find a way to reestablish the connection. It was only a matter of time. If she looks at you now with that banked fire in her eyes, just take it for what it is. Getting it on with the handyman. Passing time with the help until her real life resumes.

"I had fun tonight." She leaned her head back on the seat. "Thanks for taking me, Dan."

"You'll get the hang of small-town life after a while. Moonglow's not such a bad place."

"I'm beginning to see that." She turned her head toward him, and he couldn't help but notice a hopeful shine in her eyes. "Do you think you'll stick around? I mean, after you're finished with my house?"

"Probably not." He turned into her driveway, hoping his terse response had put an end to whatever she was wishing for that had anything to do with him. "Here we are. Home sweet home."

While Molly worked the new key in the new lock on the back door, Dan glanced at his trailer. Moonlight filtered through the live oak, dappling the Airstream's dented aluminum skin. For a minute it seemed hard to believe he actually lived in what he had come to think of as his movable squalor. For a moment it was utterly depressing to know it was only a matter of time before he was in residence there again.

It seemed so natural, following Molly into the house, watching her flip on lights and seeing her hair turn different shades of gold, depending on the wattage of the bulbs.

"I changed the sheets," she said, gesturing toward her bedroom. "And I put some extra pillows out in case you want to elevate your foot."

"Thanks."

"The clock is kind of noisy. Just put it in the drawer of the nightstand if it bothers you too much."

"Okay."

"Well…"

Only a blind man could have missed the longing that turned her light blue eyes a deeper shade. Dan readjusted his crutches and leaned down to kiss the top of her head.

"Good night, Molly."

He had a beaut of a nightmare, no doubt induced by the club soda he'd consumed. He and his partner, Carrie Gray, had just taken over escort duty from Deputies Underhill and Roarke. Hector Morales, their witness, was finishing his room service breakfast of steak and eggs, and in no particular hurry to put on the Kevlar vest that would protect his traitorous heart between the hotel and the federal courtroom where he was due to testify in a little over an hour.

As dreams tended to do, the scene shifted suddenly and they were walking down a long corridor, Carrie and Morales in front, Dan just a step or two behind them, his right hand itching as it always did in situations like this, and his brain measuring distances, delineating shadows, processing everything and labeling it threat or inconsequential, friend or foe.

Carrie pressed the down button on the elevator with the pad of her index finger, her long nail making a little clacking sound on the brass plaque behind the lit button. Then all of them—Dan and Morales and Carrie—gazed up at the light panel overhead.

Was that his mistake? Was that the moment when he let down his guard and all of his instincts failed him?

The elevator door slid open. Dan never saw the men, only the muzzle flashes—fierce, perpetual flames—from their semiautomatics. At such close range, those rifles worked with the efficiency of a Veg-O-Matic. In a heartbeat, Carrie and Morales were no longer identifiable even as they fell.

In this edition of the dream, Dan took a bullet in his ankle rather than his leg, but he continued to empty his gun into the open elevator and he put a dozen holes in the bronzed doors after they swooshed closed.

They said a woman fainted in the lobby when those doors opened on the two dead Colombians inside.

They also said that Dan was crying when the first NYPD cops arrived on the scene. *Babbling incoherently* was written in his file.

But that was never part of his dream.

Molly was glad that Dan was sleeping in. The more he slept, she figured, the less pain he'd have to endure. Also, the more he slept, the less chance she'd have of making a fool of herself again as she had the night before. She'd practically begged the man to kiss her. Now, the morning after, she was relieved he'd turned her down.

While she graded essays, she kept an ear out for the knock she was expecting at her front door. She had promised Raylene to tutor Buddy Jr. in English composition. The boy, it seemed, was mechanically inclined like his father, but unless he passed English and received his high school diploma, there would be no technical school in his future.

"Besides," Raylene had said, "every hour Buddy Jr. spends with you, Molly, will be one less hour I'll have to worry about him getting into trouble. He might even

take a look at what Danny's become and realize there's
no future in earning a bad reputation instead of a diploma.''

"There's nothing wrong with Dan," Molly had said
defensively.

"Well, I didn't say there was, honey. He's just not
exactly chairman of the board of General Motors, now,
is he?''

"Who'd want to be?" Molly muttered at her monitor.
Then, a second later, realizing what she'd said, Molly
almost laughed out loud.

As an associate professor of business, Kathryn Claiborn had spent the last six or seven years attempting to
convince her students that being chairman of the board
of General Motors was a worthy, if not the ultimate goal
for which to strive. She had lauded the glories of the
balance sheet and sung the praises of tax credits, de-
bentures and initial public offerings.

She must have been nuts, Molly thought. Or was she
disastrously off her rocker now? Had Moonglow really
changed her so much? she wondered. Or was Kathryn
merely taking a well-deserved break before resuming
her high-flying career?

Her own goal had always been to use her academic
experience to leverage herself into a cushy little firm on
Wall Street, and from there she and Ethan would form
their own cushy little firm. Now that notion seemed as
strange and stilted as the suits she'd left behind in her
closet. She couldn't even picture Ethan's face.

How had this happened? Molly hated Moonglow. She
despised every false-fronted store on Main Street, every
pickup truck parked there, every good ol' boy wearing
sideburns and hand-tooled boots, every good ol' girl
with big hair and *hon* on the tip of her tongue.

Except she didn't. She adored Raylene, who was probably the most honest person Molly had ever known. And Buddy Sr., good ol' boy or not, was sweet and soft-spoken and unashamedly in love with his wife after nearly twenty years. And Dan... She didn't even know how to begin thinking of the reasons she didn't hate Dan. She didn't dare because somewhere in the back of her brain she thought she just might be falling in love with him. People didn't fall in love that fast, did they? My Lord.

When Buddy Jr. knocked on her front door, Molly was only too happy for the distraction. The boy turned out to be a sixteen-year-old carbon copy of his father. He certainly hadn't inherited his mother's gift of gab. Buddy Jr. seemed too shy to put more than two or three words together.

Molly sat him down at the computer in her office. "Have you used one of these before?" she asked.

"Oh, sure. But just for games 'n stuff."

"What kind of stuff?"

From the way the boy's face colored, Molly figured that "stuff" had something to do with the Internet and females in various stages of undress.

"Never mind," she said, bringing up her word processing program, then typing a sentence across the screen. "Read this, Buddy. Out loud, please."

"My favorite places in Moonglow are..." he read.

"Do you have some favorite places? At least three?"

"Oh, sure. I guess."

"Okay. I'd like for you to write three paragraphs describing each of your favorite places. Decent-size paragraphs. Not just one or two sentences. Tell me why you like them, what they look like, why they're different from anyplace else. Don't forget colors and sounds and textures. It should be pretty easy. Anyway, it'll give us a good place to jump off from. Just yell out if you have any problem. I'll be close by.''

"Yeah. All right.'' Young Buddy stared at the screen, pulled the chair forward, then tapped a couple of experimental letters on the keyboard. "Okay. I get the hang of it, I think.''

"Great. I'll be back in a little while.''

Molly tiptoed past her bedroom door and then was surprised when she saw Dan perched on his crutches at the kitchen sink.

"Hey,'' she said softly, feeling her heart perform a tiny pirouette, hoping it didn't show on her face.

"Hey yourself.''

"Did you sleep well?''

He nodded. "Well enough. Who've you got stashed in your office?''

"Mr. Buddy Earl Jr. is composing an essay about his three favorite places in Moonglow, even as we speak.''

"Three places.'' Dan let out a low whistle. "I'd be hard-pressed to think of more than one.''

"Really?'' Molly cocked her head. "And what would that one place be?''

"Right here.''

A kind of silly grin worked its way across his mouth, and Molly felt her heart melt like a double dip of peppermint ice cream on a hot summer day. "This poor, pitiful pit?''

"Which reminds me,'' Dan said, putting down his coffee cup and lodging the crutches under his arms, "I've gotta pick up a few more things at Cooley's this morning. They haven't by any chance opened a bookstore in town, have they?''

Molly shook her head. "Two honky-tonks, a dozen

bars, three movie rental emporiums, but no bookstores. The library isn't too bad, though. I have a card if you'd like to borrow it.''

"Thanks. I'll just get my own."

She frowned. ''I don't know if you can without being a resident.''

"I can."

Yes, he probably could. The head librarian, Marly Eversole, was about Dan's age, which meant she'd more than likely been inducted into the Danny Shackelford Fan Club two decades before and was still carrying her membership card tucked away in her wallet. Or her heart.

Molly had had to show three pieces of identification—all newly issued by the Justice Department—to get her own library card right after she'd arrived here. Dan, she suspected, would only have to lean his crutches against the counter and flash a grin to get his.

Sometimes life just wasn't fair. Not to Molly, anyway.

"Of all the libraries in all the world," Marly Eversole said with a chuckle as she filled out a card request, "you had to walk into mine, Danny Shackelford."

"Well, you know what they say about bad pennies, Marly."

"You weren't bad, Danny," the chunky little brunette said, blinking behind her thick glasses. "You just got caught up in some bad circumstances."

"Story of my life," he said, a grimmer note to his voice than he intended as he wheeled around toward the tall stacks, wondering where the home-improvement section was and unwilling to ask for fear word would get back to Molly.

Half an hour later, he was checking out a western, a biography of Dwight Eisenhower and *The Dummies Guide to Home Repair,* which he tucked under his shirt to free his arms. Hobbling out to his car, he fully expected to hear a warning blip from the siren on Gil Watson's patrol car and then Gil's voice booming out, "I got you now, you book-stealing son of a bitch."

Dan stashed the books in the trunk of his car, then stabbed his way down Main Street in search of a tavern that was doing a brisk morning business, where he could put in a call to Houston without being overheard.

"You calling from a bodega, son?" Bobby inquired right after he'd said hello.

"Nope," Dan said. "Just got the radio turned up real loud, boss. Those glasses you hear clinking are just Molly Hansen doing up the breakfast dishes."

"I hope that's true."

"And I hope you're going to tell me that you've got a lock on whoever broke into the computer system and that you're about to make an arrest."

"No such luck," Bobby said. "Anything going on with the Claiborn woman?"

It took a second to register that Bobby was referring to Molly. And then it took an additional second for him to realize that what his boss meant by *going on* wasn't personal.

"Nothing," he replied. There was no way he was going to mention the weird phone call Molly had received and bring half a dozen deputies down on her little house. That would scare the daylights out of her, not to mention put a decided crimp in his time alone with her. Besides, he was convinced the call meant nothing.

"I'll stay in touch," Dan said.

"You do that, amigo. You doing all right otherwise?"

Otherwise was Bobby's code for "Is your head straight on your shoulders these days?"

"Fine," Dan said. *Just peachy.*

Molly returned to her office from seeing Buddy Jr. out the door. The boy hadn't done all that poorly on his paragraphs, although his spelling was a hit-or-miss proposition. Mostly miss. She didn't give him any homework, having decided he probably wouldn't do it, anyway, and told him she'd see him at the same time tomorrow.

When she wandered back into the living room, Dan was back, fooling with the phone. "What are you doing?"

"I picked up a caller ID," he said. "I thought it might be useful if Raylene's going to be gabbing your ear off. This way you can kind of prepare yourself mentally before you pick up the phone."

Molly laughed. "That's not such a bad idea." She wasn't thinking about Raylene, though. She wondered why she hadn't thought to use one of those boxes a long time ago. If she'd already had the ID device, she could have identified her mysterious caller the other night.

"I was just kidding," Dan said. "Don't look so worried."

Making a deliberate effort to iron out the frown lines in her face, she said, "The only thing I'm worried about is that if I talk to Raylene too much, I'll wind up sounding just like her. My Lord."

"There." He plugged the cord back into its outlet. "Now all we have to do is wait for the thing to ring."

"I don't suppose standing here watching it will make it do that any faster, do you?"

"I doubt it. Anyway, I'm not being paid to stand around. I'm going to tackle that leaky showerhead next." He started off in the direction of the bathroom.

"How much *are* they paying you?" she asked.

Dan's crutches came to a thudding halt. "That's kind of a personal question, don't you think?"

She shrugged. "I was just curious."

"They pay me enough, Molly. Okay?"

"Don't be so touchy, Dan. For heaven's sake. I was just wondering. It's no big deal."

"Maybe I'm just a little reluctant to compare paycheck stubs with a college professor," he said irritably. "Maybe it's an ego thing. Did you ever consider that?"

"No. I..." Molly bit softly into her lower lip. "How did you even know I was a college professor?"

He shifted his weight and glared at the floor a second before he said, "I can read, you know. I couldn't help but see that online university deal on your computer screen."

"But how did you know I was a professor?"

"You're a smart woman, for God's sake. And you're considerably over twenty-one, if you'll pardon my saying so. Hell, it never once occurred to me that you were a student."

Her frown was back. She could feel it. But her inclination was to believe him. "That makes sense, I guess."

"Good," he snapped. "Now, if you'll quit playing Twenty Questions, I'll get on with my work."

Molly watched him stomp toward the bathroom, and had to stifle a giggle. It wasn't so easy, looking aggrieved and all bent out of shape, on crutches. She chided herself for asking Dan how much he was being paid for this job. He had such a chip on his shoulder when it came to his occupation, she should have known he'd blow a gasket or two.

She let out a tiny sigh. Now that she was finding him so damned attractive, she hated that his male ego was coming between them like a barbed-wire fence. What difference did their professional status make? She wished she had told him she was only a lowly instructor now, anyway, and made a mental note to slip that into a conversation in the not-so-distant future.

In her office, she booted up her computer again. If she didn't pay more attention to business, she wouldn't even be a lowly instructor for very long.

Changing the showerhead turned out to be easy enough, even though the crutches nearly cost him his life on the slick surface of the bathtub. After that, however, Dan wasn't ready to tackle the leak in the kitchen sink without first returning to the trailer to take a look at the book he'd *borrowed* from the library.

He must have nodded off somewhere between washers and wing nuts, because when he woke, the light had dimmed considerably inside his trailer. It took a second to realize that what had awakened him was the sound of Molly screaming.

One second after that he had retrieved a key from beneath a floor panel and was taking his Glock from the metal drawer where he kept it locked away. He shoved the gun in the waistband of his jeans and was halfway across the backyard before the pain in his ankle reminded him that he'd forgotten the crutches.

As best he could determine, the screams were coming from Molly's bathroom. The back door wasn't locked, but it didn't appear to be jimmied in any way. Dan headed immediately for the bathroom. That door was locked.

"Molly," he shouted, banging his fist on the door.

Her screams had diminished to staccato curses, but that didn't necessarily mean that she was safe.

"Molly, open the door."

"I can't," she wailed.

There was no way he was going to be able to use his injured foot, either to kick or to support himself while using the other foot, so he moved back, held his automatic in his left hand, and rammed his right shoulder into the wooden door. The framing on the inside gave way with a harsh snapping noise, and, having switched his gun to the other hand, Dan lunged into the steamy little room.

The flowered shower curtain was pulled closed across the tub. Dan reached out and opened it with one quick swing of his arm, and there stood Molly in all her glistening, naked glory. Her hair was dripping soapsuds and her eyes were squeezed closed. He was momentarily stupefied by the vision of wet, firm breasts and the sleek curve of her behind before he realized that water was spraying down on her, uncontrolled, from the uncapped pipe while the showerhead he'd installed sat in several inches of foamy water in the bottom of the tub.

Dan shoved his gun into his jeans at the small of his back. With adrenaline still pouring through him, he shouted louder than he meant to. "What the hell are you doing?"

Molly was scrambling to cover herself with her arms and trying to wipe her soapy eyes at the same time. She shouted back, "I was trying to wash my hair, dammit, and the stupid showerhead came off in my hand. Now

I've got soap in my eyes and I can't see to turn the water off and I can't find my towel.'' One wet arm flailed out blindly, smacking Dan on the side of the head.

He reached in front of her to turn off the cascading water, then snapped the towel from the bar above the toilet. ''You scared the hell out of me, Molly, you know that? Come here.''

He curved a hand around her wet, soapy neck and guided her closer, then dabbed at her eyes with a corner of the towel. ''Is that better?''

Molly let out a strangled little whimper. One blue eye opened tentatively, then widened considerably. ''My God, Dan. Look at my door!'' she wailed. ''What did you do to my door?''

He shrugged while he wrapped the big bath towel around her. ''I broke it. But that's no big deal. I can fix it. Doors just happen to be my specialty. I'm a hell of a carpenter, Molly.''

A rough growl loosened from her throat and she batted his hands away, taking a firm grip on the towel. ''Well, it's a pretty good bet you're not a plumber, Dan,'' she snarled. ''Now, will you please get out of here so I can dry off and get dressed?''

Molly was running the blow dryer over her hair, standing at the bathroom sink and contemplating the shattered door frame. Dan had only been here a few days and already he'd done at least a month's worth of damage. She wondered if he wreaked as much havoc at every place he worked.

It was a nice havoc, though. Well, except the part an hour or so ago when she was blind and buck naked in the shower. Even now her face colored rosily at the memory. Dan hadn't seemed all that unsettled by it. That shouldn't have surprised her, Molly supposed. Her not-all-that-voluptuous body probably made no impression whatsoever on him. He might as well have been rescuing a wet dog.

She switched the blow dryer off, only to realize her phone was ringing, so she trotted into the living room and glanced at the caller ID.

"Who is it?" Dan came up behind her.

"I don't know. It says 'Pay Phone,' then there's a number underneath. Looks like it's local."

"Don't answer it," he said.

"Well, what if...?"

"Just don't answer it, Molly, all right? That's what the damn ID is for. No sense giving some heavy breather his jollies for the night."

It kept ringing. And ringing. At least twenty times by Molly's count. Every single ring sent a little shiver down her spine.

Chapter 4

The next morning Dan waited until young Buddy Jr. arrived for his English tutorial session before he drove the three blocks to First and Main, went back to the tavern where he'd used the phone the day before, and called Houston for a location on the pay phone number that had shown on Molly's caller ID.

It turned out to be in the back room of the pool hall right next door. No, nobody had seen any strangers around there the previous night. It had been a regular night, the proprietor told Dan, except for Clete Davis drinking a little too much Southern Comfort and tossing his cookies in the alley out back.

Dan didn't even bother to check the phone itself since he wasn't equipped to take any prints and didn't suppose any terrorist worth his salt would have left any, anyway. Hell, it was probably just some drunk who'd finally worked up enough courage to call the prettiest girl in town and ask her for a date.

That notion didn't put him in the brightest of moods as he drove back to Molly's. He'd read in her file that she'd left behind a fiancé someplace in New York, but he hadn't seen any evidence of a viable engagement. No ring on Molly's finger. No wistful sighs or forlorn expressions on her face. He couldn't imagine being engaged to Molly, then having her disappear into thin air. Why wasn't this alleged fiancé moving heaven and earth and all the bureaucracies involved to get her back?

Dan would have, by God. He gave the steering wheel a little slap for emphasis. If Molly were *his* fiancée, not even WITSEC could keep him from finding her.

She was standing in the driveway, waving goodbye to Buddy Jr. when Dan pulled up. There was a little breeze shaping her skirt to her long, lovely legs. Dan pictured those lithe limbs all sleek and soapy, and found himself swallowing a sigh as he levered out of the driver's seat and slammed the door.

"No crutches today?" she asked, moving closer to where he stood.

"I didn't have far to walk."

"Guess what?" she asked. A knowing grin inched across her lips. "I just happen to know who last night's mystery caller was. Guess who?"

He pulled his shades down his nose. "Just tell me."

"It was Buddy Jr. calling from the pool hall, trying to see if he could come by in the afternoon instead of the morning."

"Are you sure?" Dan asked.

"Positive. He just told me."

That was good news, Dan thought, and probably what he should have suspected all along. Molly's terrorists didn't exist anymore. All sources indicated that. Nobody was threatening this woman or trying to silence her. If there had been any chance of that, they wouldn't have sent Dan to keep an eye on her.

"Well, that's good news," he said. "I told you not to worry."

Her forehead creased. "Speaking of worrying, I was wondering what you were planning to work on today."

"I thought I'd have another go at that showerhead," he said. "Damned screws must've been defective."

"Molly!"

"What?" Molly called back, turning off her computer and swiveling her chair in the direction of Dan's voice.

"Come here a minute, will you?"

He was in the bathroom. Well, more precisely he was in the bathtub, a screwdriver lodged over one ear while he reached up to further adjust the newly reattached showerhead.

"Here I am," she said. "What do you need?"

"I need to know where you want this thing set so you won't be reaching up and fiddling with it and bringing it down the way you did before."

"I didn't..."

"Just tell me how you want it set."

She crossed her arms and leaned a hip against the vanity. "Well, I don't know. What are my choices?"

"Let's see." He squinted up. "There's Regular Shower. I guess that's for people who just want to get clean. There's something called Soft Pulse, which has a certain sensual appeal. The last setting, preferred by sexual deviates, no doubt, is called Pleasure Pulse." He angled his head toward her and waggled his eyebrows. "I say go for it, Molly."

She laughed. "You go for it, Dan. The regular setting will do just fine."

"Killjoy." He flipped a little lever. "That should do it. Okay. Take off your clothes and give her a try."

"I'll wait. Why don't you give her a try?"

"Okay."

He had stripped off his Hawaiian shirt and was tugging his undershirt over his head almost before Molly could react.

"Whoa. Wait a minute, Dan. I was just kidding."

He looked like a four-year-old who'd just been told they'd stopped making chocolate pudding. Forever. It occurred to her then that, living in the Airstream, Dan probably hadn't had a really good shower in ages.

"Well, I mean, if you really want to take a shower," she said, "go ahead. Here." She reached into the tiny closet for a towel. "Here's a clean towel. Just for heaven's sake wait till I get out of here, okay?"

His belt was already unbuckled and the snap on his jeans undone. She couldn't help but appreciate the muscular curves of his chest and shoulders as he reached up once more to the showerhead.

"I believe I'll have a run at the Pleasure Pulse, Molly." He winked. "I'll let you know if it's appropriate for you or not."

"I'd appreciate that no end, Dan."

Molly hastened back to her office but couldn't really concentrate for the sound of rushing water and the wet, reverberating choruses of "It's a Long Way to Tipperary."

Even though the Pleasure Pulse had been a disappointment, Dan considered himself a fairly happy camper as he dried off after his shower. Sobriety didn't feel half bad, he had to admit, and even being back in Moonglow had its advantages. Molly Hansen, for one. Maybe he'd just retire from the Marshals Service and set up here permanently as Dan the Handyman. He'd done all right on the showerhead the second time around. No telling what he could accomplish if—

"Dan!" Molly's voice came from the kitchen. "You need to come out here. Right now."

From her tone, he knew at once that it was important. Even dire. He wrapped the towel around his waist and beat a limping path in the direction of her voice.

"What's wrong?" he asked, coming through the kitchen door.

Molly was standing with her back to him, her hand gripping the inside handle of the screen door, keeping it from opening out. "There's somebody here who wants to talk to you," she said.

When Molly stepped a few inches to her left, Dan could see the barrel of a revolver waving wildly on the other side of the door.

"Get back," he said, immediately angling himself between Molly and the open door. "Lady, put that gun down before you hurt somebody," he said to the woman standing just outside.

"You don't know who I am, do you, Danny?"

He looked at her short, almost mannish salt-and-pepper hair and at the wet lines of black mascara that stained her cheeks, then he looked back at the gun. It was an old Colt Peacemaker. He hoped to hell the damned thing didn't misfire.

"Put the gun down now and then tell me who you are."

"I knew you wouldn't recognize me after all this time. How is it that you look the same after all these years and I look like some old used car? It just isn't fair."

Instead of putting the gun down, she sighted it directly at his heart. Right at that moment, it was beating so hard Dan thought a .45 caliber bullet would have a tough time penetrating it.

"Just put the gun down," he said as calmly as he could.

"Gil Watson told me you were back," she said in a voice that was increasingly high and tight. "He told me you were living with the East Coast slut." Her wild eyes focused over his shoulder at Molly. "Are you?"

Dan pushed the screen door out a fraction, preparing to grab for the Colt. "No, I'm not living here. I'm just doing some repair work."

"Sure." Her gaze strafed him from bare shoulder to knee. "And I'm Cinderella, waiting for my prince to come."

"Why don't you just go ahead and tell me your name." He edged the door another quarter inch, praying it didn't squeak.

"My name's Ginny Hoke." The woman's mouth twisted viciously. "Ring any bells?"

"Well, as a matter of fact..." Dan could feel his eyes widen perceptibly. "Ginny Hoke? Terry Hoke's little sister?"

"That's right. Doesn't surprise me you'd remember my brother better than me, either, since the two of you were thicker than thieves. Me, I was just somebody you took to the drive-in every now and then when you couldn't find anybody else. Isn't that right, Danny?"

To the best of his recollection, that was true. Dan was hardly proud of it, but he wasn't about to confess his youthful sins and beg the pardon of a woman who had a revolver pointed at his heart.

"I remember you, Ginny. You had long, pretty hair that came almost to your waist, right? And you sang the National Anthem at the baseball games. See, I remember."

"And do you remember that last night at the drive-in?" She started waving the gun again.

"Well, I... Not exactly."

"It's too damn bad you don't, Danny." Tears welled in her eyes and spilled over. She dropped the Colt against her leg, as if it were suddenly too heavy to hold. "It's just too damn bad you don't remember because that's the night your daughter was conceived."

They'd been outside an awfully long time, Molly thought, peeking unobtrusively out the kitchen window, watching Dan and Ginny Hoke sitting in the lawn chairs in the afternoon shade of the live oak. Every once in a while they leaned their heads toward each other and the sounds of soft laughter carried across the yard.

That was somewhat reassuring, Molly decided. At least the woman didn't feel like killing him anymore. She glanced over her shoulder at the nasty-looking revolver left behind on the kitchen table. The six shiny bullets that Dan had extracted from the weapon were in a little circle right beside it. Ginny Hoke's shaking fingers had arranged them that way while she sat at the kitchen table with Molly, waiting for Dan to get dressed.

"I'm sorry I called you a slut," Ginny had said. "It's not your fault that Danny's got loose morals."

Loose! Glaring out the window again, Molly was thinking Dan Shackelford was a little more than just

loose. He was two steps lower than an alley cat. A rat
of the first order. How could he have fathered a child
with Ginny Hoke and then simply gone away? It was
unconscionable.

Her feelings for him—and Molly had to admit that
those feelings had been growing these past few days
like glorious, unexpected wildflowers—seemed to
shrivel now. She could never knowingly give her heart
to a man who'd abandon a pregnant lover. Family was
far too important to her. It wasn't something she ob-
sessed about, but because her own small family had
been taken from her so violently when she was a fresh-
man in college, the idea of family had great significance
for her. Thirteen years ago, barely an hour after waving
goodbye to Molly at the university, her parents and
younger sister had been killed in a car accident.

Like Dan, Molly had pretty much been on her own
since the age of eighteen. But, unlike Dan, she'd never,
ever walked out on an obligation.

Ethan, her fiancé, didn't count, she told herself. They
hadn't even set a wedding date, and there were no children involved. In fact, Ethan had made it very clear that
he didn't want to be burdened with rug rats, as he called
them, until both he and Molly were comfortably ensconced on Wall Street. While Molly had accepted that,
she wondered, somewhere deep in her heart, if she
hadn't been perversely grateful for the terrorist bomb
that had all but broken the long engagement she hadn't
been able to break herself.

She edged back from the window when Dan and
Ginny rose and began walking toward the driveway, his
arm looped lightly around the woman's shoulder. The
fact that Dan was still limping painfully didn't bother
Molly at all. He deserved sprains and worse for what

he'd done. She hoped Ginny was going to make him pay an arm and a leg for abandoning her and their little girl.

That little girl, she realized all of a sudden, wasn't so little anymore. In fact, she was one of the children Molly had philosophized about at the hardware store when she suggested to Dan that an entire generation had been born and grown up during his absence from Moonglow. Little did she know then that she was talking about Dan's very own daughter.

She heard the thunk of Ginny's car door, followed not long afterward by the squeal of the screen door as Dan entered the kitchen.

"Ginny didn't take her gun," Molly said almost tonelessly, postponing the angry, inevitable confrontation. Her heart felt flattened. She was so disappointed in Dan, and even more disappointed in herself for misjudging his character.

"I'll see that she gets it back eventually." He palmed the bullets, shook them in his hand like dice a second before he let them fall into the breast pocket of his shirt. Then he gave a long sigh, accompanied by a brief chuckle. "Phew. That was close."

"Close!" Molly shrieked. *"Close!"* She thought the entire top of her head was going to explode. "How dare you make a joke out of something like this, Dan? How dare you snicker about letting a young girl grow up without a father? About having a twenty-year-old daughter you've never once laid eyes on?"

He had picked up the big Colt and was rolling its cylinder down his arm when he said quietly, "You don't think a lot of me, do you?"

"At the moment, no," she said. "I don't. I think you're irresponsible and shiftless and slimier than pond scum."

"Well, that might very well be, but she's not my daughter."

"She's not…?" Molly's exploding head stopped in mid-eruption while her jaw loosened a notch or two. "What do you mean?"

"I mean Ginny's daughter isn't my kid."

"But how is that possible?"

"Molly, darlin', for a professor, you're not all that bright. What did you do, skip Birds and Bees 101?"

"I need to sit down," she said, pulling out a chair at the table. "This isn't funny, Dan, and it's way too much for one person to process."

Dan twisted a chair around and straddled it. "No kidding," he said. "And you're not even the accused."

"You never slept with Ginny?"

He shook his head, moving his hand over his heart. "Never."

Molly narrowed her eyes. "Then how did she just happen to come up with you as the likely suspect?"

"Well, now, that's where the plot thickens," he said, grinning. "It didn't take me too long to remember that I did, indeed, take young Miss Ginny to the drive-in not too long before I left town. And I probably would have ravaged her, too, if she hadn't drunk too much and passed out in the back seat."

She was still skeptical. "You remember that particular night all that clearly after twenty years?"

"Oh, clear as a bell once I started thinking about it. You see, before Ginny had the good grace to pass out, she threw up all over the damned car. Miss Hannah's car. Did I mention that? That old woman just about flayed me wide open the next day when she caught a good whiff of the night before."

"Well, I suppose that would leave an indelible impression on your brain if not your backside," Molly said. "But that doesn't explain what happened to poor Ginny."

He sighed and leaned forward, bracing his forearms on the back of the chair. "Ginny just acknowledged that a wily young fellow named Cody Johnson stopped by her house that night and wound up taking advantage of her sorry state. They got married, Ginny and Cody, a few months later, as it turned out, and the little girl bore a striking resemblance to the Johnson clan, which Ginny chose to ignore once she and Cody split up."

Molly's narrowed eyes grew wider. "You mean she knew she was falsely accusing you?"

"At some level, I guess. Hell, I don't know." He upped the wattage of his grin. "Maybe it was just wishful thinking on her part."

Molly uttered something like a snort.

Dan looked decidedly aggrieved. "What? You don't think I'd make good daddy material?"

"Let's put it this way," she said. "I don't think anybody who lives like a gypsy and drinks like a fish is the world's best candidate for fatherhood. Not for a child of mine, anyway."

But even as she said the words, Molly was thinking— heaven help her—that she didn't really mean them. She'd known Ethan for years and never really pictured the children they might have together. How could she possibly be visualizing a family with Dan after knowing him just a few days?

Being sexually attracted to the man was one thing. But thinking about having his babies?

My Lord, what was happening to her?

* * *

Not for anybody's child, Dan thought as he sat on Molly's bed attempting to read the instructions with the roll of wallpaper. She'd gotten that gypsy-fish thing right, but she didn't know enough about the real Dan Shackelford to add that anybody who lived so close to danger didn't have any business being a father, let alone a husband.

Not that he'd ever cared for a woman enough to marry her, but he'd always considered it pretty senseless to ask someone to become his widow and raise his children by herself. Miss Hannah, despite her independence, hadn't done so well with his father in that regard, nor had his old man with him.

It fairly dumbfounded Dan that he kept thinking of Molly that way. If not exactly as a wife, then as a long-term, forsaking-all-others lover. He had to keep reminding himself that she was already spoken for, that whatever longing he read in her eyes was just because she'd been alone so long. She was looking for sex, not love.

He'd been alone a long time, too. My God. The two of them, if they ever came together, might generate enough pure heat to burn three square blocks of Moonglow right down to the ground. That was a thought that definitely didn't warrant pursuit. He was already way too preoccupied with notions of ravaging this woman's body when it was keeping her body alive and intact that should have been his prime concern.

He had to start from the beginning, rereading the damned wallpaper instructions, and even then the words struck him as English translated to Chinese then back again, losing all sense in the translation. Selvage? What the hell was that?

Coming so close on the heels of the incident with Ginny Hoke, it gave him a headache. Dan leaned back on the mountain of pillows on Molly's bed and closed his eyes. Maybe he didn't know the first thing about wallpaper, but he certainly knew the score when it came to sex. Zero to zero at the moment. And, too bad for him, he was currently forced to stay on the bench.

Molly didn't really need a haircut, but when she saw that Dan was sound asleep on her bed, she got her handbag, tiptoed out of the house and walked into town in the hope that Raylene wasn't booked solid for the day. If she was starting to think about Dan Shackelford and babies, she needed to ask a few questions, even if the answers did nothing more than bring her to her senses. Who better to ask than Raylene?

As it turned out, Barb Fyler, the mayor's wife, had just called to cancel her permanent.

"I figured she would," Raylene said, gesturing Molly into the chair and whipping the plastic cape around Molly's neck. "That woman keeps one appointment for every six she schedules and breaks. She must be off her medication again."

"You know just about everything about everybody in Moonglow, don't you, Raylene?" Molly asked.

"Pretty near." She dragged a brush through Molly's curls.

"I guess you know Ginny Hoke, then, huh?"

"Ginny? Oh, sure." The hairdresser gave Molly a quizzical look in the mirror. "Don't tell me she's been after Danny with that cock-and-bull story about Sarajane being his daughter. My Lord. Her imagination's more fertile than a cow pasture. One little look at

Sarajane and you wouldn't take her for anything but Cody Johnson's child.''

"That's what Dan said.''

"I should think so.'' Raylene gave a tiny *harrumph* and rolled her perfectly made-up eyes. "Danny was a wild one, but he wasn't stupid, if you know what I'm saying. My Lord. If he hadn't been careful, half the graduating class a couple of years ago would have looked just like him.'' She lifted a hank of Molly's hair. "Now, 'bout how much do you want me to take off, hon? An inch? Two?''

"Just a little,'' Molly said. "Tell me more about Dan, Raylene. What was his grandmother like?''

Raylene had reached for a spray bottle to mist Molly's hair, but she held her finger still on the trigger with the bottle itself perched on Molly's shoulder. "Miss Hannah? My Lord, honey. That was one slitty-eyed, mean old woman. I was scared to death of her, right along with half the town.''

Funny, Molly thought. Dan had described his grandmother as strong and staunchly independent, but he hadn't given the impression that she was mean or the female scourge of Moonglow.

"What was scary about her?'' she asked, closing her eyes while Raylene liberally misted her hair as well as her face.

"She was never mean to me personally. Come to think of it, not to anybody else I knew, either. I guess maybe it was just the stories I heard about her taking after Danny with whatever weapon happened to be at hand that scared me. My Lord. It's little wonder Donna Liggett lasted as long as two years, having to live in the same house with that old witch.''

"Donna...?''

"Danny's mom. I guess I should have said Donna Shackelford, but she wasn't married all that long before she took off. She and my mother were distant cousins, somehow. I never really did quite get the connection."

"Did she ever come back?"

"Not that I know of." The hairdresser took a few practice slashes in the air with her scissors before she started on Molly's hair. "Mama and I were just talking about Donna the other day, wondering whatever happened to her."

"What about Dan's father? What was he like?"

Raylene rolled her eyes again while she kept snipping. "He had a worse reputation than Danny's, that man did. I suspect that's how Miss Hannah got so slitty-eyed and mean. Those fellas must've just plain run her ragged with all their carrying on."

"It must be hard," Molly said, "raising a child all alone."

"It's not easy even when a person's not alone." Raylene measured a lock of uncut hair against a cut one. "You've never been married, have you, Molly? Seems like you would've mentioned it if you had."

"Married? No. Never." That didn't seem to be giving away any classified information, she thought, or any dark secrets that were likely to filter back to the Red Millennium and get her killed. Molly cautioned herself, though, not to get so comfortable that she started to divulge too much. Especially to Raylene, who seemed to be Moonglow's version of the *National Enquirer.*

"Bet you were engaged, though, right?"

"No," Molly lied.

"That surprises me. A sharp-looking woman like…" The phone rang, cutting Raylene off in mid-sentence.

"S'cuse me a sec, hon. That's probably Barb Fyler wanting to come in for that permanent after all."

After the hairdresser picked up the phone, Molly couldn't tell who was on the other end of the line. The conversation on Raylene's end was mostly *yep* and *all righty* and, finally, *okeydokey, bye now.*

She hung up and returned to her scissorwork, saying, "That was Danny with his shorts all in knots because you left and didn't tell him where you were going. My Lord. I could be gone a week before Buddy even realized I wasn't there, and then he'd probably only notice because his sock drawer would turn up empty one morning."

Molly frowned in the mirror, not knowing whether to be flattered or slightly appalled by Dan's possessiveness. Or even a bit afraid. If the Marshals office in Houston hadn't assured her they had indeed hired him to make repairs, she might have been suspicious that Dan had terrorist links.

"He said to keep you right here, hon, and he'll be by for you in about fifteen minutes. I oughta be able to finish you up by then." She snipped another lock of hair. "Looks like somebody just can't stand to have you out of his sight, Molly girl."

"I wouldn't exactly describe it as my shorts being in knots," Dan said in his own defense after he'd walked Molly out of Raylene's and put her in his car. "I just didn't know where you were. That's all."

"This is Moonglow, Dan, for pity's sake. How far could I have gone?"

He started the car. "So, what did Raylene have to say about Ginny Hoke?"

"I didn't ask."

"You probably didn't have to," he said. "I suspect the news is all over town by now."

"Well, Raylene said it's old news. She said that everybody always knew the truth about Ginny's daughter. And..." Molly added with a little chuckle, "she said you were always renowned for your—how shall I put it?—precautionary measures."

That reminded Dan that he ought to slip over to Idella in the next county and pick up a few precautionary measures just in case the fire in Molly's eyes burned out of control one of these nights. If he so much as glanced at a condom in the drugstore here, the town criers would have a field day. The fact that he wasn't planning to sleep with Molly, anyway, if he could help it, just made him all that more conscious of her reputation. He didn't want to hurt her in any way.

"Why don't I take you out to dinner?" he asked, heading the BMW down Main Street. "There used to be a nice little Italian place out on Route 4."

"Palazzo's," Molly said. "It's still there. In fact, I had dinner there the first week I was in town. It's pretty good."

"Not New York, though." He wanted to cut off his tongue the minute the words left his mouth. Not only did references to her past make Molly edgy, but he didn't want her asking what a ne'er-do-well handyman was doing eating Italian in New York.

"No, not New York," she said quietly. "At least, I wouldn't imagine so."

"Me, neither," Dan said, putting an end to that little blunder.

Palazzo's was Texas Italian, with strings of red chilipepper lights strung across its dusty parking lot and a pair of longhorns nailed over the front door. Inside, the tables were covered with red-and-white checkered cloths and lit with candles in red votives.

"This is nice," Molly said as she slid into a high-backed booth.

It was even nicer, Dan thought, when their waitress turned out to be not a day over twenty-one with no possible memories of him, for better or for worse. He was so relieved, in fact, that he forgot he wasn't drinking for the duration, and he promptly ordered a bottle of Chianti for himself and Molly.

It wasn't until they were halfway through their spaghetti and garlic bread and second bottle that Dan realized his dinner companion was well on her way to becoming blitzed. He refilled his glass to the rim and dripped just a few polite sips in hers.

"Drink much, Molly?"

She sucked up a long, maverick strand of pasta, then laughed as she wiped her chin. "Not lately," she said.

"Yeah. I didn't think so."

"I'd like to propose a toast," she said, lifting her glass and cocking her head toward Dan. "To Moonbeam."

"You mean Moonglow."

"That's what I said."

"To Moonglow," Dan said, clinking his glass against hers, then bolting its contents so he could pour out the remainder of the bottle before she got it.

In the meantime, Molly had begun pawing through her big straw handbag, making disappointed little clucking noises with her tongue.

"What are you looking for?" he asked.

"My wallet. I've decided, since I'm the professor and you are but a lowly carpenter, I really ought to pay for this dinner. And I would, if I could just find my stupid wallet. Now, where do you suppose it could be?''

God, she was pretty, even several sheets to the wind.

"I don't know, Professor." Dan angled his hip to reach for his own wallet just as their waitress brought the check.

"I'll take that," Molly said.

The young woman looked at Dan, as if to ask if that were all right. He nodded, deciding he'd rather fight Molly for the bill privately than have her drag the poor waitress into the fray.

"I know it's in here."

She began to empty the bag, item by item, onto the table, something he couldn't imagine her doing in a sober state. Once the bag was nearly empty, she did all but climb inside it for a final inspection. With Molly so preoccupied, Dan slid his credit card out of his wallet and handed that and the check to the waitress.

"I'll be right back, sir," she said, winking, seeming somehow relieved that the natural order of things had been maintained.

Molly surfaced from the depths of her purse. "How can I pay the bill if I can't find my wallet?"

"I got it, Molly. I'll tell you what. You can owe me."

"Okay." She picked up one of the myriad notepads and a pen that she'd produced earlier. "How much?"

"Thirty-eight dollars and fifty-eight cents."

She wrote it slowly, with the pronounced dignity of someone who doesn't want anybody else to know they're snockered. Dan was way too familiar with that. "Is that with the tip or without the tip?"

"With," he said, even as he was peeling a five from his wallet and sliding it under his plate.

While he signed the receipt, Molly refilled her bag

with the same determination with which she'd taken it all out.

"Ready to go?" he asked.

She blinked. "Are we done?"

"One of us, babe. Let's go."

Dan had to brush the rolls of wallpaper off the bed and wrench back the covers before he slung a boneless but very happy Molly onto the mattress. She landed with a breathy little *oof,* which she then turned into an elongated sigh while her arms still clung around his neck.

"Let go, Molly."

Instead of letting go, she tightened her grip, pulling him closer.

"Do you think what Raylene said is true, Dan? About you being the best kisser in the history of the world? Is that even possible?"

"Probably not." He reached up around his neck with one hand but couldn't break her iron grip.

"I think we should try it and see." She turned her head so their noses nearly collided. "What do you think?"

"I think you should get some sleep," he said. "That way you'll be rested enough to deal with the headache you're going to have tomorrow."

"Just one little kiss. Come on." She loosened one arm in order to aim a finger at her mouth, missing by an inch. "Just one little smoocheroo. Right here on the old kisser. One teensy little peck right here on the old pecker." She dissolved into soggy giggles.

"One kiss and then you'll go to sleep?" he asked.

"I swear." She sketched a messy cross over her

chest. "Cross my heart and hope to die. Stick a needle—"

"Shut up, Molly."

He covered her wet lips with his. Somebody gave a deep-throated moan, and Dan was fairly certain it was Molly, although it could quite easily have come from him. Her mouth melted at his touch, and her tongue slid against his, sending hot sparks throughout his bloodstream.

"Molly," he breathed.

"Don't stop."

For a moment, as his hand moved up under her soft tunic, up over her delicate ribs, Dan didn't think he could stop. The satin and lace of her bra barely disguised the firm warmth of her breast. His teeth practically ached to test its succulent delights. Lucky for him that Molly lurched sideways just then.

"Dizzy," she whispered.

Dan was, too, but not from the Chianti. "Here. Lie down." He settled her head against the pillows.

"That's better," she sighed. "Don't go. I'll be better in a minute."

She was sound asleep in a minute, and Dan lay beside her, knowing that, at least for this night, his dreams would be good ones, filled with sweet, seductive Molly.

Chapter 5

Molly woke up by degrees. First there was a slight consciousness, a pale dawning, accompanied by something that felt like a hatchet buried in her head. Then there was a vague but not unpleasant memory of wine and red-and-white-checked tablecloths. Finally, after she pried open her eyes, there was the stunning realization that she hadn't slept alone. Dan was snoring peacefully just a few inches away.

My God! She shot to a sitting position only to wind up having to hold her head with both hands. A bleak, sidelong glance at the clock on the nightstand confirmed one of her fears. It was nine-thirty. She had overslept by two and a half hours.

Her other fear seemed to be confirmed when Dan ran his hand along her thigh and mumbled, "Good morning."

Molly dropped back onto the pillows and stared up

at the ceiling. "Tell me we didn't," she moaned. "Did we?"

"You were great," Dan said.

"Oh, my God. We did."

He edged up on an elbow, chuckling as he gazed down at her. "Was it as good for you as it was for me?"

"I doubt it," she said. "If it had been, you'd think I'd have even some dim recollection."

"Are you telling me you were faking it? All those cute little gasps? Those soul-wrenching sighs and moans?"

Molly closed her eyes. "Oh, my God."

"Molly," he said, sounding serious now. "Nothing happened. Look. You've still got all your clothes on."

She opened her eyes, lifting her head just enough to see that it was true. She did have all her clothes on. Even her sandals. She wiggled her toes just to make sure they were her own feet and not some figment of her aching imagination. A quick glance revealed that Dan had all his clothes on, too.

"Thank you," she whispered heavenward. After a moment of silence while she pondered the plaster pattern on the ceiling, she asked, "You kissed me, though, didn't you?"

"Well, only because you asked me to."

"Damn." Even as she cursed, she smiled. "And I missed it. Now I'll never know whether Raylene was right or wrong about your world-class status as a kisser."

"You weren't too bad yourself."

"Really?" She let out a mock sigh of relief. "That's a comfort to hear. I'm considerably out of practice."

Dan lifted a lock of her hair, then brushed it against

her cheek. "You probably shouldn't take my word for it, though. I'm pretty rusty myself."

Molly didn't say so, but she found that hard to believe. Her headache suddenly evaporated, and her heart caught in her throat at the prospect of kissing Dan. Not Danny Shackelford, the greatest kisser north of the Rio Grande. But Dan.

"Maybe we could try it again sometime," she suggested. "You know. Just so we don't lose our ability altogether."

He touched her cheek. "We could do that. Sometime."

"I guess we'd be wise to wait until we brushed our teeth, huh?"

"That's always preferable."

Molly was just about to get up and race for the mint-flavored toothpaste when a knock sounded on her front door. Damn. Her headache sprang back. "Buddy Jr.," she said with a sigh. "I'm not sure I'm up to misplaced commas and dangling participles this morning."

"Go to it, teach," he said, giving her a little shove. "You've got to get out of here, anyway. I've got some serious wallpapering to do."

Dan was in serious trouble an hour later when Buddy Jr. stuck his head in the door and mumbled, "Stripping wallpaper, huh?"

"Not so's you'd notice," Dan said irritably. "Whoever put this paper up in here must've used goddamned superglue."

After at least forty-five minutes of trying, he'd managed to pull no more than a square foot of old paper from the walls, and that square foot was scattered in inch-long rips and tears on all four walls. Molly's bedroom looked as if it had been attacked by locusts.

"You need some stripping chemicals," the kid mumbled.

"What?"

Buddy Jr. quit looking at his shoes and eyed Dan instead. "I said you need some stripping chemicals, and then a spackling blade or a good putty knife."

"You know about this stuff, kid?"

"Oh, sure. My mom changes wallpaper about as often as she changes the color of her hair."

Dan could almost feel the warmth from the imaginary lightbulb that suddenly appeared above his head. "How'd you like to make a hundred bucks, Buddy?"

The boy peered into the room with a bit more interest. "Pretty big room," he said. "Probably fourteen by twelve. Lotta wall space, too. And trim. I'd do it for two hundred, I guess."

"Sold!" Dan wanted to hug him. He wanted to fall down at the kid's dirty sneakers and weep. "When can you start?"

"Tomorrow, I guess. I could stop by Cooley's and pick up some stripper. She won't be able to use this room for a while 'cause of the smell and the mess. Is that okay with her?"

"Is what okay with her?" Molly appeared behind Buddy Jr., sounding more skeptical than curious.

"I've just taken on an apprentice," Dan said. "Hell, Molly, in a week you won't even recognize this place."

Molly looked from one ripped portion of her bedroom wall to another and another. "Good," she said.

After Buddy Jr. was gone and Molly drifted back into her office, Dan came to the conclusion that he hadn't been so clever after all. He'd promised the kid two hundred bucks, but he didn't have a clue how he was going to pay him. He had about nineteen dollars in his wallet, his ATM card had disappeared weeks ago, and his checkbook was buried somewhere in the chaos of the Airstream. Even if he could find it, there was no way he wanted to cash a check here in Moonglow that featured his Washington D.C., address so prominently in the corner. It would take about five seconds for that little tidbit of information to get back to Molly.

For a minute he considered calling Bobby in Houston. Hell, Dan was on the job, wasn't he? The service could damn well come through with some petty cash for an emergency. But then, considering what his record looked like right now, Dan really didn't want any more red flags clipped to it, drawing attention to his deficiencies, monetary or otherwise.

He sighed, pulled off a couple more strips of wallpaper for good measure, then headed down the hall toward Molly's office, where he knocked softly on the door.

"Am I interrupting?" he asked, looking at the text displayed on her computer screen. "I can come back later if..."

"No. It's fine." She leaned back in her chair and ran her fingers through her long blond hair. "Young Buddy certainly didn't inherit his mother's ability with words. I'm not sure I even know how to begin to help him."

"Molly, can I borrow three hundred dollars?" Dan had already decided there was no point in beating around the bush. Anyway, she already considered him pretty much of a deadbeat.

She sat there, her eyes on the screen, not saying anything.

"I'm just a little short at the moment," he added.

"Sure," she said softly. "Three hundred? I can do that."

"I'll pay you back. You don't have to worry about that. I'll sign an IOU, if you want to write one out. In fact, I insist."

"I don't have to, Dan. I trust you."

You shouldn't, he thought. And not just about the money, either.

She smiled up at him. "I can write you a check, or if you'd rather, I'll just go down to the bank and get you the cash."

"That'd probably be better," he said. "God only knows the stories that would start up with a check. If I know anything about Moonglow, I'd say it would take about two, maybe three hours for word to get around that I was blackmailing you or something."

"Impossible," she said with a not-so-convincing little laugh. "I don't have any secrets."

"Yeah. Me, neither." Dan's laugh was just about as convincing. "What you see is what you get."

"That's a lot of money, Ms. Hansen."

The teller's nameplate read "Doris Breedlove" and the woman was peering at Molly over her glasses as if she'd just been handed a scribbled note demanding all the cash in her drawer.

"Let me just check your balance."

While Doris Breedlove's fingers tapped at her keyboard, Molly said, "Fourteen hundred sixty-five dollars and eighty-five cents."

"Yep. That's what it is, all right. Most folks come in here without any notion what they've got in their accounts. You're a right smart cookie."

"Well, I should be. I…" Molly stopped herself before she mentioned her Ph.D. in business administration. "I'm real careful when it comes to money," she said instead.

"Good girl. Now, how do you want that? Twenties all right?"

"That'll be fine."

Molly watched the teller count out the bills, make an entry on her keyboard and then recount the money, slowly, in a hushed voice, for Molly's benefit.

"Do you want an envelope for that, hon?" Doris asked.

"No, thanks." Molly folded the bills and stashed them in her bag.

"You have a nice day, now, you hear?"

When she stepped outside into the bright sunlight, however, Molly saw the sheriff's cruiser parked not far from the bank's front door, and she immediately sensed that her day wasn't going to be quite as "nice" as Doris had wished.

Gil Watson hauled his bulk out from behind the steering wheel. He gave his cap a little nudge. "Afternoon, Miss Hansen. Fine day, isn't it?"

"Hello, Sheriff Watson. Yes, it's lovely." At least it had been.

"Everything going all right at your place, ma'am?"

"Fine and dandy," she said cheerfully.

"Danny making pretty good headway on those repairs?"

"Oh, my, yes." Not that it's any business of yours, buster, she thought. Who did he think he was, anyway, the decor police?

"Glad to hear it." He touched the brim of his cap again. "You just let me or my deputy know if you have any problems, now, you hear?"

That just about did it. Molly crossed her arms. "Problems?"

Gil Watson grinned as if he'd been just dying to elaborate on his grave concerns. "Well, you're new to Moonglow, so you probably don't know that Danny Shackelford wasn't exactly one of our leading citizens when he resided here."

"That was twenty years ago, Sheriff."

"Yes, ma'am. It's been my experience that folks don't change all that much."

"You might try giving him the benefit of the doubt, you know."

"Yes, ma'am. Well, if you say he's doing a fine job, then I guess I will have to change my opinion, won't I?"

"I guess you will," she said with a snort. "Have a nice day, Sheriff."

Molly had to restrain herself from stomping away from the big lout. As irritated as she was with him, she couldn't help but worry about what the man had said. Dan wasn't doing a bang-up job with the repairs on her house. In fact, he was doing such a lousy job that he'd just had to appeal to a sixteen-year-old kid for help. Some handyman. But it made absolutely no sense to her that he'd pass himself off as one if that wasn't the case.

Of course, he couldn't very well make a living by passing himself off as the greatest kisser north of the Rio Grande, could he?

Or maybe he could, she thought, suddenly aware of the three hundred dollars tucked in her purse. Maybe he just could.

Dan was under the kitchen sink when Molly returned home. In her absence, he'd taken a quick look at his "borrowed" home-repair manual, and decided that fixing the leak under the sink would be a cinch.

Only it wasn't. He had no idea how he'd made it worse, but now what had formerly been a soundless drop per minute had increased to a definite, even loud *plip, plip, plip.*

"Oh, good. You're fixing the sink." Molly's voice had a certain amount of relief in it.

"Yep," he said, wincing as he took another cold *plip* on his cheek. "I might have to pick up another wrench, though. This one's not quite right for the job. You got something I can put down here in the meantime to catch the drips?"

"Sure."

A second later Molly's hand appeared over his head, clutching a saucer.

"Uh. I was thinking of something a little bigger than that," Dan said rather sheepishly. "You got a bucket or something?"

"A bucket! Oh, my God. Is it worse?"

"Just a little." He slid out from beneath the cabinet, grinning up at her. "No problem, though. I just need a bigger wrench."

She rolled her eyes, then handed him a dish towel. Snapped it at him, actually. "Here. You're all wet."

Dan dabbed the towel at his face and neck. "How was beautiful downtown Moonglow?" he asked.

"Wonderful," she answered, pushing him aside in order to shove a bucket under the sink. "I had a little run-in with your old friend, Gil Watson. He sends his regards."

Dan snorted. "I'll bet."

"The guy's really on your case, you know that,

Dan?'' she said indignantly. ''I'd complain if I were you.''

He laughed. ''Who should I complain to, Molly? Mayor Fyler? He probably has a lower opinion of me than Gil.''

''Well, I don't know. But it just isn't right that the man keeps acting like you're Public Enemy Number One.''

Dan shrugged. ''My coming back is probably the biggest thing that's happened in law enforcement here in the past two decades. Don't worry about it. I'm not.'' He gestured toward the sink. ''I'm more worried about how I'm going to stop that leak.''

''Plumbing really isn't one of your strong suits, huh?''

Her comment, uttered with more kindness than sarcasm, still managed to find its mark. The truth of it was that Dan wasn't sure he had any strong suits left, and he wasn't all that eager to be put to the test.

''Oh, I almost forgot.'' Molly picked up the handbag she had tossed on the kitchen table and stuck her hand inside. ''I got the three hundred in twenties,'' she said, handing the little wad to him. ''I hope that's all right.''

If his confidence had been wobbling only a moment before, it practically took a nosedive now.

''Thanks.'' He shoved the bills in his pocket without looking at them or even counting them. ''I'll pay you back just as soon as I can.''

''Don't worry about it.'' She turned her head to look longingly at the sink. ''Well, it doesn't look as if I'll be able to do much hand-washing today, so I'd better make a trip to the Sudsy Dudsy.''

''Is that place still in business?''

Molly nodded. ''As long as I have to go, want me to take along a few things for you?''

His entire wardrobe, Dan thought. ''Let me just get some things together and I'll come with you.''

Molly stared in awe at the amount of clothing and bed linens Dan was able to stuff into a single machine while she carefully sorted her own lights and darks and delicates. He poured in an unmeasured stream of her liquid detergent, then patted his pockets for change.

She reached into her skirt pocket and handed him two quarters.

''Oh, no. Thanks, but no thanks, Molly. I'm not going any deeper in debt than I already am.''

''I don't think the change machine takes twenties,'' she said, holding the quarters out to him again.

''Well then, I'll just run into Cooley's and get some change.'' He aimed a finger at his crammed washing machine. ''Watch that, now. Don't let anybody run off with my stuff.''

Instead, Molly watched Dan as he pushed out the door and passed by the laundromat's big front window. He moved like an athlete, she suddenly realized, with a graceful kind of restrained power in his stride. Even the slight limp from the sprain didn't altogether mar the impression of strength and coordination.

Well, maybe he was a marvel of speed and grace on a football field or a tennis court, she thought, but the man was still a ten-thumbed klutz when it came to anything inside a house.

Almost anything. The memory of the kiss she had missed the night before came back to haunt her. It had been a long time since she'd been kissed. Nearly a year. She thought back to the last time she had seen Ethan in her hospital room. He'd hardly been able to make contact with her through all the bandages, but even so, his rather thin, usually tightly compressed lips never did have Molly seeing stars or feeling the earth reel beneath her feet.

The letters Ethan wrote her so regularly, imploring her to get in touch, seemed far more passionate than he had ever been in the flesh. She felt another little twinge of guilt for not responding to those pleas, but by the time she had put two quarters in each of her three machines and started them up, the twinge had all but passed.

Molly was sorely tempted to put a couple quarters in Dan's machine, too, otherwise they'd be here all day. Just as she was reaching into her pocket, she caught a glimpse of Dan outside the window. His dark glasses were lodged atop his head and he was leaning against a parking meter, laughing it up with an astonishingly beautiful woman with short blond hair and unbelievably long legs.

She couldn't claim to know everyone in Moonglow, but she at least thought she had seen everyone. But not this woman. Dan certainly seemed to know her, though. And there wasn't any doubt that she knew him and was eager to resume just where they had left off twenty years ago.

There was a big lipstick smudge on Dan's cheek when he finally ambled back into the Sudsy Dudsy, but rather than the lecherous grin on his face that Molly was expecting, he looked almost grim.

"Another satisfied member of the Danny Shackelford Fan Club?" she asked, arching an eyebrow.

He didn't answer but shoved two coins in his machine to start the first cycle, then, when it didn't start up immediately, he gave it a good thump with his fist and followed it with a solid kick.

"Sorry I asked," Molly said.

Dan angled his head toward her. "That was Linda Marie Chapman," he said. When Molly merely stared at him blankly, he added, "Better known today by her married name of Linda Marie Watson."

Molly felt her blank stare solidify in a kind of horrified mask. "Watson, as in Gil Watson?"

Dan nodded. "That's Gil, as in 'You better not even look at my woman if you want to stay alive' Watson."

"Oh, jeez."

"Yeah," Dan said through clenched teeth. "Oh, jeez."

As was her habit, Molly had brought a book to read while her clothes washed and dried. For his part, Dan kept a grim silence with one eye on the garments tumbling in the dryer and the other eye on Main Street, probably expecting to see the sheriff's cruiser pull up at any moment.

He didn't seem any more relaxed two hours later when he helped her carry her clean laundry into the house. He went immediately into the living room to check for any calls that had come during their absence.

"Godammit," Molly heard him mutter on her way to the bedroom. She dropped her basket and went to see what the problem was.

"Who called?" she asked.

"Linda Watson. Twice." He swore again. "And Raylene."

"I wonder what she wanted."

"If you mean Raylene, I have no idea. If you mean Linda, I'll give you three guesses."

"Actually, I meant Raylene," Molly said. "But if I

had to guess about Linda, my first guess would be sex. My second guess would be great sex. And my third would be really great sex. Would I be right?''

He curled his lip and practically growled. "Try clandestine, illicit or lethal sex. Little wonder Gil's always prowling around town."

"Little wonder," Molly murmured, picking up the receiver and punching in Raylene's number, hoping the hairdresser wasn't calling to warn them about the sheriff.

As it turned out, however, Raylene wanted to know if Buddy Jr. could begin his wallpaper stripping job this evening rather than the next day. It seemed the boy was more than a little eager to get his hands on Dan's two hundred dollars. Molly told her that was fine, but as soon as she hung up, she realized she had just graciously ousted herself from her own bedroom, at least for tonight. The fumes from the stripping probably weren't going to make sleeping on the couch very pleasant, either.

She looked at Dan and smiled. "I've never slept in a trailer before."

Molly had never felt so content as she sat sipping a lemonade and watching Dan tending the hot dogs on the grill. The sun was going down, turning her little corner of Moonglow a luscious gold. A breeze overhead riffled the leaves of the live oak. She hadn't felt this calm in a long time. Maybe never.

"I hope the potato salad doesn't taste like wallpaper stripper," she said. "It's permeating everything in the house."

"Guess that means young Buddy knows what he's doing, then," Dan said.

His green eyes were mellow from the sunset hues, even if his disposition seemed less so. Molly assumed he wasn't thrilled about sharing his trailer with her. She, on the other hand, was looking forward to it, even though she was a bit nervous. It was a little like anticipating a date with the wildest boy in class. Maybe, she thought, she'd finally find out about his reputation as a kisser. Maybe, she thought, Moonglow wasn't such a horrible place after all. How could it be when she found herself suddenly so happy here?

"What are you grinning at?" Dan was staring at her, his head tilted quizzically to one side.

"Was I?" She sipped her lemonade, using the glass to hide the smile she couldn't suppress. You'd have thought she was in Manhattan, about to dine on rack of lamb with a gorgeous investment broker, rather than in Moonglow and about to eat hot dogs with an itinerant handyman.

No. Not just a handyman. Dan. In some strange way she felt as if she'd known him forever.

It wasn't like her at all to become so mesmerized, so infatuated, by a man so quickly. Use your head. Slow down, she told herself. Stop, for heaven's sake.

Only Molly wasn't listening. At least, not to her head.

"Well, come on in if you're coming," Dan said an hour after dinner, not bothering to disguise his irritation. Other than himself, nobody had been inside his trailer before. He'd grown oblivious to the clutter, but he dreaded seeing the shambles of his life through somebody else's eyes. Through Molly's eyes.

She couldn't very well have slept in her house, though. That was obvious after Buddy Jr., wearing a fumigator's mask and CD headphones, had started applying the stripper solution to the walls. And, as Molly had predicted, her potato salad had tasted suspiciously like the chemical fumes in the house. Other than letting her sleep in his trailer, Dan's only choice would have been accompanying her to the nearest motel, the Sweet Dreams Inn, out on Route 12. If memory served, that dive was even worse than his Airstream.

He turned on a battery-powered hanging lantern, illuminating the messy interior, then discreetly checked to make sure the drawer, where he'd stashed his gun, as well as his badge and Marshals Service ID, was still securely locked.

"Mi casa es su casa," he said in his best Tex-Mex accent when she stepped hesitantly over the threshold, wearing a tightly cinched plaid flannel robe and clutching the pillow she'd brought with her as if it were a little girl's teddy bear.

"This is cozy," she said, gazing around as if she'd just arrived on another planet. "Oh, look. There's even a little kitchen in here."

"It's purely for decoration," Dan said, using his foot to push a pile of clean laundry aside.

"A refrigerator, too!" She opened its small square door. "But how does it run if you're not hooked up to electricity?"

"Portable gas tank on the front of the trailer."

She opened the door to the bathroom, glanced around, then closed it again. "Reminds me of an airplane."

"Same principle," he said while he shook out a clean sheet for the air mattress. "Only you don't get Mile High Club privileges."

Molly raised an eyebrow. "You'd know about that, I'm sure."

Dan tucked the sheet tightly under the edges of the mattress, then reached for another. "You take this," he said, "and I'll just bed down here on the floor."

"That doesn't seem fair, Dan. When I invited myself, I didn't intend to be putting you out of your bed. I'll sleep on the floor. I don't mind. Really."

"Well, *I* mind." He smoothed the top sheet out, then snapped a blanket over it. "There. All set."

When Molly's mouth set in a stubborn line, he took her by the shoulders and sat her down on the mattress. "My trailer, my rules," he told her, reaching up to snap off the lantern.

She grumbled a little as she fought her way out of her robe in the close quarters, then Dan heard her legs sliding between the sheets and had to warn himself immediately to forget the sound of that sleek flesh colliding with the cool cotton, and the way she kind of thumped around, her backside carving out a comfy, warm niche in the mattress while her head settled deeply into her pillow.

He found himself looking forward to sleeping in those same sheets tomorrow night and nights to come, breathing in the sweet scents of Molly's lotions and perfumes. A pretty pitiful state, he thought, when a man was fantasizing about sleeping in an empty bed while a woman like Molly was currently filling that very bed.

Dan sighed roughly and shifted positions atop the sleeping bag he'd slung out on the floor.

"I really wish you'd change places with me," Molly whispered.

"This is fine. Go to sleep."

"I don't think I can while I'm feeling so guilty," she said. "It really isn't fair at all that you—"

"Shh," he hissed, levering up on his elbows and cocking his head toward the window.

"I'm serious, Dan. It isn't—"

"Shh." He sat all the way up, leaned to his left and clamped his hand over her mouth. "Be quiet, Molly, will you? I think I hear somebody outside."

"Who?" she croaked.

No sooner was the word out of her mouth than there was a soft rapping on the trailer's door and a woman's voice calling, "Danny, are you in there?"

Dan recognized the voice immediately, and let out a blue stream of whispered curses.

"Who is it?" Molly asked.

"Linda Watson." He cursed again.

Molly made a little gulping sound. "The sheriff's wife?"

"Da-a-anny," the woman cooed. It sounded as if she were running her fingernails along the Airstream's aluminum siding. "I know you're in there."

"What are you going to do?" Molly asked.

Dan could only shrug. Other than pretending he was deaf or dead asleep or just plain dead, he didn't have a clue.

"Da-a-anny."

"All right," Molly snapped. "That does it. I'm going out there and tell that female tomcat to get lost. Where's my robe?"

Her hand slashed out in the darkness, clipping Dan's jaw. He thought about restraining her, but then decided against it. If the big Crown Victoria cruiser was lurking somewhere nearby, better Gil Watson should see Molly confronting his wife than Dan being confronted by her. Granted, it put Molly's reputation at stake, but having been in law enforcement for as long as he had, Dan knew the degree of damage a small-town sheriff was permitted to get away with, and he really didn't feel like having a bruised kidney or a couple of broken ribs at the moment. In the end, that might be more detrimental to Molly than a bruised reputation.

"Go for it, Rocky," he said, lying back down and cocking his arms behind his head.

Molly swung open the door of the trailer and stomped down its little stairs. She cinched her flannel robe tighter as she looked around for Linda Watson, who was leaning casually against the rear bumper, striking a match to light the cigarette that dangled from her lips.

In the flare of the flame, Molly got a good look at the woman, from her big gold hoop earrings to the gold lamé sash at the waist of her white jumpsuit, all the way to her gold sandals. She couldn't help but think how much Raylene would have loved the outfit. My Lord.

"Excuse me," Molly said. "People are trying to sleep here, if you don't mind."

Linda shook out the match and dropped it. "Oh, I don't mind, hon. Tell Danny I'm here, will you?"

Molly felt her jaw come unhinged and her mouth drop open idiotically. That hadn't been the response she was expecting. She'd had visions of the Watson woman mumbling an embarrassed apology once she realized that Dan already had female companionship, then slinking away into the night. Any decent person would, after all. Instead, Linda Watson stood her ground, regarding Molly as if she were as much competition as a bowl of chopped liver.

"Tell him," Linda said, gesturing toward the door.

"I won't tell him any such thing," Molly replied. "He's in bed. I mean, he's not awake."

Linda blew out a stream of smoke, then glanced at her wide gold watch. "At ten-thirty? What'd you do, honey, put him to sleep?"

Molly's mouth gaped wider. Ordinarily, she wasn't a person who lost her temper easily. She liked to think of herself as calm and reasonable, cool and completely logical. But suddenly something sort of ripped loose inside her.

"Put him to sleep?" She laughed. Well, it was closer to a cackle. "Maybe I wore him out, *honey.*"

Now it was the other woman's turn to look surprised. She recovered fairly quickly, however, glaring at Molly hard before flicking her half-smoked cigarette onto the ground so close to the hem of Molly's flannel robe that she had to jump back.

"Never mind," Linda said, then raised her voice in the direction of the Airstream's open window to add, "Danny can find me down at the Blue Moon whenever he's in the mood. See you around, honey."

"Not if I see you first," Molly muttered childishly at the woman's sashaying backside. "Witch," she added under her breath.

She slammed back into the trailer.

"I can't believe that woman!" she shrieked. "Did you hear her? Did you hear what she said?"

"I heard," Dan said.

He didn't sound too outraged, though, Molly thought. More than anything, he sounded amused.

"I don't know what you think is so damned funny," she snarled as she felt her way through the darkness toward the air mattress.

Somewhere near her knees, Dan chuckled. "You wore me out, Molly?"

She located the little bed and flopped on it. "Well,

what was I supposed to say to somebody who was looking at me like I was about as sexy as a dead armadillo on the side of the road?''

"I think you're sexy," he said.

Molly blinked. "You do?"

"Uh-huh. Way more than a dead armadillo on the side of the road." He yawned. The sleeping bag rustled as he turned on his side. "G'night, Molly."

Chapter 6

Dan pressed the accelerator to the floor on his way to the little town of Idella just across the county line. It had been a while since he'd unwound the big engine in the BMW, and the raw speed felt as good as an ancient brandy blazing down his throat. He blew by mile after mile of mesquite and prickly pear and one dead armadillo by the side of the road.

The sight of that unfortunate critter made Dan smile, almost against his will. It was because of Molly—the sexiest woman he'd ever known, although he hadn't told her so—that he was beating a fast path to a secluded pharmacy for the protection he swore he wouldn't need. Telling himself, again and again, that you didn't take a woman like Molly to bed unless you had a lot more to offer her than a few wild and steamy nights wasn't doing much good to cool his ardor. Sadly, nothing was going to accomplish that except to get this damned assignment over and get away from temptation. Away from Molly. Far away.

He'd left her this morning in the safe young hands of Buddy Jr., not that he expected any terrorists to emerge from the woodwork. In fact, what Dan was really expecting at any moment was notification from the service that the crisis was over.

He could already hear Bobby's laid-back voice when he called him with the news. "All's well, amigo. Time to quit screwing around and get back to some real work. You ready?"

Was he ready? As Dan dropped back to the speed limit on the fringes of Idella, he was glad that today wasn't the day he had to make that particular decision. Once inside the pharmacy, it was all he could do to decide which protection to buy from a huge and multi-colored array.

He tossed the turquoise-and-black package as casually as possible on the counter, then studied a display of mini flashlights and key chains while the female clerk rang up his purchase. Still without making eye contact, Dan handed over a twenty dollar bill.

"You look so familiar," the clerk said. "You're Daniel Shackelford, aren't you?"

A silent little sigh broke in his throat. He thought he'd be safe in Idella. What did he have to do? Wear a wig and a pair of thick glasses with a false nose? Now he noticed that the clerk was a pretty brunette with frank gray eyes, probably not too much younger than he was. He offered up a quick little prayer that he hadn't slept with her.

"I don't mean to be intruding," she continued, "it's just that if you are Daniel Shackelford, you were one of my mother's favorite students."

"Mrs. Booth?" he asked, astonished. "The history teacher?"

"Right. Mildred Booth."

"It should have clicked as soon as you said Daniel," he said. "Mrs. Booth is the only person in the world who ever called me that. How is she? Still teaching?"

"Oh, no. She retired about eighteen years ago. She's seventy-eight now, but still going strong."

Dan couldn't help but chuckle. "Tough lady, your mom. She could turn a kid's blood to cherry Popsicles with one of her stares."

"Don't I know? Remember, I had to live with her." She handed Dan his receipt and change. "It was good seeing you, Daniel. I can't wait to tell my mother. She'd be thrilled if you stopped by for a chat. She's still in the same house in Moonglow. Right behind the elementary school."

"I'll do that," he said, shoving the change in his pocket. "Good seeing you."

"You, too." She held out a small plastic bag. "Here. Don't forget your…um…your purchase."

On the drive back to Moonglow, Dan held to the speed limit and thought about Mildred Booth, the only teacher who'd ever treated him like a human being instead of a Shackelford. He could still picture her, a mountain of a woman whose face could harden like Mount Rushmore or soften like a pale pink rose. Mrs. Booth hadn't just taught him history. She'd taught him he was a worthy individual. It was because of her belief in his abilities that he'd gone on to college after the Marine Corps, and it was her letter of recommendation that had probably been at least partly responsible for his acceptance in the U.S. Marshals Service. If it hadn't been for Mrs. Booth, he thought, he probably would be an itinerant handyman right now, or worse.

Too bad he couldn't stop by and see her while he was working undercover. Too bad he couldn't take Molly to meet her. The two of them would really hit it off.

On the other hand, he wasn't so sure he wanted to see his iron-clad mentor now that his career was on the skids. She'd see right through him, too. She always did. He didn't think he could bear to see one of her disappointed looks.

When he arrived at Molly's, he stashed his purchase in the trailer, locking the condoms in the drawer with his badge and gun, before going into the house to check on Buddy Jr.'s progress. Amazingly enough, the kid had two walls completely stripped and was just beginning on a third.

"Nice work," Dan said from the doorway, squinting as the fumes got to his eyes.

Buddy Jr. uttered a muffled thanks from behind his fumigator's mask.

"Where's Molly?" Dan asked.

"Dunno. She said something about the library."

Dan slapped the doorjamb and muttered a curse. He'd told her not to go anywhere until he got back, hadn't he? But then, in all honesty, why would any woman do what her resident repairman told her unless it suited her mood? Dammit. He was half tempted to tell Molly the truth just to protect her pretty neck.

On the other hand, since that pretty neck apparently wasn't in any danger, he'd just keep up the stupid charade. If she barely bought his act as a handyman, she'd probably fall down laughing if he told her he was a federal agent.

* * *

Marly Eversole waved from the front desk when he walked into the library. "Looking for Molly Hansen?" she asked in a loud whisper.

Dan nodded, wondering bleakly if the whole town already knew about the incident with Linda Watson last night.

"She's back in the stacks," Marly said, pointing to the back room crammed with shelves where Dan had filched the home-repair book a few days before. It occurred to him he'd have to sneak it back pretty soon before he left town. Or maybe he'd keep it as a souvenir and just send Marly a nice-size check to cover his transgression.

"Thanks, Marly."

He found Molly sitting cross-legged on the floor, paging through an old *Moonglow Monitor* yearbook.

"Hey," she said softly when he settled beside her. "Look at this." She flipped back a few pages.

Dan rolled his eyes. He didn't even remember looking like the gawky kid in his senior picture. "Looks like an alien," he muttered.

"You've improved considerably," Molly said. She flipped a few more pages. "Here. Read what it says under 'Where will they be in twenty years?'"

He scanned the list for his name and read aloud, "'Serving ninety-nine to life.' Yeah. That's about right. I probably disappointed a hell of a lot of people showing up here after all these years without hand and leg cuffs." He narrowed his gaze on Molly's face, irritated that she'd dredged up his past once again. "What are you doing with this, anyway? Nobody looks at other people's high school yearbooks, Molly."

She smiled, undaunted by his glare. "I was just curious. I wanted to see what all the fuss was about way back then.'' She thumbed back to his photograph and traced a finger over it. ''I think you were pretty cute.''

''Cute,'' Dan grumbled. ''Just some idiot kid who imagined himself an outlaw. It's a wonder I didn't wind up serving ninety-nine to life.''

He hauled himself up off the floor and held out a hand. ''Are you ready to get out of here?''

''I guess.''

Molly closed the book and slid it back onto the shelf before she took Dan's hand and let him pull her to her feet. Once she was standing, though, she didn't back away. There was barely an inch between them when she tipped her grinning face up to his.

''I'll bet you made out like a bandit back here in the stacks,'' she said. ''Where I grew up, the library was always the best place for stealing a few kisses.''

''Oh, yeah?'' Dan lifted an eyebrow. ''Hung out at the library a lot, did you?''

''Well…'' she drawled, ''I studied, too.''

''Uh-huh. When you weren't sneaking back into the stacks to be kissed.'' As he spoke, his hand rose to cup her neck beneath her long blond hair. ''I know your type, Molly Hansen.''

''Do you?''

Her face moved closer to his, and Dan wasn't sure if that was his doing or hers. About the only thing he was certain of was that her smile had somehow changed from simple amusement to pure seduction, and that her blue eyes had taken on a darker, sensuous cast.

He swore softly as his mouth came down on hers, then it took all of ten seconds for the kiss to ignite and burn completely out of their control. While his hand was angling up under her loose cotton top, Molly's right leg was climbing up his left. A moment later, after he'd reached around for a handful of her backside, Molly's other leg came up, clamping around his hips, while her arms encircled his neck.

Dan couldn't get close enough and neither could she, but Molly's back was already jammed against a bookshelf, and while he moved against her, books started toppling onto the floor. A few at first, like a gentle rain, then more, volume after volume, harder and harder. Molly didn't seem to notice. Dan noticed, but he didn't have the presence of mind to care.

"What in the world is going on back there?" Marly Eversole's voice carried through the stacks.

Dan tore his mouth away from Molly's. Her legs were still locked around his hips. "It's okay, Marly," he called. "We're just doing a little research. I think we found what we wanted."

"Well, I hope so, Danny," the librarian called back. "We're closing in five minutes."

Molly was trying her best to stifle a giggle in the collar of Dan's shirt, but she wasn't all that successful.

"This is a library, people," Marly said just before her footsteps echoed on their way back to the main desk.

By now Molly had unwound herself from him and stood blinking at the book-strewn aisle.

"Some kiss," Dan said.

Molly shook her head. "Some mess."

She really had gotten herself into a mess, Molly thought as she and Dan walked the several blocks back to her house. Good grief. She hadn't even been able to look Marly Eversole in the eye. She'd just sort of slunk out the library's front door after she and Dan had re-

placed all the books that their sudden, explosive encounter had sent toppling to the floor.

Nothing like that had ever happened to her before.
Or maybe, more accurately, no*body* had ever happened
to her before the way Dan Shackelford had happened
back there in the stacks. Admittedly, it was she who'd
come on to him first, but she'd really only expected a
brief sample from the greatest kisser north of the Rio
Grande. She hadn't expected her entire body to start
fizzing and then to explode out of her control.

"What are you thinking, Molly?" Dan asked, breaking the silence between them.

"Oh, nothing." *Liar. Liar.*

"Really?" He sounded surprised, perhaps even disappointed.

"Really." *Pants on fire.* My God, she thought,
wasn't *that* the truth?

"You know what I was thinking?" he asked.

"No." She tried to sound casual, as if she could care
less about what was on Dan's mind after the fireworks
in the library.

"I was thinking maybe we should cool it. Not that I
didn't like kissing you." He reached for her hand and
brought it to his mouth for a quick brush of his lips.
"Believe it or not, Molly, nothing quite like that ever
happened to me before."

Molly was inclined to believe it. How, she wondered,
could any human being sustain repeated sexual encoun-
ters like that and not be reduced to a little pile of smoking ashes? "Me, neither," she said.

Dan laughed. "Really? And here I was thinking you
shimmied up every man who kissed you as if he were
a telephone pole."

She looked away, feeling her face ablaze with color.

"I'm just teasing you," he said. "I just think we need to be careful. Me, anyway. I'm not exactly in a position to get involved with anybody right now."

Molly sucked in a breath. He must be married! Why hadn't she considered that from the get-go? Men as gorgeous as Dan were never single. Not in her experience, anyway. His itinerant lifestyle had misled her. She felt like such a jerk.

"I'm really not in any position to get involved myself," she said. "There's a man...well, we've been sort of engaged for a long time."

"Oh, yeah?"

She couldn't tell if Dan sounded relieved or irritated, but there was definitely an emotional timbre in his voice.

"Yes," she said. "I probably should have mentioned it before." *The way you should have at least hinted that there might be a Mrs. Dan Shackelford, you creep.*

"All the more reason to cool it, then, don't you think?" he said.

"Definitely." Molly forced a little laugh, hoping it didn't sound too brittle. "Besides, without a decent bookstore in Moonglow, I really don't want to risk losing my library card."

Dan knew it was too much to hope that Buddy Jr. would be finished with the wallpaper stripping by the time he and Molly got back from the library, and that the house would be free of fumes, allowing Molly to resume sleeping in her own bed. No such luck. The fumes just about bowled them over the moment they entered the house, and the kid still had a whole wall to go, plus nerve enough to ask for an advance on his two hundred dollars.

Dan took five bills from his wallet. "You pretty sure you'll be finished with the stripping tomorrow?" he asked the boy.

"Oh, sure. Tomorrow, easy. Then it'll be another day or two for the place to start smelling okay again."

"Great," Dan said.

Great. Another couple nights with Molly in his trailer was just what he was looking forward to, especially now that she'd divulged her engagement. Once again, Dan found himself wondering about the guy's intelligence, letting a woman like Molly just disappear from his life.

He went into the kitchen to empty the bucket from under the sink only to find that Molly had already done it. She was just putting the bucket back when he came in.

"Still dripping?" he asked, earning a pretty frosty look from Our Lady of the Sink. He couldn't wait to see her expression when he told her about the perpetual fumes. "Buddy says he'll be done tomorrow, but the smell will take another day or two to dissipate."

"Maybe I'll just go to a motel," she said.

"That doesn't make sense. Not when you can sleep for free in the Airstream. Unless, of course, you think your fiancé would object."

"Actually, I was thinking more about the objections of Mrs. Shackelford."

He blinked. "Who?"

"Mrs. Shackelford. You know. Your wife?"

"My…?" He laughed. "I don't have a wife. Where'd you get that idea?"

Now it was Molly who was blinking. "Well, you said you weren't in a position to get involved, so I naturally assumed…"

"Wait a minute." Dan held up his hand. "Wait just

a minute. I said I'm not in a position to get involved because I'm me and you're you. Not because I'm married.''

The hint of a smile passed across her mouth. ''You're not?''

''No. Never have been, either.''

''Oh.'' There was definitely a smile now, but Dan wasn't sure what it meant. ''Well, that's different, then,'' she said with a little shrug. ''I accept your generous invitation.''

''What about this fiancé of yours?''

''He won't mind,'' she said breezily. A bit too breezily in Dan's opinion.

''I meant what I said, Molly, about not being in a position to get involved,'' he told her sternly.

''Dan, I really don't think sleeping on your air mattress qualifies as *involved,* do you? For heaven's sake.''

Having said that, she walked past him with a few little clucks of her tongue, leaving Dan to wonder whether or not she thought wrapping those long legs of hers around a guy's waist and making him half crazy constituted involvement.

For the rest of the day, Molly wasn't sure whether she was avoiding Dan or vice versa. She took her laptop out on the front porch, but spent most of the time thinking about Dan rather than working.

The fact that he wasn't married shouldn't have made such a difference to her. If anything, it should have served as a warning that this was not a man who was prone to settling down or establishing any meaningful sort of relationship.

How had he phrased it? *He wasn't in a position to get involved.* Well, neither was she, Molly thought.

There was no way she could have anything but a superficial relationship as long as she was a protected witness with no past and nothing in her present but lies. She wasn't looking for a serious involvement, and if she were, it certainly wouldn't be with an itinerant handyman.

She didn't know what she was looking for, actually. She just kept thinking about that kiss in the library. That mind-altering, body-slamming kiss. The mere memory of it did funny things to her stomach and made her toes curl and her fingers hit a succession of nonsensical letters on the keyboard.

In an effort to get her mind off Dan, Molly wandered into the kitchen to empty the bucket under the sink. After she poured it into the bathtub, she peeked in the bedroom to see how Buddy Jr. was coming along.

"Well, you're getting there," she said.

The boy took off his earphones and pulled the black mask down from his face. "Did you say something, Ms. Hansen?"

"I said you're coming right along, Buddy. Good job."

"Oh. Thanks." He looked down at the floor a moment. "Say, I was just wondering. I couldn't help but notice that the doorjamb in the bathroom is all busted. You got somebody to fix that for you? 'Cause if you don't, I'd be happy to make a little more cash."

She started to say that Dan was going to fix it, but changed her mind. Raylene would be thrilled to have her son working hard and staying out of the pool hall. "How much would you charge?" she asked.

Buddy shrugged. "Wouldn't take much lumber or paint. I'd do it for seventy-five bucks."

"Okay. You've got a deal."

"Great." He put his earphones on again, settled the mask over his mouth and nose, and went back to stripping paper.

Molly took the bucket back into the kitchen and shoved it under the sink, wondering if she should hire Buddy Jr. to fix the leaky pipe as well. She wondered if whoever in the Marshals Service had hired Dan would be checking with her afterward to see if he'd done a satisfactory job, and the thought almost made her laugh out loud.

What choice would she have except to tell them "Quite satisfactory. The man has wonderful hands."

Those hands, she couldn't help but notice when she walked outside, were busily washing the black BMW. Anything to avoid real work, she thought churlishly.

"Want some help?" she asked, squinting at the bright sunlight reflecting off the wet chrome on the car.

"No, but I'd like the company."

He gave her one of those smiles that made her stomach do a quick flip, and Molly had to warn herself not to allow her gaze to linger on his appealing mouth. She leaned against the side of the house. A sliver of peeling paint jabbed her arm and reminded her that housepainting also seemed missing from Dan's repertoire of skills.

"How long have you been doing this, Dan?"

"Washing the car?" He aimed the hose at the soapy windshield. "About twenty minutes."

"No, I mean the home-repair racket."

"Racket!" With his free hand he dragged his dark glasses down his nose and glared at Molly. "Are you saying you're not pleased with the progress I'm making on your house?"

"Well..."

"It's moving along," he said defensively. "Home

repair isn't something you do in the blink of an eye, Molly. There's a certain amount of organization in the beginning. A thorough assessment of damage. A proper regard for easily overlooked details.''

"Don't forget the patient accumulation of tools," she said, her tongue firmly in her cheek.

"Exactly."

"And the cautious hiring of sixteen-year-old subcontractors."

"That, too," he said, reaching to scrub a spot on the windshield.

Molly pulled another paint chip from the siding, breaking it into tiny white fragments. "Okay. Tell me the truth. You're not really a handyman, are you?"

He held the hose away from the car and stood there a long moment, as if deep in thought. The silence made Molly nervous. Fearing his answer, she was almost sorry she'd asked in the first place.

"All right," he finally said. "I guess you've figured it out, so I might as well confess. I'm not a handyman, Molly. I lied about that."

She swallowed hard, dreading his next words, wishing she'd just played along. He was handy enough. Besides, what did she care about repairs on a house that wasn't even hers to begin with?

What if he wasn't a handyman, but an ex-convict, maybe an armed robber just out on parole? What if…dear God…what if he were a member of the Red Millennium? No. If that were true, she'd already be dead.

Dan's glasses were back in place now so she couldn't see his eyes when he said somberly, "I'm sorry I lied. Do you forgive me?"

"That depends."

"On what?"

"On what you really are."

He sighed as he gazed down at the running hose, then shifted it from his left hand to his right. "I work for the government, Molly."

She let out a little laugh. "Oh, yeah. Doing what?"

"I'm an itinerant hose inspector." A grin slashed across his mouth as he aimed the nozzle in her direction. "And this one works just fine."

Molly shrieked. She shoved away from the wall and lifted her hands to shield herself, but there was no getting away from the relentless spray. In a matter of seconds, she was soaked.

"You're going to be sorry," she said, laughing as she advanced through the oncoming water. "Quit it, Dan. I can't see."

"You don't have to see. Just trust me. This hose is in perfect working order. I give it my highest approval rating."

Molly lunged for the hose, but Dan changed it to his other hand, moving it out of her reach but still keeping the water directed at her.

"Give me that," she demanded, trying to reach around him. She couldn't see a thing for the soggy hair that was falling over her face.

"Give you this?" He was laughing now. The wretch. "I don't think you're qualified, are you? Do you have a license? A learner's permit? Something with your picture on it?"

With his arm around her shoulder, Dan somehow maneuvered the hose down the front of her shirt, thoroughly dousing whatever dry spots remained.

"That's cold!"

"Good. That speaks well for the insulation. I believe I'll upgrade it from a Double A to a Triple A."

"Uncle!" she screamed. "Uncle! Uncle! Uncle!"

The back door squeaked open and Buddy Jr. called out, "Hey! Are you okay, Ms. Hansen?"

Dan pulled the hose from her shirt just as Molly turned to view her savior. The boy was looking at them with an expression that was part curiosity, part disapproval, as if the two of them were mischievous toddlers.

"Are you okay?" he asked again. "You're all wet."

"No kidding," Molly replied, using both hands to shove her dripping hair from her face.

She could see Buddy Jr. clearly as a result, and could see his expression change significantly. Instead of looking disapproving, the boy began to grin. Molly couldn't imagine why, nor did she know why Dan was suddenly grabbing her shoulders and whirling her around to face him rather than her rescuer.

"What is wrong with you?" she snapped when his arms wound around her and water from the hose started cascading down her back.

"Nothing's wrong with me," he said, his lips close to her ear. "It's you, darlin'. Our young friend just glimpsed the winner of the world-class wet T-shirt contest." Then he called over Molly's head, "She's fine, kid. We're just fooling around. Guess you better get back to work."

"Yeah. Okay." Buddy Jr. didn't sound too enthusiastic, but a second later Molly heard the screen door open and then bang closed again.

"Is he gone?" she whispered into Dan's shoulder.

"Yep. Very reluctantly, too, I might add."

Molly took a small step back, then looked down at the wet cotton fabric that was molded to her chest. She might as well have been naked. "Oh, my God," she moaned. "Look what you did to me, Dan."

He *was* looking, Molly realized, but his intense gaze didn't even come close to being a leer. There was far more hunger than lust in his expression. More elemental need than momentary desire. Her heart took a flying leap into her throat just as Dan dropped the hose and reached out for her, one hand sliding around her waist, the other curving around her neck.

"Molly." Her name came out as a kind of rough growl just before his mouth covered hers.

She was hardly even aware that her right leg was inching up Dan's left until he chuckled softly against her lips.

"You're shimmying again, Molly."

"I can't get close enough to you," she answered with what little breath she had left after the kiss. "I want you, Dan."

He drew back his head and his green eyes burned into hers. "And damn the consequences?"

She bit her lip as she nodded.

When Dan's eyelids sank closed, Molly wasn't sure whether he felt the same way. For a panicky second she was afraid he was going to be reasonable and sane and back in control, all the things she wasn't at the moment. She thought if he rejected her, she'd never be able to look him in the eye again. She'd melt into an indistinct little puddle right here on the driveway. She'd wither and die and...

Dan let out a rough little curse, then he stepped away from her and strode to the faucet on the side of the house where he gave its little wheel a few brusque turns to shut off the water.

"I just hope we both live to regret this," he muttered,

swinging Molly up in his arms and heading for the
trailer.

He let Molly's wet body slide the length of his, but
her feet had hardly touched the trailer floor before those
long legs of hers were inching up his again. He only
stopped kissing her long enough to whisk the wet T-
shirt over her head, then shrug out of his own damp
shirt.

He'd never wanted a woman the way he wanted
Molly. Her mouth was custom-made for his, and he
tried to take his time with those lush lips and that eager
tongue, with her sweet, succulent breasts, with the sensuous swell of her belly and the dip of her navel and
the damp, musky places below.

"Molly. Molly." He heard himself saying her name
like a prayer.

Dear God, if there was salvation to be had, he was
about to find his in her sweet, hot depths.

"Molly."

The only thing Dan regretted was that he had stashed
his little package from the pharmacy in Idella in the
locked drawer where he kept his automatic, necessitat-
ing an abrupt halt to their lovemaking while he floun-
dered for the key. It didn't help that his hands were
shaking when he tried to fit it into the lock.

With the blinds closed tight, it was dark in the trailer.
Hot as hell, too, although that didn't seem to bother or
even deter Molly. Her skin was damp and cool from
her recent dousing, unlike his which felt scalded every
place she touched him with her roving hands and those
long, promising legs.

Neither one of them, it seemed, had any brakes. Or,
if they had, neither one of them chose to use them. They

were like two planets hurtling through blank space, colliding, melding in a sudden, sharp display of fireworks, then falling back to earth. Spent. Completely undone.

Dan exhaled a long, almost languorous sigh as he dropped his head into the damp crook of Molly's neck.

"Oh, my," she whispered.

"Too heavy?" He began to shift to his right, but those lithe legs clamped tighter, keeping him in place.

"Just right," she said with a sigh of her own. "Don't move."

"I wasn't sure if I could, anyway."

She laughed softly, but Dan wasn't kidding. He couldn't recall ever having such an intense sexual experience. Only part of it was because of his recent abstention. The rest—most of it—was pure Molly.

"That was fast," he murmured a bit sheepishly.

"That was great."

"Was it?"

He lifted his head, straining to bring her face into focus, wondering if she was just saying that in order not to bruise his ego. Her eyes were at half-mast and her lips were curved in a warm and sated and utterly convincing smile.

He felt the strong flow of desire course through him again, less urgent now but not to be denied.

"The only good thing about fast," he whispered, tasting a corner of that smile, "is that it leaves plenty of time for slow."

"Mmm."

"And slower."

When Molly opened her eyes, she realized that the darkness inside the trailer wasn't because the blinds were closed. It was night. She sighed, curling more closely against Dan's warm back, feeling every muscle in her body protest as she moved, willing that body to savor the afterglow without letting her mind intervene.

But the more she told herself not to think, the more disquieting thoughts tumbled through her brain. She dispensed with the *What have I done?* readily enough. She'd just had the greatest sex in the history of the world. It was the *What do I do now?* that couldn't be so easily dismissed.

She wasn't the sort of woman who slept around, who made love to men with whom she couldn't imagine a future. And right now she couldn't imagine her own future, much less one with Dan, the not-so-handy handyman. Why in the world would he even want a future with her when he had his pick of every woman in Moonglow, and most probably all of Texas, as well?

She let out a soft, forlorn sigh.

"Quit thinking, Professor."

Dan's voice surprised her. She thought he was fast asleep.

"I wasn't thinking," she said.

"Yes, you were." He chuckled. "I could hear all those mental gears clacking and grinding and trying to work themselves into Reverse."

He turned to her, drawing her close, whispering, "There is no Reverse, Molly, darlin'. Not for us anymore." His hand smoothed up the inside of her thigh. "There's just Play."

Her body reacted instantly to his touch even though her mind was loathe to go along. She was thinking there ought to be a forward gear, and then she wasn't thinking at all when Dan's touch became more intimate, more insistent.

"Sweet, sweet Molly, I can't stop wanting you," he breathed in her ear.

Before she could answer that she felt the same, there was a loud metallic banging on the trailer's door and Gil Watson's voice boomed out, "Danny Shackelford, you in there? You best come outside. I need to talk to you. Now."

Dan was up and halfway into his jeans almost before Molly could react with a stifled groan of "What now?"

"Get dressed, Molly," Dan whispered, "but stay in here. Lock the door behind me, all right?"

She opened her mouth to argue, but he cut her off immediately.

"Don't argue. Just do it."

"All right. All right," Molly muttered.

After Dan went outside, she fumbled around in the dark for her clothes while bits of conversation drifted through the window. The sheriff sounded like his arrogant, officious self when he said, "The Brenneman place out on the old State Road was broken into sometime this morning, Danny. There's cash missing. A lot of it. I need to know just where you were between, oh, let's say eight and noon."

Chapter 7

Dan knew exactly where he'd been between eight and noon, mostly driving to and from Idella. He had a receipt to prove it, too. There was just one little problem. The receipt from the pharmacy was itemized, and there was no way in hell he was going to let Gil Watson see it.

"I was around," he told the burly sheriff. "I met Molly Hansen at the library about noon. Marly can vouch for that."

"What about earlier?"

"Look, Gil. I didn't break into the Brenneman place. Okay? Hell. That's kid stuff. Have you rousted any of Moonglow's resident juvenile delinquents?"

The sheriff rested a beefy hand on the butt of his revolver. "I know how to do my job, Danny. That's why I'm asking you where you were."

It had been a long time since Dan had been on the receiving end of a shakedown. He felt a kind of heat rip through him, and hoped to hell he could control his temper. He did his best to make his voice affable and just nervous enough to appease this asshole behind the badge.

"I was here, Gil. Honest. You can check with Molly Hansen tomorrow, if you want."

"He can check with me right now."

The angry voice belonged to Molly, who was stomping down the trailer's short flight of stairs looking downright perturbed.

She also looked like a woman who'd been made love to recently and thoroughly. Her blond curls were disheveled at best. Her lips were slightly swollen and—dammit! Dan cursed himself for not shaving earlier. Her cheeks and chin showed a mild whisker burn, evident even in the moonlight. She looked fierce and fragile and he wanted her all over again even while he was wishing she had kept that lovely and well-loved kisser behind the locked door the way he'd told her to.

"Ma'am." Gil Watson gave her a nod and a long look that said he pretty much knew what she'd been up to in the trailer. His sideways smirk at Dan confirmed it.

"What's the problem, Sheriff?" she demanded, jutting her pink chin in Gil's big face.

"Molly," Dan said, "go back inside. I'll take care of this."

She stiffened just enough to let him know she wasn't used to taking orders, then she refocused her glare on Watson. "Dan and I have been together for most of the day," she said.

"Is that right?" the sheriff drawled. "Well, it's not that I don't believe you, Miss Hansen, but I still think I'll ride ol' Danny here over to my office for a little one-on-one.'' He turned to Dan, dismissing Molly entirely. ''You gonna get in my car nice and easy, son? I hate to bother with cuffs if they're not necessary.''

The last thing Dan wanted was to be hindered by a pair of handcuffs if push came to shove, and he had no reason to suspect it wouldn't. He drew in a long breath, trying to prepare himself for the inevitable ''one-on-one.''

''You don't need cuffs, Gil. Let's go. The sooner we get this straightened out, the happier we'll both be.''

''Dan!'' Molly exclaimed. ''You don't have to go with him. For heaven's sake. You haven't done anything wrong.''

''Inside, Molly.'' He took her arm and propelled her toward the door, then up the steps while he called over his shoulder, ''Give me a minute to get my shoes on, will you, Gil?''

Once inside the trailer, Molly started buzzing around like a wet honeybee.

''This is nuts, Dan. That big gorilla has absolutely no right, none at all, to cart you off in the middle of the night. You do know that, don't you? This isn't Nazi Germany, for heaven's sake.''

''No, it isn't.'' He yanked his shoelaces tighter. ''This is Moonglow, Molly, where there's nothing more permanent than a bad reputation. That's why I asked you to stay the hell in the trailer.''

''I know, but...''

''Just be quiet and listen a minute.'' His other shoe tied, Dan stood up and drew her against him. ''I won't be gone all that long. I want you to promise me you'll stay here with the door locked till I get back. Will you do that?''

''But I...''

He tightened his arms around her. "No buts. You hear me?"

There were a couple hard knocks on the side of the trailer. "You 'bout ready there, Danny?" Gil called.

Molly nearly choked on an oath, and just before she blasted the lawman with her unqualified opinion of him or called him a Gestapo pig, Dan silenced her with a kiss. A long, deep, toe-curling kiss.

"Don't go," she whimpered when he finally let her up for air.

"I have to," he said, tracing a thumb down her soft cheek, then gently across her wet bottom lip. "Stay in here and keep the door locked. Promise me."

After she nodded, albeit rather glumly, Dan kissed her forehead. "That's my girl."

Then he stepped outside, listened for the lock to click securely while he wondered exactly where—between Molly's place and the Sheriff's office—Gil was planning to unofficially *interrogate* him.

When Molly awoke on the air mattress, sunlight was seeping through the blinds, giving a bronze cast to the inside of the trailer. She had no idea what time it was. The only thing she knew for certain was that Dan was still gone.

She raced for the house, hoping she'd find him there—under the sink, maybe, making it worse in another disastrous attempt to fix it. His car was still parked in the driveway just where they'd left it yesterday. The back door still squealed like a stuck pig when she jerked it open. No Dan under the sink. Just a bucket, filled nearly to the brim.

Hurrying to the bedroom, Molly came upon Buddy Jr. who was measuring the door frame in the bathroom.

"Buddy, have you seen Dan this morning?" she asked loud enough to make herself heard over whatever was playing on his headphones.

"Probably out in his trailer," the boy said.

"No. No, he's not."

Buddy Jr. shrugged. "Maybe he's in town."

Maybe he's in jail, Molly thought. A little shiver of fear ran through her. She hoped he was in jail. That seemed like a very safe place when she considered alternatives, such as lying in a ditch somewhere out on the old State road or dangling from a rope someplace. God only knew what that gun-belted, tin-starred Gil Watson would do to a man he suspected of fooling around with his wife.

Fooling around. The thought brought Molly up short. She and Dan had made love last night, and there had been no "fooling around" about it. It had been hot and wild and more intense than anything Molly had ever experienced. They'd just about burned to a crisp in each other's arms.

Dan was a generous, patient lover, at least after their first combustible encounter. She could still hear his voice whispering in her ear, encouraging her, goading her, inspiring her to heights of physical pleasure she'd never known before. Good Lord. He'd stripped away her inhibitions as completely as Buddy Jr. had stripped the wallpaper off her bedroom walls.

She thought about the times that she and Ethan had made love, how she'd always held back, how her fiancé never seemed to notice, or if he noticed, didn't seem to mind. Poor stunted Kathryn.

Lucky, lucky Molly. She couldn't imagine being Kathryn again. Kathryn didn't have Dan Shackelford in her life. Molly did. And she intended to keep him.

She changed out of her slept-in clothes, told Buddy Jr. to keep up the good work and was on her way down Second Street barely ten minutes later. The Sheriff's Office was a one-story asbestos-shingled building, wedged between the volunteer fire station and Pike's Saddlery. She pushed through the front door with both hands.

A uniformed young man sitting at a desk put down his copy of *Field and Stream,* eased his lanky bones to a standing slouch, and drawled, "Morning, ma'am. It's Ms. Hansen, right?"

"Yes, it is," Molly said brusquely. "Is Sheriff Watson in?"

The man, apparently a deputy, shook his crew-cutted head. "No, ma'am."

Molly's plan had been to confront Gil Watson directly to find out what had happened to Dan. Now, in light of the sheriff's absence, she felt knocked off course. She raked her hair back from her face.

"I'm looking for Dan Shackelford," she told the deputy. "Any idea where he might be?"

His gaze dropped to the desktop for a second as he shifted his weight from one long leg to the other. "Well, ma'am, I'm really not—"

"Where is he?" Molly raised her voice. Her hands curled into fists at her sides. "I demand to know where he is."

The deputy angled his head toward a door. "In there. In a cell."

"In a cell?" She'd considered the possibility, but the fact left her nearly speechless. "In jail?"

"Yes, ma'am."

"Why?"

He shrugged. "You'd have to ask the sheriff about that. I haven't seen any paperwork on it yet."

Feeling as if she'd been punted back to square one, Molly stepped closer to the desk. "I want to see Dan." She pointed toward the door. "Right now."

"I'm afraid I can't do that, Ms. Hansen. You'll have to ask the sheriff."

"All right, I will. Just tell me where he is. I'll go ask him. Better yet, I'll call him and we can resolve this immediately."

When the deputy mumbled something she couldn't understand, she gave the leg of the desk a little kick and told him to speak up.

"He's at the hospital." Again, the young man's eyes evaded Molly's. "Mrs. Watson had a little accident last night."

Probably driving under the influence after she left the Blue Moon, Molly thought uncharitably. "Well, I'm sorry about that, but I still need to talk to him. Where is he? County Hospital?"

When he nodded, she reached for the phone on the desk. "What's the number?" she demanded, then stabbed the numbers as he gave them to her one by one.

It took a full ten minutes of being transferred from one department to another at the hospital before Sheriff Watson came on the line, only to tell Molly that the deputy could have easily beeped him. She pitched a dark look across the desk as she continued to talk. When she told the sheriff she wanted to see Dan immediately, he surprised her by saying, "Sure you can see him. You can even take him back to that dented tuna can where he lives. Hand the phone over to Jess and I'll tell him I said so."

Jess, the deputy, nodded and uh-huhed and okayed,

then put the receiver back in its cradle and reached in a drawer for a set of keys. "Chief says your friend is as free as a bird. Follow me."

Molly didn't know what to expect when he opened the door and ushered her into a narrow, dark hallway. All she knew was that the smell—a mix of sweat and vomit covered by a thin veneer of Pine Sol—nearly bowled her over as she followed the deputy down a line of empty cells no bigger than closets. He stopped at the last one, turned a key in a lock and pushed the door in, banging it hard against the cement-block wall behind it.

"You're free to go, Shackelford," he said, then to Molly he added, "Tell him he can pick up his wallet out front. No rush. Take your time, ma'am. I'll be out at the desk."

After the deputy brushed by her on his way out, Molly edged forward until she could see into the cell. As soon as she saw Dan, her heart squeezed tight. He was sitting on a metal cot, leaning back, his head tilted against the wall and his eyes closed. One of those eyes was puffy and there was a nasty cut on his cheek.

But it wasn't the sight of those physical injuries that affected Molly so deeply. It was something else. Something she couldn't quite identify in Dan's demeanor. A look about him that signified utter dejection, total defeat.

"Dan?" she asked softly, tiptoeing into the cell.

His eyes opened, but for a second he didn't even seem to recognize her. Then his mouth quirked in a half grin. "Hey," he said.

"Hey, yourself." Molly sat beside him on the cot, lifting a hand to touch his face. "My God. What happened to you? You look awful."

''I accidentally ran into Gil's nightstick once or twice. It's not as bad as it looks.''

''Well, it looks pretty bad. Do you think you ought to see a doctor?''

He shook his head.

''Okay.'' She sighed as she took his hand. ''Let's go home and put some ice on that eye.''

They had walked half a block from the Sheriff's Office when Molly stopped and said, ''I can run back to the house and get the car, if you want. I really think I should.''

Dan gritted his teeth. It was bad enough that he felt like a punching bag, but now Molly was treating him like a ninety-year-old man who probably wouldn't live to see ninety-one. She kept babbling about bruises, internal injuries and X rays, when she wasn't blathering about corruption, injustice and civil rights.

''Just keep walking, Molly, will you?'' He took her hand and tugged it. ''I'm okay. I swear. All I need is a long, hot shower and a couple hours' sleep.''

''And a lawyer,'' she added grimly, matching her steps to his.

''Never mind about that.''

What he needed was to get away. From Molly. From Moonglow. From everyone and everything. He needed to get back to that whiskey-soaked limbo he'd been living in where he didn't feel anything.

Dan wasn't quite sure how it happened, but last night Gil Watson's nightstick and big fists had done more than merely bruise him. He had taken the pummeling because he didn't want to blow his cover or risk his ability to remain in Moonglow to protect Molly. But those blows had felt strangely like a punishment he deserved, and they had jarred something loose in Dan's head or maybe even his soul.

All night long, after Gil had shoved him in the cooler, he'd sat with his eyes closed while visions of his last assignment played through his mind like a never-ending film. Rated X for hard-core violence. His partner, Carrie, died again and again. His witness, Morales, bled until every surface of the dream scene was slick and red.

Being with Molly, he decided, had only been a brief vacation from the reality of his failure. Lovely as it had been, it was over now. During the night in the cell, he had made up his mind to call Houston and resign, effective as soon as Bobby could send a replacement. Somebody good. Somebody better.

When they walked in the house, Dan was relieved to discover it nearly free of fumes. He glanced at the puddle in front of the kitchen sink where the bucket was overflowing. He probably ought to tell Bobby to assign a deputy who was as good with a wrench as he was with a gun. Hell, it wouldn't hurt if the guy was single and halfway decent-looking, too, for Molly's sake.

The sudden thought of somebody taking over for him not just in Molly's house but in her bed burned in his gut. He shouldn't have slept with her. He should have had more discipline, more sense. And she should have been a whole lot smarter than to fall into bed with some bum she didn't know the first thing about.

That thought irritated him enough that he stiffened slightly when Molly wound her arms around him and leaned her head against his chest.

"Poor baby," she said. "I'll go get the shower started so it's nice and hot by the time you're out of your clothes."

"You don't have to." He rested his chin on the top of her head, letting his arms remain at his sides. Damned if he'd hold her and watch all his good resolutions go down the drain.

"I know. And I don't have to tuck you into my bed after that, but I'm going to." She lifted her head up a bit and sniffed. "No more stripper fumes, thank goodness."

"I'll sleep out in the trailer, Molly. Thanks, anyway."

"I wish you wouldn't." She hugged him tighter, causing his battered ribs to protest and his breath to whistle in sharply. "I'm sorry," she squeaked, letting go and stepping back. "Dan, are you sure you don't need to see a doctor? We could be at County Hospital in a few minutes."

A sudden frown crossed her face and she swore softly.

"What?" he asked.

"Oh, I just remembered that's where the sheriff was when I spoke with him this morning. Apparently his wife had some kind of accident."

He let out a sharp little laugh. "I doubt if it was an accident. Gil probably did the same thing to her last night that he did to me. *Interrogated* her."

"Beat her up, you mean?" Molly sounded shocked.

"Wouldn't surprise me."

"What should we do?" she asked. "Shouldn't we report him to somebody?"

"What do you want to do, Molly? Call the police?"

He sounded as cynical as he felt, then regretted it immediately when Molly's pretty face crumpled and tears filled her eyes. Against his better judgment, he reached out and pulled her into his arms.

"It's not your problem, sweetheart. And there's not a damned thing you can do. Guys like Gil Watson usually get what they deserve sooner or later."

"I hope in his case it's sooner," she said.

He pressed his lips to her warm hair, knowing how he'd miss the feel of her in his arms, how he'd miss the incomparable sweetness of her body beneath his. Get over it, he told himself, knowing he never would.

Molly stood at the kitchen sink, listening to the pipes clank in her little house, hoping that a hot shower truly would be the best medicine for Dan. After she'd turned on the water for him and put out a clean towel, she'd come back to the kitchen to empty the brimming bucket and wipe up the floor.

What a mess. If she had any sense at all, she'd tell Dan she no longer required his services. It was stupid for him to hang around here, accomplishing nothing. Well, no, that wasn't exactly true. He'd accomplished a good deal in the week he'd been back in Moonglow, mostly rekindling old flames and stirring up ancient resentments, not to mention turning her own world upside down and inside out, playing havoc with all the adjustments she'd made in the past year.

He'd made her feel alive again after a year of living in limbo. He'd made her forget to mourn the demise of Kathryn Claiborn and to take delight in Molly Hansen. If he left—*when* he left—she was going to feel like nobody again.

She swore, reaching for a glass and turning on the faucet, only to hear the water run relentlessly into the bucket below. Suddenly, she didn't know whether to laugh or cry at her miserable plight, so she bent her head and did both.

"Are you okay, Ms. Hansen?"

Wiping her eyes, Molly turned to see Buddy Jr., his arms full of various lengths of wood, a leather tool belt slung around his narrow hips, and the ever-present earphones circling his neck.

"I've got these pieces for the door all measured and mitered," he said. "Once I nail them up, there's just the painting left. Want me to go ahead with it now?"

"Sure."

The boy had already angled through the door on his way to the bathroom when Molly remembered Dan in the shower. She started to call out to Buddy, then decided he'd figure it out for himself once he saw all the steam drifting out from the broken door. He could just stack the lumber in the hallway and come back later.

"Ms. Hansen?" he called out to her.

"I know," she called back. "You can finish up later this afternoon if that's all right with you."

"Well, yeah. But I think you better come in here. Something's real wrong with Mr. Shackelford."

Molly's feet barely touched the floor between the kitchen and the bathroom. She brushed past Buddy, waving steam away from her face as she entered the little room, half expecting to find Dan lying in a pool of blood on the floor. Instead, he was standing in the tub, both arms braced on the wet tile wall, while hot water poured over his head and cascaded down his naked body from the unadorned, uncapped, headless shower pipe above.

Under other circumstances, Molly might have laughed or even made some kind of sarcastic remark about his plumbing skills, but one look at the expression on Dan's face told her that this wasn't the time for levity. His mouth was twisted in a brutal, anguished curve, and even though his eyes were squeezed closed, she could tell that not all of the moisture pouring down his cheeks was from the shower. Some of the wetness was tears.

She reached out and turned the hot and cold handles off. For a second the only sound in the little room was the gurgle of water in the drain. Dan didn't move. He simply stood there, eyes closed, dripping. When Molly snapped open the towel and began drying him, he didn't even seem to be aware of it.

"Dan," she said with some urgency, "what's wrong? Tell me."

He dragged in several rough breaths, then mumbled something she couldn't quite understand. It sounded like *I killed her,* but that didn't make any sense at all to Molly.

"What's wrong? What's the matter?" she asked again, rubbing him harder with the towel as if that would somehow clear his head.

"Is he okay, Ms. Hansen?" Buddy Jr. inquired hesitantly from the doorway.

Molly had nearly forgotten he was there, but the boy's voice seemed to bring Dan out of whatever hellish trance he was in. He twisted his head and snarled, "Get out of here, kid."

"Go on, Buddy," Molly said quietly. "Come back tomorrow."

"Well, if you're sure—"

"Get the hell out," Dan yelled. Then he opened his red-rimmed eyes, finally focusing on her. "Molly?"

"Yes. It's me, Dan. Tell me what's wrong. Are you hurt? What is it? Let me help you."

He shook his head, then blinked.

"No one can help me," he said.

* * *

Get a grip, Dan kept telling himself, but there was nothing to hold on to. Even Molly's arms, as she led him out of the bathroom, felt too fragile to keep him from sliding closer and closer to the edge. The harder he tried to pin his consciousness to the here and now, the more he kept flashing back to that corridor and the second just before the elevator doors opened.

That's it. Move up so you're between Carrie and the doors. No. Not that. Do it different. Screw the elevator. Take the stairs. Morales will bitch all the way down, but that's okay. He'll end up in the lobby alive.

"Dan, here. You're shivering. Get under the covers."

"We need to take the stairs," he said. "The damned stairs."

"All right. Just get into bed and rest for a minute. We'll talk about that later."

"Not later. Now, Carrie. Do it now, dammit."

"Look at me, Dan. It's me. Molly."

He knew that. Dammit. He knew where he was. In Moonglow. In Molly's woebegone, stripped bedroom. He'd just watched her whisk the covers back on the bed. He could see her face all crimped with worry and her mouth flattening in a stubborn line. She wanted to help him. She didn't know he was way beyond that.

"It's okay," he told her, trying to sound in control. "This doesn't have anything to do with you."

"That's where you're wrong," she said. "The minute you bashed that stupid trailer of yours into my house, Dan Shackelford, everything about you became about me, too."

"Well, get over it, sweetheart." He tried to sound cold. The tough guy. Bogey brushing off Bacall.

"You get over it, Dan." With surprising strength, she

pushed him down onto the bed and whisked the covers over him. "Now, stay here while I figure out what to do."

There was nothing to do, he wanted to tell her, but she was already gone when he finally framed the thought from the wreckage in his head.

Molly headed straight for the phone, then stood there stupidly staring at it. Who could she call? And even if she knew who, what could she say? That there was a man in her bed who seemed to be coming apart at the seams?

If she were back on the Van Dyne campus, she'd call the Health Center's hotline. But here in Moonglow? She didn't even know if they had a shrink on staff at County Hospital.

There was a knock on the back door just then and a *Yoo-hoo! Anybody home?* that made Molly want to cry. Raylene! Molly dashed to the kitchen. If angels had pink hair and incredible busts, then an angel had suddenly appeared.

"I'm so glad you're here," Molly said.

"Well, what's going on, hon? My Lord. Buddy Jr. just came home looking like the sky was falling, babbling something about Danny losing his marbles in the shower."

"I don't know what's wrong. Gil Watson roughed him up last night and threw him in jail, and now Dan just..." Molly lifted her hands helplessly. "I just don't know."

"Yeah, I heard about that," Raylene said. She was digging in her huge black leather handbag, not looking at Molly as she spoke. "Nobody'll be surprised if one of these days Gil walks into a bullet from his very own gun, and likely as not it'll be his wife's finger on the trigger.''

Molly sighed. As much as the thought pleased her at the moment, it didn't help Dan's situation.

"Did Gil hurt him?" Raylene asked. "Any bruises? Anything broken?"

"No, I don't think so. Nothing more than a few cuts. He's just...I don't know...confused, agitated. His head's messed up. I wish I could get him to sleep."

"Ah-ha!" Raylene's hand emerged from her bag, clutching a small plastic container. Despite her long pink nails, she efficiently popped the cap off the little bottle, then shook out two capsules which she pressed into Molly's hand.

"Those babies are extra-strength," she said. "You give Danny both of those, tell him they're sleeping pills, and I guarantee you he'll zonk out for the next ten or twelve hours."

"Thanks, Raylene."

"Sure thing. A good sleep's the best medicine there is for a messy head. You look like you could use forty good winks yourself, Molly. Here, hon."

She started tapping out more capsules, but Molly stopped her.

"Thanks, anyway, but I think I better keep my eyes open and my head on straight for a while."

"You sure?"

Molly nodded. "I'm sure."

"Well, all right, then. You call me if you need any help. You got the number of the shop?"

Again, Molly nodded. "I can't thank you enough, Raylene."

The hairdresser shrugged. "Then don't, hon. That's what friends are for. My Lord." She adjusted the shoulder strap of her voluminous handbag across her voluminous chest and moved toward the door. "Everything'll be just fine tomorrow. You'll see."

With a glass of water, Molly carried the little capsules to the bedroom, hoping she'd find Dan already asleep. He wasn't. He was lying right where she'd left him, staring vacantly at the ceiling.

"I brought you something that will help you sleep," she said, edging a hip onto the mattress beside him. "Dan? Did you hear me?"

He shifted his gaze. As earlier in the jail cell, he didn't seem to recognize her at first. Then he said very slowly and distinctly, "Call Houston, Molly. Tell them I quit. Tell them to send somebody else."

"Don't worry about that now," she said. "It's not important. Here. Sit up a little so you can take these. They'll help you sleep."

To her surprise, he did exactly as she asked. Docilely. Unquestioning. Like a trusting child. Then he dropped his head back on the pillow.

"Maybe I won't dream," he murmured, staring overhead again. "These dreams. God. They're wearing me out."

Molly smoothed his rumpled hair off his damp forehead. "You'll have good dreams," she said. "Sweet dreams."

"Call Houston," he said again, the focus fading from his eyes.

"All right."

"It's important."

"The house can wait," she said softly.

"I can't do it, Molly. Tell them I can't do it."

"Shh."

Chapter 8

The bullets thunked almost silently into the wall a foot or so above the headboard. The first one stirred the part of Dan's brain that was always on alert. By the time slugs five and six hit, he had shoved the deeply sleeping Molly off the bed and was sprawled on top of her on the floor.

It was dark. That was about all he knew as he struggled to the surface of his capsule-induced stupor. What else? Dan prodded his dulled senses. A slight current of air grazed his bare back so he knew the bedroom window was open. No glass had shattered. There had been little or no concussion. That meant somebody using a silencer had fired from close range, and it meant he hadn't missed. The shots had been intended as a warning. But whether that warning was for him or for Molly, he didn't know.

Molly twisted beneath him. "Dan, what in the world

do you think you're doing? Get off. You're crushing me.''

He rolled off, positioning himself between Molly and the window, deciding there was no reason to worry her until he knew just what was going on. ''Sorry,'' he said. ''I guess I must've had a nightmare or something.''

''I guess you did,'' she said, elbowing up. ''You were talking in your sleep for the longest time. Hours. Crazy stuff.''

''Crazy dreams. That's all.'' He got to his feet. ''I'm going to get some clothes on. Don't turn on the light yet, okay?''

''Okay, but…''

''Just don't, Molly,'' he said sternly.

In the bathroom, Dan flipped on the light and caught a glimpse of his face in the mirror, instantly recognizing the fierce concentration that came with the more intense moments of his job. Despite the pallor and the blood-shot eyes, it was the look of a hunter. A warrior, even.

Old habits died hard, he thought, stabbing his legs into his jeans. Old visions died harder, he realized, as his dead partner's bullet-riddled body appeared before him. Or was it Molly? His heart seized up, and it took nearly every ounce of his will to shunt the bloody image aside.

Back in the bedroom, Molly was rearranging the bed-covers and plumping pillows in the dark. Dan wanted her out of there, not just for her own safety, but so he could inspect the bullet holes in the wall above the bed. He closed the window and drew the curtains closed before turning on the lamp on the dresser.

''Oh, my God,'' Molly softly exclaimed.

Dan studied the direction of her gaze, hoping it wasn't toward the area directly above the white wicker headboard. Still, considering the condition of Buddy Jr.'s stripped walls with their stains and gouge marks, he doubted she'd notice the six little holes that stood out so clearly to him.

"This place looks like a war zone," she said. "And the bed! I swear, Dan. How can one person, sound asleep, wreak so much havoc?" She shook her head. "Those must've been some nightmares, my dear."

"They were. I think I'll just stay up for a while," he said. "Are you tired?"

"No. I slept a little while you did. In between bad dreams."

"How about making some coffee, then?"

"Sure." She adjusted one of the pillows. "I might even consider scrambling some eggs even if it is near midnight. Are you hungry?"

"Yeah. That'd be great, Molly. I'll come help as soon as I get the rest of my clothes on."

Her gaze, fully trained on him now, turned soft. Her blue eyes glistened with moisture. "You're better, aren't you, Dan? I mean, really better? I was so worried about you."

At the same moment he opened his arms, Molly hurried toward him. Her arms circled his waist and her cheek pressed against his chest. "Really worried," she said again, while he stroked her hair.

"Thank you," he whispered, meaning it as much as he'd ever meant anything in his life. "I'm okay. Honest. It was just a lot of memories, all of them zapping me at once. Being back here in Moonglow is just tougher than I anticipated." It wasn't the whole truth, he thought, but it wasn't exactly a lie, either.

"Tougher, indeed. No thanks to *some* people."

"Hey, that's my problem," he said. "Not yours."

He tilted back his head and urged up her face with a finger under her chin, then smiled a smile guaranteed to elicit one from her. "Your problem at the moment, woman, is how to feed a starving man."

She smiled, as he knew she would. "No problem."

After Molly left for the kitchen, Dan quickly shoved the bed and headboard away from the wall in order to inspect the bullet holes. With the nail file he found on the nightstand, he carefully dug out one of the slugs, examining it in the palm of his hand. He wasn't a ballistics expert by any means, but he'd seen enough expended bullets to be fairly certain that this one came from a .357 Magnum. Not such an unusual pistol, especially here in gun-toting Texas. Gil Watson wore one on his ample hip. But then, so did his deputy and God only knew how many other Moonglow residents.

Of course, not everybody in Moonglow wanted Dan out of town. That narrowed it down some.

And even as he resisted the notion that the warning shots had been meant for Molly, Dan was mentally rehearsing his appeal to Bobby for an immediate, well-qualified replacement.

Molly stood at the kitchen counter, unable to remember how long it had been since she'd fixed an omelette this late at night, although she suspected it had been for Ethan during the early days of their courtship.

While she chopped onions and diced green peppers, she tried to remember those early days and nights with her fiancé, but they were just a blur for the most part, the same way Ethan's face was a blur. Every time she tried to picture him, the only face she could conjure was Dan's.

How was it possible, when she'd known Ethan for

years, when she'd planned to spend her entire life with him? How was it possible that Dan, after barely a week, was indelibly etched on her brain?

It was ludicrous. Kathryn Claiborn was a successful academic. Professors didn't fall in love with handymen. Did they?

She stopped chopping, standing there with the knife poised over the cutting board and the onion fumes wafting up into her eyes, wondering all of a sudden where Kathryn Claiborn had gone, and why Molly Hansen seemed more real to her now than the woman she'd been for the first thirty years of her life.

"Kathryn?" She whispered the name, bewildered, finding it awkward and unfamiliar on her lips, beginning to cry even as her mouth twitched in a baffled smile and her heart seemed so full it threatened to spill over, just like the tears in her eyes.

She *was* Molly Hansen. Kathryn, the cool and calculating professor, was gone. She was truly Molly, living here in dusty Moonglow, in this dratted, falling-down house, and she was wildly in love with a falling-apart handyman named Dan Shackelford. It was the damnedest thing that had ever happened to her. She stood there, laughing out loud while the tears streamed down her cheeks.

"What's so funny?"

Dan was suddenly behind her, his warm breath close to her ear. Her heart rose up like a helium balloon with a happy face on it. She loved him! How did this happen? He'd think she was insane if she said so.

"Onions," she said instead.

"I thought those were supposed to make you cry," he said.

"I'm doing that, too." She turned in the circle of his arms. "See?"

Beneath his rumpled hair, his brow worked into deep furrows, and those deep green eyes of his went soft with concern. For a second, she could have almost sworn it was love.

"Aw, Molly," he said. "What's wrong?"

"Nothing." *I love you. It's crazy. Maybe I am, too.*

"Something." He swore softly. "You were doing just fine until I came along and messed everything up for you. I'm sorry, honey." He bent his head so his forehead touched hers, then closed his eyes as he spoke. "You won't have to put up with me much longer. I promise."

She stepped back, her fingers tightening on the knife handle. "What does that mean, Dan?"

"It means that as soon as the company can send a new man, another repair guy, I'm outta here."

"Oh." Molly's heart—that happy balloon—went pop inside her chest. "Just like that?" She snapped her fingers.

"Just like that," he answered in a voice that seemed oddly rough. "That's what I do, Molly. I leave. Hell, ask anybody in Moonglow."

"They don't know you," she said firmly. "Not the way I know you." *They don't love you the way I love you.*

Something flickered in his eyes, something soft and warm, then it disappeared just before his face hardened like cement. "You don't know the first thing about me."

"I know how I feel. I wouldn't have made love with you if I hadn't cared. A lot." She reached up to touch his cheek, hoping to soften his expression, but he deflected her hand.

"Quit it, Molly. You're a grown woman. A professor. Just take what we did for what it was. Two people having a little roll in the hay. Nothing more."

Despite the harsh tone and the cruel words, she didn't believe him. Whether it was denial or some sort of intuition, Molly wasn't sure. She only knew that her instincts were right. Dan cared for her, too, and just as deeply, only something wouldn't allow him to admit it.

"Is it because of the differences between us?" she asked. "Because of the disparity in our careers?"

He let out a coarse laugh. "What? You think it would bother me that you've got academic degrees up the wazoo, including a Ph.D. in finance and a promising career on Wall Street while all I've got is a toolbox and a maxed-out MasterCard?" He ripped his fingers through his hair. "Why, hell, Molly, I never gave that a thought. It never entered my mind."

"How did you know that?" She felt her throat constrict.

"How did I know what?"

"About my degrees. About Wall Street."

"You told me," he said with a shrug. "That's how."

"No, I didn't." Suddenly the air in the kitchen seemed warmer, nearly stifling, and Molly found it difficult to breathe. She was sure she hadn't told him that much about her former life. She hadn't told *anybody* during this past secretive year. They'd warned her not to say a word.

Dan, she decided, was looking positively shady, as if he knew even more than he'd let slip. Had he gone through some of her hidden papers or other personal effects? she wondered. When? Why?

"Yes, you did, Molly," he said now, then shrugged again and gave her one of his mind-altering grins. "Hell, maybe not. I don't know. Maybe I'm just psychic. Miss Hannah used to read palms. Maybe I inherited it from her."

"Yeah, that's probably it." She turned back to the sink, applying knife to onion again, unable to look at Dan and sort out her fears at the same time. She needed to think.

"Mind if I use your phone while you're fixing the eggs?" Dan asked.

"No. Not at all. Help yourself."

Think, she ordered herself. It wasn't such an easy task when all the blood seemed to have drained from her head.

Dan punched in the number of the Houston office. It was going on one o'clock now, but he knew there was always a skeleton crew on duty, maybe even more during this computer crisis.

Bobby wasn't in.

"Could you speak up, sir?" the agent on the other end of the line asked him. "I'm having a hard time hearing you."

"Look," Dan whispered into the mouthpiece. "Let me have Bobby Hayes's home number, will you? This is important." Bobby and Eileen and the kids had moved sometime in the past year from their town house to a pretty, two-hundred-acre spread west of the city. Dan couldn't remember their new unlisted number, if he'd ever known it.

"I'm afraid I can't do that, sir."

"Hey, buddy, this is..."

Instead of finishing the sentence, Dan slammed the

receiver down. He'd call Bobby tomorrow. Ten or twelve hours wouldn't make all that much difference. Even twenty-four. He could hold it together for Molly's sake that long. Assuming he didn't make any more stupid mistakes like that remark about Wall Street and her degrees.

He sauntered back into the kitchen, prepared to tell her more lies when what he really wanted to tell her was the truth, that if it was possible to fall in love in a week, that was just what he'd done, and that he was going to miss her for the rest of his life.

On the counter, the chopping board was piled with neat little mounds of diced onion and green peppers. A dozen eggs sat untouched in their cardboard carton. Water plipped into the bucket under the sink. The back door was open.

And Molly was nowhere to be seen.

Molly sniffed, then stepped inside the Airstream. Apparently during her last visit there she'd been wearing a good deal of perfume or else had been too lost in the throes of lust to notice the unpleasant odor of the trailer. It struck her as a locker-room blend of beer, dirty socks and who knew what else.

She was snooping. If Dan knew the facts of her life, she'd decided to find out some facts about his. She didn't even know what she was hunting for, but she knew she had to hunt quickly, before he got off the phone. Sleuth that she wasn't, she had no idea where to begin.

It was almost too dark to see anything. Not wanting to turn on a light, Molly reached for the cord of the venetian blinds on the window and adjusted the slats until stripes of moonlight fell across the dark interior.

Now that she could see, her gaze skimmed across a row of books on a shelf beside Dan's bed.

Mystery. Mystery. Histories of the American Revolution and the Civil War and Vietnam. Drugs in America. Drugs in Central America. Terrorism. Terrorism today. Terrorism tomorrow. More terrorism. Dan's taste in reading had a decidedly violent bent, Molly thought.

While she was trying to make some sense of that, her gaze strayed to the locked drawer near the air mattress, the drawer from which Dan had retrieved the little square packet the night before when they'd made love.

He had rummaged around on the floor, she remembered, for the key. Doing the same, she found it quickly enough under a loose piece of carpet, inserted it in the little round lock and turned it, then eased out the drawer a few tentative inches. With no interior lights, it wasn't easy to see, but there was enough illumination to distinguish, just to the right of more foil packets, the metal butt and trigger of a very lethal-looking handgun.

A gun! Molly inhaled a sharp gasp and shut the drawer just as the door of the trailer opened behind her. She whirled around to see Dan standing there, looking less than pleased and more than a little suspicious. Almost dangerous. Definitely dangerous. Her heart started pumping harder.

"Find what you were looking for, Molly?" he asked, coming toward her. Before she could answer, he reached down to lock the drawer and then pocketed the key in his jeans.

"I wasn't..." She swallowed audibly. "I didn't..." She swallowed again, then blurted, "You've got a gun, Dan."

"Yeah. I've got a gun. Me and just about every other

guy in Texas.'' He crossed his arms. ''So what? No big deal.''

''Well, no big deal except every other guy in Texas usually has his gun mounted across the rear window of a pickup truck,'' she said. ''What in the world do you need that nasty-looking weapon for?''

He arched an eyebrow while one side of his mouth quirked up. ''To protect my valuables?''

Molly, less fearful of him now, gave the interior of the Airstream a cool once-over. ''Valuables. Right. Try again, Dan.''

That half grin revved to full throttle as he shrugged and turned up his hands. ''To defend myself from wild, insatiable women in the middle of the night?''

In spite of herself, Molly laughed. That was probably true, she thought, remembering Linda Watson's recent nocturnal visit, not to mention her own fairly wild and insatiable behavior the night before. The mere memory of their lovemaking was enough to raise her temperature one or two degrees.

As if he sensed the sudden, sultry increase, Dan cocked his head. ''That wouldn't be why you're out here, would it? Feeling a little wild and insatiable, Molly? Huh?''

''Well, I...''

She was embarrassed to admit that she was, but it struck her as a far better excuse for her presence in his trailer than snooping.

''Maybe,'' she said, putting a bit of velvet in her voice, then passing the tip of her tongue across her lips for emphasis. There was nothing contrived, however, about the heat spiraling through her or the ache of desire deep inside. It didn't seem to matter that she didn't trust this man. She wanted him all the same.

"Maybe," he echoed softly as he closed the distance between them and drew her against him. "Maybe we should do something about that."

When his mouth came down on hers, *wild and insatiable* didn't even begin to describe how Molly felt. Every thought in her head disappeared, and every caution in her heart gave way as her senses surrendered to Dan's kiss, to the slow, warm pleasures of his lips and his tongue and his teeth.

Somewhere on the edge of her consciousness, there was an insistent ringing. It took a moment to clear her head enough to realize it wasn't the sound of her own blood singing in her veins, but the telephone in her house across the yard.

"The phone," she murmured against Dan's mouth.

His response was somewhere between a growl and a groan of pleasure.

"I should probably answer it," she said without much conviction as the phone kept ringing, now on its fifteenth or twentieth ring. "This late at night, you never know. It could be important."

"As important as this?" His hand slid around her back, and with a single, expert flick, he undid the clasp of her bra. "Or this?" The hand curved beneath her breast while his lips trailed down her neck, her collarbone, her eager flesh.

Molly's head lolled back. Her eyes sank closed as pleasure coursed through her. "No," she whispered. "Nothing's as important as this."

Even in the haze of passion, Dan knew damn well who was on the other end of that urgently ringing phone. Bobby. They'd IDed Dan's earlier call in the Marshals office and then alerted the boss immediately.

Tomorrow would be soon enough to take himself off
this assignment, to walk away from Molly, who was all
warm and willing, wild and insatiable and perfect in his
arms.

Stupid. He'd only meant to distract her from the dis-
covery of the gun, to deflect her curiosity with a kiss
or two. He should have known he couldn't stop once
he'd had even the smallest taste of her. Thank God he
still had the presence of mind to retrieve the key from
his jeans, unlock the drawer and fumble for some protection. As he did, he was relieved to know that his
U.S. Marshals ID and badge were still stashed well back
in the drawer, out of Molly's sight when she'd looked
inside.

It would hurt her less in the long run to think she'd
been abandoned by some jerkwater handyman than a
misfit, over-the-edge officer of the law.

For now, though, he couldn't get enough of her. She
was wild and insatiable, as if she knew—as he did—
this would be their last time. Almost insatiable. Her
body was so perfectly familiar in spite of their short
time together that he knew just where to touch her, exactly how to play her—slow, fast, hard, then harder—
to bring forth every keening, resonant chord of her cli-
max. And his own.

They fell asleep, satiated, spent, their limbs tangled
and their separate breaths blending as one being. Dan's
last thought was that he'd never come this close to
heaven again, no matter how long he lived. Funny, finding heaven here in Moonglow.

Hours later, when Dan woke to stripes of sunlight
coming through the trailer's blinds and the sound of the
door quietly clicking closed, it took him only a blink to

realize that Molly was headed into the house, no doubt to finish preparing their interrupted omelette, but only after she consulted the ID box on the phone for last night's unanswered call. Bobby's call—he was certain of that—with the Houston area code prominently displayed on the box.

By the time he'd dressed and sprinted across the yard and into the house, she was standing just where he'd anticipated, frowning at the phone.

"What's up?" he asked, glancing over her shoulder at the number just before Molly hit the erase button.

"Nothing," she said.

"Who called?"

She shrugged. "I dunno. Wrong number, I guess."

What he guessed was that she knew damned well the call was from the Marshals office in Houston, but there was no way she was going to share that information with her handyman. What she didn't know, though, was that the call was meant for him, not her.

"Are you hungry?" she asked, attempting to change the subject.

"Famished."

Once Molly was in the kitchen, Dan punched in the numbers he knew by heart, asked the operator for Bobby, then waited, silently rehearsing his exit lines. The minute he heard Bobby's voice, however, that brass-tacks, we've-got-trouble tone, Dan sensed that his own agenda had suddenly been blown to smithereens.

"We've got a line on that hacker," Bobby said without preamble.

"Oh, yeah?"

"If we're right, it looks like those upstate New York boys might have patched together their old network."

Dan's heart skipped a beat before it froze completely.

"Upstate New York? What do you mean? Not Kathryn Claiborn's…?"

"Maybe." Bobby cut him off. "Maybe not. This guy we've got in custody up in Albany isn't the most reliable son of a bitch ever to come down the pike. If he's just blowing smoke, we'll know soon enough."

Dan mouthed a deep curse into the receiver while his gut corkscrewed and his mouth went dry and every nerve in his body snapped, not with the old adrenaline that said he was ready for anything, but with the fear that signaled he wasn't, he couldn't, he—

"I need backup, Bobby."

"Whoa now, amigo." The voice on the other end of the line dropped to a low and unyielding tone. "We're still pretty short-handed. What you need to do is keep your eyes open and the Claiborn woman's head down. You hear what I'm telling you, Dan?"

He muttered a grudging "I hear you."

"All right, then. I'll keep you apprised."

Bobby hung up, and Dan stood there listening to dead air for the longest while, trying to breathe, trying to disregard the images of death that preyed on his brain, trying to figure out how he was going to keep Molly alive, if it came to that.

"You've hardly touched your omelette," Molly said, mopping up the last of hers with a wedge of toast, thinking that she'd been so hungry this morning that even the rubbery eggs with the desiccated onions and peppers had tasted divine.

One of these days she'd get the hang of cooking on this electric stove with its temperamental burners. It was probably too late to add that to her list of things that needed to be fixed. As if Dan could.

He sat across the table from her, looking tired, disheveled and even a little glum. The tired part didn't surprise her because neither of them had slept all that much the night before. And in his tattered jeans and rumpled Hawaiian shirts, he was disheveled more often than not. But glum?

In spite of being tired, Molly felt so incredibly alive and vibrant she could hardly sit still. Even knowing the U.S. Marshals Service in Houston had been trying to contact her last night didn't cast too much of a pall over her current mood. Those ''check up on the witness'' calls came occasionally. Last night's was probably from some deputy working late and looking to keep busy.

She'd even managed to convince herself that the gun locked in Dan's drawer posed no threat to her at all. The weapon was just what he had claimed—it was for his own protection. And Dan Shackelford, she decided, was exactly what he was billed as—a traveling handyman and the greatest kisser north of the Rio Grande. Maybe even north of Antarctica. She felt her lips slide into a silly, smitten kind of smile that she was helpless to conceal.

''So, what are the plans for today?'' she asked, fairly sure that he wouldn't say he was leaving. How could he after last night?

He put down his fork on the barely touched plate of eggs and toast. ''I thought we might try to scare up a decent plumber,'' he said with a slight nod toward the leaky sink. ''Either that or try to find a bigger bucket.''

Molly laughed, scooping up his plate and carrying it to the sink. ''I never thought I'd hear you admit defeat.''

''I just know my limitations.''

There was nothing flippant in his tone. In fact, it

struck Molly as completely serious, perhaps even a little sad. It matched the expression on his face. As irritated as she'd been with his earlier devil-may-care attitude, she suddenly longed to see it reappear.

"Hey." She sauntered toward him across the warped linoleum floor that he still hadn't gotten around to fixing, then nudged his arms aside so she could sit on his lap. "I haven't noticed any limitations. None of any importance, anyway."

Instead of smiling, he frowned all the more.

"Dan? What's the matter? I know there's something troubling you. It's practically written on your face." She traced a finger across his forehead, down one cheek, along his angular jaw.

"Oh, yeah?" He avoided her eyes as he spoke. "What does it say? Here lies Danny Shackelford. He used to be good?"

"You *are* good. My God, Dan, you…"

His lips slid sideways in disgust as he brushed her hand away from his face. "I'm not talking about bed, Molly."

"Neither am I," she shot back. "You're a good person. You're warm and you're witty and you're smart as a whip when you aren't trying to disguise it behind that good ol' boy demeanor. Who cares whether or not you can fix a showerhead or repair a leaky pipe or wallpaper a room? None of that's important. What's important is…"

Molly stopped, the words *I love you* teetering on her tongue like a first-time, frightened diver on the high board. She cleared her throat, dragged in a deep breath, then let it out with a frustrated "I don't know. Maybe you're just in the wrong line of work. Did you ever think of that?"

"Frequently," he snapped.

"Well?"

"Well, what?"

"What are you going to do about it?"

"This." Without warning, he separated his legs, thus eliminating the lap on which Molly was perched, but caught her before she slipped through. "First things first, Professor. Let's go find us an honest-to-God, card-carrying plumber. I need to go out to the trailer for a minute, so I'll meet you at the car."

In the trailer, Dan checked the clip in his gun before settling it in the waistband of his jeans, against the small of his back. On the off chance that it would be necessary, he jammed his Marshals badge and ID in his pocket. That left just a few lonely little square packets in the drawer. He swore softly as he closed it.

From a lower drawer, he pulled out Kathryn Claiborn's file and quickly studied the half-dozen pictures of the men known to be members of the elite terrorist group known as the Red Millennium. Four of them were dead, one of those having been blown to bits in the chemistry lab explosion Kathryn had witnessed, and the other three having perished when their small plane went down in a storm in the Florida Keys.

The two who remained at large—Ahmad Sharis and Jorgen Metz—had ceased all activities during the past year. Their whereabouts were unknown, but one thing was for sure. If either the big Egyptian or the albino Swede showed up in Moonglow, they'd sure as hell be noticed. It was time now to see if anybody had done any *noticing,* especially given the bullets fired last night.

Molly was waiting for him beside the BMW, but she wasn't alone. Dan had forgotten about Buddy Jr. and his remedial English lessons. The kid was leaning a hip against the rear fender, looking as if he'd rather drink hemlock than spend another long morning at Molly's computer.

"I forgot about Buddy's lesson," Molly said apologetically when Dan reached the driveway. "You're going to have to find that plumber without me, I'm afraid."

"No problem," Dan said. Actually, he was glad not to have Molly tagging along while he tried to find out who was in town and who wasn't, and, more important, who had fired those shots. Buddy Jr. might not be the perfect bodyguard, but Dan was fairly comfortable leaving Molly with him for a little while.

"You need a plumber?" the boy asked, suddenly looking alive, even keenly interested as he straightened his lanky frame.

Molly laughed. "Don't tell me you do that, too?"

"I help my dad," he said. "Why don't you show me what you need done. I bet I could fix it cheaper than anybody else in town, and I sure could use the cash."

Molly looked at Dan. "What do you think?"

"Sure," he said. "Give it a shot, kid. I'd rather pay you than some guy with his pants half down to his knees."

"Great." Buddy Jr. started for the back door.

"I'll be right there," Molly called, then asked Dan, "Are you still going out?"

"For a while. I won't be gone long."

She lifted on tiptoe to kiss his chin. "Don't get waylaid by any wild and insatiable women, okay?"

"Not if I can help it, darlin'," he said, hoping the wild women of Moonglow would turn out to be the worst of his problems.

Chapter 9

Some sources were better than others in Moonglow, so Dan went straight to the best. Raylene. To his enormous relief, her shop was empty when he arrived, so he was able to slide into her purple vinyl chair without a wait. Raylene smiled while she draped the pink plastic cape around his shoulders and snapped it tight at the neck.

"It's about time you dragged your shaggy self in here, Danny," she said. "My Lord. When was the last time you had a haircut? 1988?"

"Thereabouts." The pink-haired beautician was looking a little too eager, so he added a quick, "Don't take off too much, okay?"

"Trust me," she said, getting to work with her spritzer in one hand and a comb in the other.

Dan closed his eyes. "What's new?" he asked.

Half an hour later he had learned more than he ever wanted to know about the goings-on in Moonglow. Buddy Sr. had a hernia in addition to his continuing

battle with acid reflux. Buddy Jr., when he wasn't hustling games at the pool hall, was taking every job he
could in order to save enough money to buy Henry
Young's old Harley. Laverne Catton was going ahead
and having the triplets even though she was separated
from that no-good Jake, and last but hardly least, Linda
Watson was going home from the hospital this afternoon.

"I guess you heard about her *accident*," Raylene said
with a roll of her eyes and a tell-tale emphasis on the
final word. "Gil hasn't left her side. Not for a second.
I'd almost feel sorry for him if I didn't suspect he was
the one who put her there."

"Gil always did use his fists more than his brain,"
Dan said. "Are you sure he's been at the hospital since
yesterday?"

"Positive. Cindy White, that's Carleen Carter's old-
est girl, is working at the hospital and she said so. You
remember Carleen, don't you? She married Dewey
White."

Dan nodded, but all he was thinking was that if Gil
Watson had been at the hospital all that time, then who
the hell had fired the warning shots into Molly's bedroom wall?

Raylene pushed his head forward, ordered him to
hold still, then took a few snips at the base of his neck
before she said, "There. That's better. I'm sure Molly
will be glad to see there's a right good-looking man
under all those snarls and split ends. You two are getting to be quite an item, Danny."

"Is that right?" Dan surveyed his haircut in the mirror, grateful Raylene hadn't left him bald, or worse,
blond.

"Somebody was asking about you and Molly yesterday morning at the Bean Crock when Buddy Sr. was having breakfast. He just happened to overhear.''

"Who was asking?"

She combed his cowlick, without much success. "Buddy didn't say. Just some guy he'd never seen before, is all. He said he seemed real curious about whether or not Molly was from here." She sighed, frowning at the untamed strands of hair. "You want me to put some gel on this, hon?"

"No. Thanks, Raylene. How much do I owe you?"

"Oh. Whatever. It was an easy cut and I wasn't doing anything, anyway." She unsnapped the plastic cape, then removed it deftly, shaking off the hair.

Dan slid a hand into his pocket and eased his wallet past his badge, then extracted a twenty dollar bill, which he slid under the blow dryer on the counter. "The Bean Crock," he said casually. "Where's that? Breakfast doesn't sound half bad."

"It's the old luncheonette just across from City Hall. You remember. Where we used to sneak off to on Fridays when they had fish sticks for lunch at school." She laughed. "The kids still do. At least that's what Buddy Jr. tells me. My Lord. Except for the color of my hair, nothing ever changes around here, does it?"

Although Dan laughed and said he agreed, he was worried that things in Moonglow were suddenly about to change. Dramatically.

By ten o'clock the breakfast crowd had disappeared, so there weren't too many customers in the Bean Crock. But there wasn't much information, either. Sally, the young waitress, hadn't worked the day before, and Zeke, the cook and owner, had been much too busy with his grill to notice anybody who didn't look as if they belonged. As a result, Dan was fairly sure that neither the swarthy Ahmad Sharis nor his fish-white partner, Jorgen Metz, were in town. That didn't mean they hadn't sent an emissary, however, or even hired a local thug to do their dirty business.

Before going back to Molly's, he swung by County Hospital to make a few discreet inquiries about the sheriff, only to find that Raylene had been right. Gil, according to two nurses and one aide, had been glued to Linda all night. Presumably, Gil's big .357 Magnum had been glued right there with him, too. So much for the long arm of the law.

Molly's house looked quiet when he pulled into the drive. He gave a quick, disgusted glance at the pile of guttering in the side yard, thinking maybe he could get Buddy Jr. to fix that as well since the kid was so hot to earn some cash toward that Harley he had his young heart set on.

When he walked inside, it surprised him a little not to see Buddy Jr.'s long legs sticking out from under the kitchen sink.

"Anybody home?" he called, wishing like hell that Molly would keep her doors locked, but not wanting to frighten her and knowing that anybody who really wanted to get to her wouldn't be stopped by a locked door. Or, he thought glumly, by a has-been federal agent.

"Just us mice," Molly answered from her office.

Suddenly he couldn't wait to wrap his arms around her, to feel her heart beating against his, to possess all that willing, generous warmth once more. Dan hurried down the hallway, but stopped dead in his tracks when he passed Molly's bedroom where Buddy Jr. had begun wallpapering. The first strip was already up, dead center on the wall behind Molly's headboard, right over the bullet holes. It was as if the kid were trying to hide them.

He walked in the room and tapped Buddy Jr. on the shoulder. The boy tugged off his earphones.

"Looks good," Dan said, gesturing toward the wall.

"Thanks."

"How come you started here? In the middle?"

Buddy looked confused for a moment. He stared at the wall, then he lifted his narrow shoulders in a shrug. "That's where the wall is straightest. Only place I could plumb a good line."

"Oh." It sounded reasonable enough to Dan, who didn't know any more about putting wallpaper on than he knew about taking it off. The boy probably didn't even notice the holes, he guessed, or he would have mentioned them. "Okay." He gave him a little congratulatory slap on the back as he turned to leave. "Keep up the good work, kid."

In her office, Molly's back was to the door and her attention totally focused on her glowing monitor. Dan slipped his arms around her from behind and buried his face in her warm, fragrant neck. She responded with a pleasured little mewing sound, turned off her computer and lifted up her arms to cradle his head.

For a brief second, there was a lump in Dan's throat and his emotions rose so close to the surface that he thought he might start crying. No woman—no human being, for that matter—had ever made him feel so welcome before, so essential, as if he belonged right here and nowhere else.

He lifted his head and saw their faces, side by side, reflected on the glass of the monitor. His heart shifted in his chest. He loved her! The notion nearly brought him to his knees. He loved her, and, if it was true that the Red Millennium had located her, he might lose her.

"Let's get the hell away from here, Molly." He swiveled her chair around so she was facing him. "Now. Today. Let's just go."

"Dan!" She laughed in surprise. "I can't just pick up and go. I've got a job. Papers. Students." She gestured toward the computer. "Remember?"

"You can take your laptop. Hell, put the whole computer in my trailer. I can make room for it. Where do you want to go? East? West? How about Mexico?"

"Dan!" She simply stared at him, a sweet smile on her lips, her eyes happy and bright. "Hey," she said finally. "You got your hair cut."

He ripped his fingers through the newly shorn locks. "What's that got to do with it? Come on, Molly. Say yes. Let's go. Today." Dan shook her chair a little for emphasis.

"I can't."

"Yes, you can."

She looked away, but just before she did, Dan saw something in her expression that nearly made him sick. He couldn't quite give it a name. Distrust? Disappointment? Maybe a kind of despair? It was a look that said he'd gone too far, that he'd breached some unspoken barrier, that he was a handyman and she was a professor, that their worlds might touch for a while, even create some sparks, but anything beyond that was not merely unthinkable, it was impossible.

"You don't understand," she said. "I can't just up and leave."

He did understand. That was the problem. Anyone accepting the benefits of witness protection was required to keep the Marshals office apprised of their whereabouts. For Molly to leave Moonglow, she'd have to call Houston first. But her rejection of his offer wasn't just about a phone call and a little red tape. It was about Kathryn Claiborn and Dan Shackelford and the differences between them.

Hell, maybe it was even about that fiancé of hers back in New York.

"Just think about it, okay?" he told her, letting go of the chair.

She nodded in reply, but the gesture was one of grave reservation rather than enthusiasm. And then the phone rang.

"I'd better get that," she said, sounding almost relieved for the interruption.

After Dan stomped off in what Molly would have described as a good impression of a huff, she stood with her hand over the phone, knowing the call was from Houston, dreading the impending news, whatever it was. Whether it turned out to be good news or bad news or even no news at all, it would still be just one more secret she was obliged to keep from Dan. She hated that.

Her fingers were trembling noticeably when she finally picked up the receiver and offered a tentative hello.

"Is this Molly Hansen?" asked the voice on the other end of the line.

"Yes."

"Ms. Hansen, would you please call our office back at the usual number?" The man, presumably a deputy marshal, hung up before Molly could reply.

She had forgotten the drill. Her calling back was for security purposes, to reassure her that she was indeed speaking with her sponsors in the witness program rather than with anyone trying to hunt her down. She placed the call, and the phone was answered immediately.

"This is the U.S. Marshals Service, Deputy Marshal Kevin Holt speaking."

"This is Molly…well…Kathryn Claiborn."

"We'll use Molly Hansen," he said. "How are you, Ms. Hansen?"

"Fine," Molly said. Or was she? "At least I think I'm fine. Why don't you tell me, Deputy Holt?"

He laughed, a short and muffled bark, but, all in all, the man didn't seem truly amused. "We wanted to alert you to the possibility of new activity in the Red Millennium. This isn't meant to alarm you. It's just a standard precaution."

Despite his words and his reassuring tone, Molly was alarmed. Very alarmed. Her heart started to pound. "What do you mean *new activity?*" she asked. "Here? In Moonglow?"

"Well, I'm not at liberty to divulge that information, ma'am. But I can tell you that there's nothing going on in Texas that we know of at the moment."

Nothing that they knew of. Molly didn't find that very consoling. "What should I do?" she asked, her mounting panic evident in her voice.

"You don't have to do anything, Ms. Hansen. We already have a deputy there keeping an eye out for you."

"Here? You do?"

"Yes, ma'am." She could hear him riffling through papers before he continued. "That would be Dan Shackelford."

Molly almost laughed. "No, Deputy Holt. I think

you've got the wrong information. Dan Shackelford is here making repairs on my house.''

''Yes, ma'am.''

The guy wasn't getting the point, so Molly raised her voice. ''He's a repairman, for heaven's sake. You people need to send a deputy, a trained agent.'' The cavalry, she nearly shrieked. Not some bumbling handyman.

''Deputy Shackelford is a trained agent, Ms. Hansen. We just didn't want to alarm you unnecessarily. That's why he took that cover.''

Molly's mouth opened, but only a puff of air came out. She was truly speechless. Finally she managed a surprised little ''Oh.''

''I wouldn't worry too much,'' the deputy said. ''We're only taking the standard precautions. But call us anytime if you have any questions or concerns. Or just ask Deputy Shackelford, ma'am.''

Ask Deputy Shackelford! Molly was already framing a long list of questions as she hung up the phone, beginning with why the hell had he been lying to her, to be followed immediately by how the devil was he planning to protect her from the terrorists of the Red Millennium when he couldn't even replace a confounded showerhead.

''Ms. Hansen?''

Startled, Molly whirled around to see Buddy Jr. a few feet away. She had forgotten he was even here.

''I didn't mean to scare you,'' he said. ''I just thought you might want to take a look-see at the wallpaper. I've got two strips up now.''

''Oh, sure.''

She followed the boy into the bedroom, silently fum-

ing, and hoping that at least one of those strips was
composed of Dan Shackelford's hide.

Dan sat in his rickety lawn chair in the shade of the
live oak, glaring at the back of the house and the pile
of fallen guttering that seemed to taunt him now. *Loser,*
it fairly screamed. *How are you going to take on an
agent of the Red Millennium if you can't even tackle a
few lengths of aluminum or a few strips of wallpaper?
How can you keep Molly safe and sound if you can't
even do an adequate job on her house?*

He wanted a beer in the worst way. Two of them.
Three. A six-pack to blur his brain and take him to that
fuzzy place where his memories dimmed and his deficiencies were all but forgotten.

The irony was that he didn't blame Molly one bit for
refusing his plea to run away. Hell, in some deep corner
of his heart, he even applauded her for being sensible.
Not that she knew she was rejecting anything more than
a misbegotten handyman who still knew a thing or two
in bed. But she hadn't let their explosive, nearly stellar
lovemaking be a factor in her decision, smart woman
that she was. If she'd fallen for Danny Shackelford, at
least she hadn't hit the ground. Not the way he had,
anyway.

He wanted to forget that, aside from being a loser
professionally, he'd also been a fool personally to let a
woman get into his heart the way that Molly had. He
couldn't imagine his life without her now. Couldn't
imagine not holding her hand, not kissing her generous
mouth, not sleeping with her warm body curled in his
arms. There had never been a woman he couldn't walk
away from. Until now.

When his head started to ache as if it were trapped

in a vise, Dan closed his eyes. He didn't know how much time had passed when he became aware of someone slowly approaching. He blinked in the bright sunlight, but it didn't take more than a second to recognize his former history teacher, Mildred Booth.

With the ample fabric of her dress billowing in the breeze, Mrs. Booth moved across the lawn like a great ship coming into port, considerably slower than she'd moved twenty years ago, but no less commanding. Her hair was white now rather than the steel-gray that Dan remembered, but her expression hadn't altered one whit. Her gaze was steady and stern, perhaps even forbidding, but tempered by a trace of amusement pulling at the corners of her mouth.

He felt as if he was seventeen all of a sudden, about to be sent to the principal's office. Shooting up from his chair, it was all he could do not to salute the woman.

"I was wondering just how long it would take you to drop by and see me, Daniel," she said. "Then I got tired of wondering, and decided the mountain might as well come to Mohammed."

Now he felt fifteen and guilty as hell, just on general principle. His throat automatically constricted, making him sound like a kid. "Hi, Mrs. Booth."

"Hi, yourself." She eyed the lawn chair he'd vacated. "Do you suppose that thing will hold a woman of my stature?"

Quite honestly, Dan wasn't sure. Mildred Booth had always been a large woman, about five nine and at least two hundred pounds. She seemed even larger now. Monumental. He steadied the chair as she lowered herself into it, and didn't let go until both Mrs. Booth and the chair appeared secure.

For a moment she sat quietly, then calmly asked,

"How are you, Daniel?" as if she'd only seen him a week or two before, as if twenty years hadn't intervened since he'd left Moonglow and his past and Mrs. Booth behind.

Great, he started to say, but the word caught in his throat when she gave him that gray-eyed, all-knowing look he remembered so well. She didn't brook lies.

"Not so great," he answered, blurting out the truth almost before he realized he'd spoken.

"That's what I've heard," she said. "There aren't many secrets around here. Some people have very big mouths." Her tongue clucked softly. "Especially people with pink hair."

"Yeah," he murmured in agreement, wondering just what Raylene had told her.

"I brought something to show you," she said.

It was only then that Dan noticed the thick, leather-bound album on her lap, nearly lost in the folds of her dress.

"Do you have another chair?" she asked, and then sighed and said, "Or why not just pull up a piece of ground and take a look at this."

Dan sat cross-legged, opened the book, then stared at the first page where a newspaper article was carefully centered and glued. Its headline read Texas Marine Wins Corps Honors. The article, dated nearly sixteen years ago, detailed the ceremony at Camp Pendleton when he was awarded several ribbons for marksmanship and hand-to-hand combat.

He flipped the page to see another article from the *Washington Post.* U.S. Marshal Testifies Against Drug Lord. There were more. Page after page. There was a picture of him in Miami leaning against the front bumper of a confiscated Rolls-Royce. There he was in a crowd shot in the Rose Garden, not too far from the vice president and the attorney general. There were notices of awards and page after page of articles about his citations and successes. It was like watching his entire career flash before his eyes.

"Where did you get all these?" he asked, looking up.

Mrs. Booth was contemplating something in the distance. "I've subscribed to a clipping service for years," she said matter-of-factly. "In over four decades of teaching, I only had two students whose careers I found interesting enough to follow. You and Annabeth Tate."

"The poet?" Dan shifted on the ground. "I didn't know she was from Moonglow."

"Well, now you do."

He chuckled softly at Mrs. Booth's reluctance to waste words. His gaze dropped to the album again. "I'm sorry I didn't stop by as soon as I got back in town."

"You had more important things to do," she said, clearly meaning it, for there wasn't a hint of sarcasm in her tone.

"Yeah. Well…" He flipped to the back of the album where the headline screamed Deputy Marshal and Witness Gunned Down in Manhattan Hotel. The pages that followed were blank. He supposed they'd remain that way, or else one page would eventually be devoted to a brief obituary.

"I'm proud of you, Daniel," the woman said quietly, reaching out a hand, liver-spotted and crooked with arthritis, to gently touch his head. Not a lingering touch. More of a tap. Then she drew back her hand, clasped it in her lap and added, "I must be getting sentimental in my old age, but I thought you ought to know that."

In all the years she had pushed and prodded young Danny Shackelford to succeed, to make something of himself, to rise above his name and circumstances, Mrs. Booth had never given him a compliment. Not directly, anyway, even though her letter of recommendation to the Justice Department years ago had been a testimonial so glowing it fairly lit up half of Washington.

Now, out loud, the woman had said she was proud of him, and all Dan could think was that he didn't deserve it. He didn't know what to say in response, and even if he'd known what to say, he wasn't sure *how* to say anything because of the tight knot in his throat.

Then Molly's back door squealed open and slammed back on its frame, and Molly rounded the corner of the house, coming toward him with her hands fisted and fire in her eyes that was evident even at fifty feet. Dan was instantly grateful for the reprieve with Mrs. Booth even if it did mean Molly was mad as hell with him about something. He handed the album back to his teacher, then stood, not merely to be polite, but for self-defense.

Molly had cooled off perceptibly before she arrived, however, probably after seeing the elderly woman sitting in the lawn chair.

"Hi, Millie," she said with a little wave. "What brings you here?"

"Oh, I was just out and about," Mrs. Booth said almost breezily.

"You two know each other?" Dan looked from Molly to his teacher and back. Had he heard right? Had she actually called this forbidding woman, this institution-in-a-dress, Millie?

"We met at the library right after I came to town," Molly said, "when we were both looking for *Lady Chatterly's Lover.* Funny, huh?"

Both women laughed like witches in a coven while Dan felt himself breaking out in a cold sweat. They actually held hands for a moment. If there was more to this story, he really didn't want to hear it.

"I meant to return those books you lent me, Millie. I'm sorry. Dan arrived last week to work on my house, and I totally forgot."

"That's quite understandable," Mrs. Booth said. "Well, I'll leave you two alone now." She braced both hands on the flimsy arms of the chair in order to rise. Dan and Molly each took an elbow to assist her. The leather album slid from her lap onto the ground, and when Molly promptly picked it up, Dan snatched it from her hand.

"Don't forget your book, Mrs. Booth," he said, offering it to her. "And thanks. Thanks for everything. Can I drive you home?"

"You're welcome, Daniel. And no, thank you. I enjoy the walk." Album in hand, the big woman began her slow progress across the yard. "Come see me," she called back. It was more of a command than an invitation. "Both of you."

Dan watched her go, feeling an odd mix of emotions. Sadness. Nostalgia. A momentary touch of pride that gave way to regret. He sighed, then turned toward Molly, whose hands had gone to fists again as she glared at him.

"Not now, Molly. Okay?"

He grabbed the lawn chair, snapped it shut and stalked to the door of the Airstream.

"Now, Dan."

Molly pulled the trailer's door closed behind her. It

took a minute for her eyes to adjust to the dim interior, another minute for her nose to adjust to the less-than-fresh atmosphere. The disarray around her suddenly made her even more angry with Dan. Why was he living like this?

"I just spoke with a deputy U.S. marshal in Houston by the name of Holt," she said.

Dan was shoving the collapsed lawn chair into an overhead rack at the back of the trailer. "Never heard of him," he answered gruffly.

"Well, he's certainly heard of you."

The lawn chair displaced a stack of magazines on the already crammed rack, and they tumbled to the floor in a glossy avalanche. Dan swore.

"You lied to me, Dan," Molly said.

He swore again.

"Is that all you can say?" She repeated his curse at double the volume.

"Okay. I lied. It was part of the job. Can we stop arguing now?" He squatted down and began slapping magazines into a pile.

Molly had worked up far too much of a head of steam to let it go at that. "When did you plan to tell me? Or didn't you? Was that it? Was it just 'Hang around the ignorant little witness for a while, Deputy, but don't give her any information that might possibly save her life'?"

"It wasn't like that." He stood and shoved the magazines back in the overhead compartment. "It wasn't like that at all."

"Well, tell me what it *was* like." Molly sat hard on the air mattress, crossing her arms, biting her lower lip to keep from crying hot, angry tears. "I'm in big trouble, and suddenly I feel like I'm all alone." She didn't add that she was also in love and suddenly she didn't even know who she was in love with. Some stranger. Some lying jerk.

"You're not in big trouble," he said, sitting beside her, his arm touching hers. "And you're not alone. I'm here. Hell, I've been here. You just didn't know it. There was no reason to worry you when nobody had any idea whether or not you're in any danger."

"But am I? The deputy on the phone said—"

"I don't care what he said. Nobody knows, Molly. That's the bottom line. The WITSEC files were compromised. Nobody knows who did it or why. It could've been some kid, some hacker who just got lucky. But precautions had to be taken."

Still chewing her lip, Molly nodded. She didn't know if she believed him or not. She wanted to believe him.

"You were a low-priority witness, and I was close by on..." He paused for a second. "Well, I was on vacation, so they sent me. It was never any big deal."

"I see." The terrified witness part of her longed to believe him, but at the same time in her heart she was afraid that the *no big deal* label might also extend to their relationship. That was something she didn't want to believe for a second.

"And the rest?" she asked hesitantly, fighting back tears.

"What rest?"

"Us? You and me? Was that also no big deal?"

He slid his arm around her, pressing her head against his shoulder. "Molly," he said softly. "That was a very big deal, sweetheart. The biggest."

"Was?" she whispered.

"There's a lot you don't know." He sighed.

"That's not exactly fair, is it? I mean, you probably know just about everything about me. About Kathryn Claiborn, anyway."

He nodded. "Pretty much."

"And I don't know anything about you. Not really."

"Sure you do. You know plenty," he said, chuckling softly. "You know every dark detail of my wicked, misspent youth. You know I'm no great shakes as a handyman. And you know I'm a hell of a kisser."

Molly was hard-pressed not to smile as she nestled her head closer against his shoulder, then asked only half in jest, "Yeah, but are you any good with a gun?"

Dan didn't laugh in response. In fact, when he replied, there wasn't a hint of humor in his voice. It was as hard as steel, nearly as cold.

"Yes, Molly. I'm *very* good."

Chapter 10

"I'll bet you know why I'm here," Molly said to Mildred Booth, accepting the glass of lemonade the big woman handed her.

She had slipped out of the stuffy Airstream during Dan's deep, postcoital sleep, then quickly showered and headed even more quickly toward the small bungalow next door to the high school where she found the retired teacher rocking on her shady front porch. Millie didn't seem particularly surprised by the visit. In fact, it was almost as if she'd been expecting Molly to appear.

"This, no doubt." Millie brought a hand from behind her back, producing the leather album that Molly had seen earlier. "Enjoy," the woman told her while she lowered herself into a substantial wicker rocker.

Molly didn't open the book immediately, but rather traced her fingers across the grain of the leather and the elaborate gilt scrolls at each corner. "You think a lot of Dan, don't you, Millie?"

"Yes, I do," she replied. One white sliver of eyebrow arched over the frame of her glasses. "Don't you?"

"I hardly know him." Molly's frustration was evident in her tone.

"Well, you will. Go on. Open it. I'll just sit here and watch the traffic while you read."

After twenty minutes, only two or three cars had passed the little house, but Molly had learned more about Dan Shackelford than she'd learned in all of the previous week. Especially after reading the final article pasted in the album.

She knew he was brave and responsible and quite good, perhaps even the best, at his chosen profession, altogether different from his bumbling handyman persona. In several photographs, she witnessed expressions on his face that she'd never seen before. There was the cool look of mastery in one. In another, taken while he leaned against a Rolls-Royce, he wore a smile of such blazing confidence, it almost took her breath away.

"He doesn't know how to cope with failure, does he?" she said quietly, her gaze meeting Millie's.

"I'm not a psychologist," the elderly woman said, continuing to rock in her chair, returning her eyes to the street, "but that would be my guess."

Molly snapped the album closed. "Well," she said, "I'll just have to do something about that, won't I?"

"I should hope so, dear."

But what could she do?

That was the question gnawing at Molly after she left Mrs. Booth's. When a man's confidence was shattered, how did one put it back together? Was it even possible?

It had been a good while since the incident in Manhattan when Dan's partner and the witness he was protecting were gunned down. If he were due for a miraculous recovery, Molly was pretty certain it would have happened by now.

He'd told her that he'd been on vacation when he was ordered to Moonglow to watch over her, but she suspected it wasn't a vacation at all. More likely he'd taken a leave of absence from the Marshals Service and hidden out in his stupid trailer, avoiding everyone and everything. Wallowing in recriminations and self-pity and beer. Digging himself deeper and deeper into depression and despair.

She thought about the student health services back at Van Dyne College with their highly qualified counselors and psychologists, and wondered if there was a decent therapist here in Moonglow, but then decided Dan had probably already been offered the services of the best shrinks in the government, and had most likely turned them all down.

Get him back in the saddle. That's what she had to do. Just like when somebody fell off a horse. Only how was she going to do that? Dan had already assured her she wasn't in any danger from the Red Millennium, so there weren't going to be any bad guys for him to fight.

Unless...

Molly smiled.

Unless she conjured up an antagonist or two to lure her fallen knight back into the fray.

Dan had no idea how long Molly had been gone, but the shower curtain was wet, along with her oatmeal soap and towel. He was fairly confident that even the most polite of assailants wouldn't have given her time to

shower before abducting her. Still, he wished she'd
awakened him and let him know her plans. Dammit.

The kid wasn't around, either, after putting up two
more strips of wallpaper and replacing the leaky metal
pipe under the kitchen sink with a substantial length of
PVC, something Dan couldn't have done even if it had
occurred to him. Buddy hadn't emptied the drip bucket,
though, so Dan lugged it outside.

He was just about ready to jump in his car and go
hunting for Molly when he saw her coming down the
street with a grocery bag in her arms. The late-afternoon
sun was gilding her hair and her skirt was molding itself
to her long legs with every step she took. He wondered
if Kathryn Claiborn had ever been even half as lovely
as his Molly.

Meeting her at the end of the driveway, he took the
heavy grocery bag from her arms. "What's for dinner?" he asked. "Bricks?"

"I thought we should celebrate the new pipe under
the sink, so I'm fixing linguine with my special white
clam sauce," she said before adding, "well, sort of."

"Sort of?"

Molly blew a strand of hair out of her eyes and
laughed. "You don't actually think they sell clams
down at the Pick 'n Pay, do you?"

"I'd be surprised," Dan said. "So, what's for dinner,
then?"

"Linguine with my special white clam sauce," Molly
repeated, "only the linguine is spaghetti and the clams
will be masquerading as tuna."

"Sounds good," Dan said, rolling his eyes behind
her back as he followed her through the door and into
the kitchen.

As it turned out, though, the ersatz clam sauce was

terrific, as well as the California Chablis that Molly had found to go with it.

"This is nice," she said halfway through the meal.

"What?"

"Being able to talk about the past, not having to worry that I'm going to spill the beans about the *real* me."

Dan nodded while he twisted a few strands of mock linguine around his fork. "It's hard being in WITSEC, I know. A lot of people can't hack it, even for a few months. Especially the people who have to leave big families behind."

"Well, I guess I was lucky, not having a family to leave," she said a bit wistfully. And when Dan asked, "Wasn't there anybody?" her reply was a quiet but adamant "No, nobody."

He took a sip of the cool Chablis. "What about your fiancé?"

Molly shrugged. Dan couldn't tell whether the gesture was meant to indicate affection or indifference, or if it meant she just didn't want to talk about the guy.

"What a jerk," he said, a bit more forcefully than he'd intended.

Molly's eyes narrowed, zapping him with two blue flames across the table. "You don't even know him."

"I don't have to," Dan countered.

"To know he's a jerk?"

"That's right."

Molly drained the wine in her glass, setting it down with a little thump. "And just how do you know that?" she asked, reaching for the tall green bottle and pouring more. "Are you omniscient? Psychic? What?"

"No," he said. "I'm here. With you." Dan grinned. "And he's not."

She burst out laughing. He'd caught her right in the middle of delicately sipping her wine, and she proceeded to splutter it all over herself and the table, as well. Dan leaned back in his chair, crossing his arms, cocking his head, still grinning.

It was all he could do not to say *I love you.* Certainly a hell of a lot more than that jerk back in New York.

After dinner, Molly stood at the kitchen sink, enjoying the warmth of the soapy dishwater, but wishing Dan hadn't closed the curtains on the window. She much preferred gazing out into the backyard to staring at a bunch of gathered blue gingham.

Her scheme to get her errant knight back on his charger hadn't gone as planned. She'd had such a good time during dinner telling the truth about her past that she hadn't wanted to ruin it with a lie about some suspicious character she'd seen in town. The fact that Dan had called Ethan a jerk didn't even bother her. Maybe her fiancé was a jerk. Molly hadn't really thought about him much in the past year.

She rinsed a plate under the stream of hot water, glad that Ethan wasn't here and that Dan was, oddly happy that she herself was here, in a crummy little house in a backwater town where she couldn't even buy canned clams or a decent pinot noir, doing dishes in a rust-stained sink, and loving Dan Shackelford with all her heart.

The back door squeaked as Dan came in from taking out the trash, and the next thing Molly knew his arms were around her and his lips were tantalizing her neck. When his warm breath covered her ear and he whispered sexily, "I'll dry. Where's the dishtowel?" he might as well have been whispering erotica for the sensual effect it had on her. Her heart drummed an extra beat and her bloodstream heated up a few degrees.

"No, don't let go," she said, putting the rinsed plate down in order to clasp his arms more tightly around her. "This is so nice. So sweet. So…I don't know. So domestic."

From his silence, Molly immediately knew she'd chosen the wrong word—*domestic*—to describe her bliss. Stupid. Stupid, stupid, stupid. She could practically hear the workings of Dan's mind—*Domestic? Marriage? Me?*—and especially the squeal of the mental brakes as he applied them.

His embrace loosened perceptibly. "Molly, honey, my life's pretty messed up right now. I…"

"Silly. I didn't mean that the way it sounded," she said quickly and brightly, cutting him off, reaching for another plate to scrub and rinse. "All I meant was that it's nice to finally feel comfortable here after hating this place for a year. That's all. The dish towel's right over there, by the way."

She angled her head toward the metal bar near the refrigerator at the same time she cursed herself for spoiling the moment. It only made sense that a man who considered himself on the skids would be reluctant to deepen a relationship, no matter how much he cared about a woman. He cared. She knew he did. It was time, Molly decided, to pull her little scheming rabbit out of the hat.

"Here." She handed him a plate. "Something really odd happened today while I was at the Pick 'n Pay. I forgot to tell you."

He frowned. "What was that?"

"Well, for just a split second, I thought I saw Jorgen

Metz passing by, out on the street. You know who I mean, right? That eerie-looking albino with the—''

''I know who you mean,'' he said gruffly. ''Why didn't you tell me this before?''

She shrugged. ''I didn't exactly forget, I guess. I just didn't want to spoil our dinner by having you get all bent out of shape.''

''Dammit, Molly.'' He took a last swipe at the plate and put it down on the counter. ''We're not kindergartners playing hide and seek, here. This is serious.''

''See! You *are* all bent out of shape. That's why I didn't tell you before. Here.'' She handed him a wineglass. ''Dry this.''

When he glared at her, she added, ''It was probably just my imagination. I mean, he's such a creepy guy, it certainly would have registered more if I'd really seen him.''

''Well, just what did you see?''

She gave a thoughtful pause, as if searching her memory when what she was actually doing was trying to invent a plausible story. ''I can't say that I saw him, exactly. It was more of an impression. Fleeting. There he was, and then there he wasn't. Like that.'' She snapped her fingers, but because they were slippery with soap, it wasn't quite the cavalier gesture she'd intended.

''But you saw enough to believe it was Metz?''

''Well, yes.''

''Okay.'' He put the dry wineglass down, then handed Molly the dish towel. ''Dry your hands. Pack a quick bag. We're going to Houston.''

''Dan!'' Good grief. She'd wanted to get *him* back in the saddle, for heaven's sake. No way was she going to Houston. No way would she let him foist her off on another agent there.

"I can't leave," she said. "I told you that before."

"You're leaving. With or without a bag. It's up to you."

"No, Dan, I..."

His hands clamped her upper arms like two vises. His eyes were practically shooting sparks when he said, "And you can ride in the front seat with me, or in the trunk. That's up to you, too. But, Molly, you *are* leaving."

"All right. All right," she said, pulling out of his grasp. "I'll go toss a few things in a suitcase and get my laptop. But I think you're overreacting, Dan. I really do."

"Yeah, well, that's what I get paid for," he grumbled as she left the kitchen. Then, as she made her way down the hall, he yelled, "And close the curtains in the bedroom while you're in there."

"Fine," Molly shouted back. And after she closed the curtains, if she even bothered with the stupid things, she'd have to find a different rabbit to pull out of a hat. The albino one obviously hadn't worked.

While Molly packed, Dan sat at the kitchen table, drumming his fingers on its top. He had his car keys in his pocket and his gun was still nestled in the small of his back so there was no reason to go out to the trailer. The minute Molly was ready, they'd get in the car and go.

He'd wait to call Bobby from someplace down the road, just in case there was a bug on Molly's phone. In a little over three hours, he'd have her in Houston and out of danger. Assuming she *was* in danger. At this point, Dan didn't care if he wound up looking like a hysterical, overreacting idiot, or turned into the butt of deputies' jokes for the next ten years. All that mattered was Molly's safety. And he wouldn't be around to hear the jokes, anyway.

"Molly," he called. "Are you almost ready?"

"Just about."

"Well, hurry the hell up."

Just then he heard a car pull into the driveway, followed immediately by the slamming of two doors. He was already reaching for his gun when he heard Raylene's unmistakable voice.

"You get your sorry butt in there, young man, and you apologize for all you're worth. Do you hear me?"

Dan was already at the door when he heard Buddy Jr. whimper "Yes, ma'am. Ouch!" to the woman who was pulling him along by one ear. Dan glanced at the car they'd just parked behind his, blocking his exit, and decided to get rid of them quick. Whatever the kid was supposed to apologize for, Dan was ready to graciously and promptly accept, then send them on their way.

"Hey, Raylene. What's up?" he asked, pushing open the screen door.

"Tell him, Buddy. Go on." She cuffed the boy and sent him stumbling across the threshold into the kitchen before coming inside herself. "My Lord, Danny. I'm so ashamed of this child of mine, I could just curl up and die."

"It can't be that bad," Dan said.

"That's what you think," the beautician said while she was rummaging around in her oversize handbag. "What about this?" She pulled a .357 Magnum from the depths of her bag. There was a silencer screwed to its muzzle.

Dan took the revolver from her before she blew his

head off. "Where did you get this, Raylene?" he asked, making sure the safety was on.

"It's Buddy Sr.'s," she said, then turned to her son, who looked as if he was about to cry. "Go ahead. Start talking, mister. Nice and loud. Danny's waiting." She tapped a high-heeled sandal on the floor. "We're all waiting."

Buddy Jr. dragged in a breath. "I'm sorry I fired those shots the other night. I only meant to scare her."

"Whoa. Wait a minute," Dan said. "*You* fired those six slugs into the wall?"

"Yessir."

Dan stared at the gun a moment. "Where'd you get the silencer, kid? These are illegal, you know."

"Yessir. I know."

"Tell him, Buddy," Raylene said. "You tell him every bit of it, or I'll…"

Dan held up a hand, cutting her off. "This is important, Buddy. You need to tell me everything. Now."

The boy's eyes, already red, brimmed with tears. "I was only trying to get enough money to buy Henry Young's old Harley. That's why I was working here, for Ms. Hansen. You know. Only I still needed more. Seven hundred bucks. So I met this man…"

"What man?" Dan asked, believing he already knew the answer. "What did he look like?"

"Creepy," the boy said. "Real pale. Like a dead fish."

Dan breathed a hot oath. Jorgen Metz. Molly really had seen him.

"He knew I was working here," Buddy continued. "He gave me the silencer and two hundred dollars. But I fired into the wall above the bed. I couldn't hurt Ms. Hansen. I wouldn't do that."

"My Lord!" Raylene exclaimed. "I can't believe what I'm hearing. I can't believe this is my own flesh and blood talking here. My baby."

"What happened next?" Dan asked calmly. He believed the boy was telling the truth. He'd interrogated enough suspects to know the signs. Only he wished the kid would make prolonged eye contact, just to be sure. "Look at me, Buddy. Tell me what happened next."

Tears were streaming down his cheeks now. The kid could hardly speak. "He got real mad at me. Then he said it was okay, to forget about the gun. He had something else. Then he told me he'd hurt my mom and my dad if I didn't…"

"Didn't what?" Dan urged. He was noticing now that Buddy's gaze kept returning to the same place. The cabinet beneath the kitchen sink. Something was wrong, but Dan couldn't quite make the mental leap.

"If you didn't what?" he asked again, more urgently this time.

"If I…if I didn't put in that…that piece of plastic pipe he gave me." He was staring at the spot below the sink now, crying harder. "There. That one."

Dan could almost feel the tumblers clicking in his brain as everything fell into place. He should have seen it before. He should have guessed. He should have known.

"Molly," he screamed. "Get out of the house. Now."

Molly wrenched the zipper closed on her suitcase and called back irritably, "I'm coming. I'm coming. Just give me a minute to—"

"Now." Dan came through the bedroom door,

grabbed her by the wrist and yanked her into the hall-way.

"Dan! My suitcase! What are you...?"

"There's a bomb in the house, Molly." He pulled her along faster, his fingers digging into her wrist. "Don't talk. Just run."

"Oh, my God."

She didn't need to be told twice, but her knees had already turned to liquid and she couldn't have moved at all if Dan hadn't been leading her along the hall, through the living room and out the front door. Raylene and Buddy Jr. were standing in the driveway, looking confused. No, they looked terrified. What was happening? It felt to Molly as if she were suddenly caught in the dark, rushing currents of a nightmare, being swept along, unable to understand or to wake up.

"I'm so sorry, hon," Raylene said as Dan pulled her past the beautician.

"What?" Molly asked, even more confused.

"Never mind about that," Dan said. "Raylene, you and Buddy meet us at the Sheriff's Office. Get in the car. Now." Then he jerked open the back door of his car and told Molly, "Get in. Get down on the floor."

When she started to say something, he shouted, "Do it, dammit," and pushed her in, slamming the door behind her.

The BMW's engine roared to life and the tires squealed when Dan pulled out of the driveway and accelerated down the street. Then, a moment later, Molly felt the car swerve, then stop. Dan cut the engine. She heard him slap the steering wheel, ram his fist into the dashboard, then loose a string of curses that filled the interior of the car.

"I should have known," he said. "Dammit. I should have seen it right there in front of me."

Molly elbowed up from the floor, then slid onto the back seat. "Should have seen what?" she asked.

"The bomb. Under the sink. Sitting there all that time and looking like an everyday piece of PVC. They finally did it." He slapped the steering wheel again. "Those bastards finally did it."

"Who? What? Dan, I don't know what you're talking about."

"The Red Millennium," he said. "Metz and his partners have been working for years, trying to come up with a nonmalleable plastic explosive that was stable enough to be molded into something like a pipe or a switch plate or other construction material. That explosion in New York—"

"My explosion?" she asked. "The one I was in?"

He nodded. "Yeah. At Van Dyne. They were getting close, but they weren't there yet. They had the rigidity, but they couldn't make it stable."

After she got out of the hospital, Molly had made a concerted effort not to read anything about the explosion. It gave her nightmares. Now she thought ignorance was probably not the best policy, especially considering that her survival seemed to be at stake.

"Why weren't they content just to use plain old tried-and-true bombs?" she asked, feeling even more ignorant because she didn't even have a vocabulary that included terrorists and explosive devices.

"Too easily detected," he said. "Too risky to put in place. But if they could actually build the explosive compounds into the building, in the plumbing or the electrical work, then they could just sit back and wait. Months. Even years."

"My God," Molly breathed. "That's brilliant."

"No kidding," Dan said sourly.

"But how did the bomb get under my sink?"

"Buddy Jr."

Molly's breath whistled out through her teeth.

"You were right about Jorgen Metz, Molly."

Oh, no, she wasn't, she thought as Dan continued.

"Metz is here. In Moonglow. He paid Buddy, then threatened him. I doubt the kid even knew what the pipe was when he installed it."

She saw his glance cut to the rearview mirror, then realized he'd been doing that repeatedly as he spoke. It suddenly dawned on Molly that Dan wasn't simply her friend or her lover. He was her protector, as well. And perhaps, with no help from her at all, he was truly back in the saddle again.

"You saved my life, Dan," she said quietly, reaching out to touch the back of his head. "Thank you."

He started the car, gave another glance in the rearview mirror, then fixed his eyes on Molly's face in the mirror. "It isn't over yet, you know," he said, trying but failing miserably to offer her a reassuring grin. "Just keep your head down, babe."

After hustling Molly inside the Sheriff's Office, Dan was relieved to see Raylene and her son already there. On the other hand, Gil Watson's bulk ensconced behind his big desk was no relief at all. He had hoped that Gil would still be at Linda's side, leaving him to deal with young Jess, the deputy.

"What's this about a bomb, Danny?" Gil said almost as soon as Dan walked in the door. "I told you you'd best keep your nose clean while you're in town, didn't I?"

Dan sighed while he reached into the pocket of his jeans for his credentials. "How's Linda?" he asked.

"Better," Gil said. "Didn't I tell you to watch your step?"

"Yeah, Gil. That's what you told me." Dan tossed his photo ID onto the desk. "Take a look at that and then we'll start this conversation again."

"What the hell is this?" the sheriff asked, picking up the ID in his meaty hand, squinting at the photo. "Is this supposed to be you?"

Molly, who had been standing just behind Dan, charged forward. "Dan's a deputy U.S. marshal, Gil. You big—"

Dan cut her off. "Thanks, Professor. I'll take care of this." As he spoke, he was clipping his badge to the pocket of his Hawaiian shirt. "Before we discuss anything, I need to use your phone."

Gil looked from the ID in his hand to the phone and then to Dan's face. His big Adam's apple jerked in his throat. "Long distance?"

"Yeah, Gil. Long distance." It was all Dan could do not to laugh as he picked up the receiver. "But the Justice Department's good for it. Trust me."

Once he got Bobby on the line, Dan turned his back on the sheriff's desk and lowered his voice. It didn't take him long to fill Bobby in and to detail just what he needed. Backup from the Marshals office. An ATF bomb squad. All of them on their way to Moonglow in helicopters yesterday, if possible. And a good lawyer on call to represent Buddy Jr.

"You got a handle on it for now, amigo?" Bobby asked, his tone confidential, his meaning more than clear.

"Hey. No problem," Dan said, then broke the connection. *No problem*. Ha! That was a joke.

He turned back to the desk and put the receiver back in its cradle. "Gil, I'm going to need you to send your deputy to pick up Buddy Earl and bring him into protective custody."

Gil's lips slid into a sneer. He cocked his head toward Raylene and her son. "Buddy's sitting right over there, Danny. Or didn't you *detect* him?"

"Buddy Sr., dammit." Dan slammed both hands on the desk. "I need your help, Gil. If you can shove all that high school crap out of your head for a few hours, I'd appreciate it. And we can debate jurisdiction then, too, if you want. But right now, if you don't do exactly what I tell you, somebody's going to get killed. And if that happens, by God, I'll see you in prison for obstructing a federal officer in the course of his duty." Dan took a breath. "Do you understand me, mister?"

The sheriff sat up a little straighter in his chair, rolled his beefy neck, looked at his watch, then drawled to his deputy, "Drive on over to the Earls', Jess. See if Buddy Sr.'s there. If he is, why don't you just go ahead and ask him to come on back here with you." His gaze moved slowly back to Dan's face, then his eyebrows lifted as if to casually inquire, "There. Are you satisfied?"

"Thank you, Sheriff," Dan said. There was no sarcasm whatsoever in his tone. He meant it. He needed all the help he could get just then. "I've got people coming in. Deputy marshals and the ATF bomb people. Anybody you could bring in right now, Gil?"

"Maybe. First I'd like to know what's going on in my town, though. That is, if you don't mind, *Deputy* Shackelford."

"Right. Okay." Dan settled a hip on the edge of the desk and began to explain.

For security, Dan had moved Molly, Raylene and the two Buddys into one of the windowless cells in the rear of the sheriff's office, but Senior had immediately grabbed Junior and ushered him into an adjacent cell for a tongue-lashing that was still going on an hour later.

Molly was still having a hard time believing that the Swedish terrorist she'd conjured up for Dan's benefit was actually here in Moonglow. Maybe Buddy Jr. was wrong. But it didn't make sense that the boy was lying. And how in the world could an albino Swede be a figment of Buddy's imagination? The kid hardly even had one.

"My Lord," Raylene whispered from her perch on an upper bunk where her legs dangled over the side. "This is like being in a movie, isn't it, Molly? I keep half expecting Bruce Willis to come rushing in."

Molly tried unsuccessfully to mount a smile in response. She was so worried, for all of them, but mostly for Dan. Each time she peered down the narrow corridor toward the office, she could just glimpse his shoulder as he sat at Gil's desk. Everyone else was out. Gil and Jess and the two cops who had come over from Idella. And while they searched for Jorgen Metz, Dan remained behind, protecting his witnesses.

"Well, if he does come rushing in," Molly said, "I hope he's on our side."

"You know," Raylene continued, "I never did believe that Danny was just a traveling repairman. I knew he was way too brainy for that." She tapped a long pink fingernail against her temple. "Plus it didn't make sense that a smart cookie such as yourself would fall head over heels for the Maytag repairman. You know what I mean?''

Molly knew what she meant, but she also knew the beautician was wrong. She thought she'd probably fallen in love with Dan the minute he backed his stupid trailer into her house. She couldn't remember ever *not* loving him. Worse, she couldn't imagine any kind of future that didn't include loving him.

''I'm probably not as smart as I look,'' she said.

''You're a professor, Molly. My Lord. And from New York. You must've just about lost your mind being stashed away here in the armpit of the universe.''

''No,'' Molly said. ''I didn't. Well, maybe at first. But I like it here, Raylene. I really do.''

Raylene gave a little snort and shook her head in dismay. ''You like it here in Moonglow.''

''Yes. I do. Don't you?''

''Honey, I'm *from* here. I have to like it. But you...''

There was a commotion in the front office. Raylene jumped down from the bunk and both women rushed out into the corridor to see what was going on.

Molly heard Dan ask, ''So you found him? You've got him in custody?''

''We've got him in custody, all right,'' Gil Watson replied. ''Permanent custody. The son of a bitch is dead.''

Chapter 11

"Well, that's good, isn't it?" Molly asked Dan, giving the back of his shirt a tug to get his attention. "It's good that Metz is dead. Right?"

It was nearly dawn, and because she'd refused to remain behind in the cell at the Sheriff's Office, she was slumped low in the front seat of Dan's car, parked in her own driveway, while members of the ATF bomb squad were taking their sweet, slow time with the pipe under her kitchen sink.

She was so tired. But even so, she was monumentally relieved that her terrorist pursuer was dead. Gil and Jess had located Jorgen Metz at the Lone Star Motel, but the man had "eaten his gun," as Gil so vividly put it, rather than be taken prisoner. It seemed like a blessing to Molly. She couldn't figure out why Dan didn't seem happier about it.

"Dan!" She gave his shirttail another yank. "Answer me. It's good, right?"

"Yes and no, babe." He turned and squatted down, taking her hand in his. "Metz took a hell of a lot of information with him when he croaked. They're going through his stuff now, but it doesn't look like they'll find very much."

She sighed. "Well, at least he's not going to be able to hurt anybody ever again. That's something."

He drew her hand to his lips. "No, he won't hurt anybody again," he said.

"You look exhausted." Molly brushed his hair back from his forehead, then touched his unshaven cheek. "How much longer will they be in there?"

"As long as it takes to get that pipe out safely."

She shuddered, thinking of Buddy Jr. installing the disguised bomb, not even aware of the danger. "What's going to happen to Buddy now?"

Dan shook his head. "The kid's in deep, but for the time being he and Raylene and Buddy Sr. will go into the WITSEC."

Molly blinked. "Why? The only terrorist he saw is dead."

"We don't know that for a fact, Molly." He dragged his fingers through his hair, and his voice became rougher. "We don't know what Buddy saw or who he met. We don't know if Metz was acting alone or with a partner. This isn't over by a long shot."

"I thought it was," she said quietly.

Another helicopter buzzed close overhead, making it impossible to hear whatever it was that Dan said next. Then he stood and walked away, joining a group of men by the back door. Molly saw one of them gesture toward the Airstream, then all of them laughed. All except Dan.

* * *

It was late afternoon before they finally let Molly back in her house. The bomb people and their dogs had pretty much torn the place apart, searching for more explosive devices. Dying of thirst from sitting out in a hot car most of the day, the first thing she did was turn on the faucet in the kitchen to get a drink, and, with no pipe at all underneath, not even a leaky one, water had poured all over the cabinet and onto the floor.

Not knowing whether to laugh or cry, she was doing a little of both, along with swearing a blue streak when a tall man with close-cropped hair knocked on her back door.

"Ms. Claiborn, I'm Chief Deputy Robert Hayes from Houston. Mind if I come in?"

"No, not at all. Come in. I hope you can swim," she muttered, getting down on her hands and knees to sop up the water.

"Sorry for the mess," he said. "Here. Hand me some of those paper towels." He squatted beside her, and between the two of them, they made quick work of the wet floor.

"I'll see that somebody comes to repair that," he said, angling his head toward the sink. "If you decide to stay, that is. That's what I came to discuss with you. Have a seat, Ms. Claiborn." He pulled out a chair at the table.

"Hansen," Molly said, tossing a wad of wet paper towels into the trash can before taking a seat.

"I beg your pardon?"

"Hansen. That's my name."

He laughed as he lowered himself into a chair across from her. It was a warm, friendly laugh, Molly noticed. Not what she would have expected from a man who looked lean and mean as a drill sergeant. Unlike most of the other federal agents she'd encountered that day, Robert Hayes wore a well-cut suit and an expensive tie. Funny, she thought. She'd almost come to think of Hawaiian shirts as standard apparel for deputy marshals.

"It's okay, Ms. Claiborn. I'm one of the good guys. My office gave you the name." He glanced around the kitchen. "And this house, too, although I'm not so sure I want to admit it."

Molly looked around, too. "It's not so bad," she said with a little shrug. "Actually, it's kind of grown on me. Along with my name."

"That's what I wanted to talk to you about," Hayes said. "At this point, it's too early to say just how much jeopardy you're in. Quite frankly, I don't know. But I've just been informed that we've got a good lead on Ahmad Sharis from some papers we found with Jorgen Metz's body. They might even be picking Sharis up right now in New York."

"That's good," Molly said.

"Better than good. If they do pick him up, with any luck we can get him to trial in six or eight weeks. So, really, we're only talking about another two months in our protection. We'll keep you in WITSEC, naturally, through the trial, but I suspect after that you'll be able to return to New York and your former employment and everything and everyone else you left behind."

He crossed his arms and leaned back, awaiting her reaction.

Molly felt as if the man had just yanked a rug out from under her feet, or rammed his fist into her solar plexus. Go back to New York and her job at Van Dyne? Back to Ethan? That was impossible. Unthinkable.

"I don't *have* to go back, do I?" she asked.

"Well, no." He looked uncomfortable, like somebody who wasn't accustomed to surprises. Like somebody who smelled smoke, but wasn't quite ready to yell *Fire!* "No, of course you don't *have* to. Most witnesses do."

"Good," she said, trying not to show her enormous relief. "I guess I'm not most witnesses."

"You must like it here in Moonglow," Hayes said.

"Very much."

He cocked his head slightly. "And you've been getting along all right with Deputy Shackelford?"

"Fine," she said. "Just fine."

Now his eyes took on a hard, investigative look, narrowing, zeroing in. "I was thinking of pulling him off protective duty."

"I can't imagine why." But she could imagine. Dan's superiors must have been aware of his crisis, of his loss of confidence. After all, they were the ones who'd sent him to Moonglow, never expecting anything to happen here.

"He's done a wonderful job," Molly insisted. "Look! I'm alive. Deputy Shackelford has been thoroughly professional. Really. A true credit to the Marshals Service. He…"

As if on cue, the screen door squeaked open. Dan backed across the threshold, his attention obviously fixed elsewhere as he lifted his hand in an obscene gesture and called, "Yeah, well, blow it out your ear, Kowalski."

Then he turned, grinned at Molly and quit grinning the second his gaze fell on Chief Deputy Robert Hayes.

"Hey, Bobby," he said.

"Dan," Bobby Hayes said, then the chief deputy rolled his eyes in Molly's direction. "Thoroughly professional, hmm?"

"Well, most of the time," she said, squirming. "You know."

"I'm afraid I *do* know." Hayes shoved his chair back and stood up. "I intended to pull you back to regular duty, Deputy Shackelford, but our witness has requested your continued presence. Do you have any problem with that?"

"Fine with me," Dan said.

"Good." He was quiet a moment, gazing idly around the dismal kitchen, then he asked, "Do the two of you have any plans for dinner?"

Molly and Dan looked at each other, then at Bobby Hayes, both shaking their heads in unison.

The chief deputy's rather stony expression cracked into a smile. "Great. I'm famished and I heard there's a pretty decent Italian place out on Route 4. Care to join me?"

Palazzo's was more crowded than Molly had ever seen it, what with all the federal agents who had descended on Moonglow and all of the locals eager to get out and trade tales about the recent events. Nothing this exciting had happened in Moonglow since…well…ever.

Molly could hardly see the red-and-white-checked tablecloths for all the plates and pitchers and elbows on the tables. The restaurant was so packed that she and Dan and Bobby Hayes had to sit at the bar for half an hour waiting for a table.

Even the bar was packed, and Molly found herself perched on a tall stool, wedged between two pairs of broad shoulders, one of them in pressed glen plaid and the other a wrinkled riot of palm trees. She ordered a club soda, not wanting to repeat her last performance here when she'd gotten drunk on Chianti and the sight of Dan across the table from her. Dan, much to her surprise, ordered a club soda, too, but he hardly had time to take a sip because people kept coming up and slapping him on the back.

While Dan was politely enduring the back-pats and the congratulations from people who seemed to think he'd miraculously changed from bum to hero in the space of twenty-four hours, Molly and Bobby tried to carry on a conversation, but it was nearly impossible with all the noise around them.

"I'm sorry. I didn't hear that," Molly said, missing his last statement entirely.

"I said this is quite a homecoming."

Molly gave a little snort. "It's a bit overdue."

The gray-haired man leaned closer. "You don't have to be concerned about your safety, Ms. Hansen. You're in good hands." He angled his head toward Dan.

"I know that," Molly replied.

"*He* doesn't."

She looked long and hard into the chief deputy's somber gray eyes. Suddenly she sensed how much this man cared about Dan, truly cared, far more than a mere professional concern, and suddenly she trusted Bobby Hayes implicitly. Enough to say out loud what she'd never spoken before.

"What can I do? I'm in love with him, you know."

"Yeah. I can see that." He took a thoughtful sip from the bottle in his hand, then shook his head slightly and said, "Damned if I know what you can do. Just keep loving him, I guess. Maybe that's all he needs."

"Maybe," Molly said. But she didn't think so. She could give Dan all the love in the world, but she didn't know how to give him an ounce of confidence.

* * *

It was quiet in the trailer. Thank God, Dan thought. It was a welcome relief after the past twenty-four hours of nonstop noise, whether it was from federal agents shouting back and forth, or the dense static of walkie-talkies, or townsfolk clamoring to congratulate the local boy who "turned out all right, by God."

After Bobby dropped them off following dinner, both Dan and Molly had been so exhausted they'd just flopped, fully dressed, on the air mattress in the trailer. Molly had fallen asleep almost the second her head touched the pillow, but Dan wasn't quite that lucky. He couldn't stop all the recent events from playing over and over in his brain.

Just before she fell asleep, Molly had nestled closer to him and whispered, "You did good, Deputy Shackelford."

"We were lucky," he replied, knowing that if Raylene hadn't happened across the silencer on that gun and hadn't wrested the truth from her son and then dragged him across town for an apology, that pipe would still be under Molly's sink. If Jorgen Metz hadn't died, he might have had time to set it off. If Molly hadn't been walking through the Chemistry Department at Van Dyne at precisely the wrong time… If he hadn't been positioned behind his partner when that elevator opened… *If. If. If.*

"Lucky," Molly echoed sleepily. "Yes. I think we are."

She slept in his arms like a trusting child, unaware that her trust was misplaced. And he, coward that he was, continued to let her do it. He was going to stay even when he knew he ought to leave. Because he couldn't bear the thought of another man watching out for her. Because he couldn't stand the idea of leaving her. Because there would be no life for him after Molly. Because he was no damned hero, but just a man who'd fallen in love.

Bobby, who knew as well as Dan did that there were no medals forthcoming for finding a bomb only after somebody had literally pointed it out, had pulled Dan aside earlier tonight at the restaurant and asked, "Are you okay about staying on here, amigo?"

Dan had tried to sound casual in reply. "Sure. No problem."

"In case you don't know it yet, the lady tells me she's in love with you," Bobby said, then speared him with those steel-gray eyes of his. "Unprofessional as it is, compadre, I'm guessing you feel the same."

He nodded. There was no use denying it. At the same time, he tried to suppress a startled, goofy grin. He *was* in love!

"Okay," Bobby said after a long, deliberate pause, meant to put Dan on the sharpest of tenterhooks. "Just don't let that get in your way."

He levered up on an elbow now, tracing the warm curve of Molly's flank with the palm of his hand, listening to her soft breathing, questioning his ability to keep her alive, but knowing, by God, he'd die trying.

He was drifting in and out of sleep, trying to keep one step ahead of bloodred dreams, to keep the elevator door from opening, to keep Molly out of harm's way, when she turned within the circle of his arms and softly brushed her lips against his.

"Are you sleeping?" she whispered.

"Not importantly." He chuckled softly, pulling her closer.

"Love me, Dan," she whispered, edging away from him just far enough to whisk her shirt over her head. "Please love me."

He was ready, even before she undid the snap and her soft hand slipped under the waistband of his jeans to find him.

"My pleasure, darlin'," he murmured, kissing each dimpled corner of her lips before taking full possession of her sweet, willing mouth. "Always my pleasure. I love loving you, Molly."

"Do you know what I wish?" she asked, her voice riding on a long and nearly breathless sigh.

"What, sweetheart?"

"I wish we could stay here forever. Right here. Just like this."

Her words trailed off in a muted *ah* as his hand moved from the slope of her breast, over the dip of her navel, down, threading the maze of cotton skirt and silk panties until he reached the slick, hot essence of her. The secret place where he could stay, where he wished he could lose himself forever. Right here. Just like this.

"I wish," she said, "I wish I could seal the door and the windows to keep us in and everybody else out. To keep the whole world out."

"You and me, welded in an Airstream," he murmured, his mouth following the track his hand had blazed along her flesh.

"Two sardines in our own comfy tin." She sighed. "Wouldn't it be nice, Dan? Wouldn't it?"

"Nice." He knew from sweet practice just where, just when, just how to use his tongue to send a deep shudder through her.

"Oh, that's nice. Oh, how I wish..."

"Molly," he whispered, "Shut up, darlin'."

Later, she lay beside him, catching her breath, still wishing aloud, this time that tonight would never have to end.

Dan was at a loss for a proper response, one that wouldn't sadden her. In his experience, everything ended. Nights. Days. Loves. Lives.

He tucked her head into his shoulder and kissed the top of her hair. "We'll have plenty of nights," he told her, hoping it didn't sound dismissive.

Molly was quiet then for a long while. Dan thought she'd fallen asleep until she whispered softly, "You make me feel so safe, Dan. I love you. Do you know that?"

Ah, God. He didn't answer. Instead he let his breathing deepen, feigning sleep.

I love you, too, Molly. I wish you were as safe as you feel.

Over the next few weeks, Molly came close to getting her wish of being hermetically sealed inside the Airstream with Dan and long, luxurious nights of making love that left them both bleary-eyed the following mornings. It was a little like a honeymoon, she thought.

Well, not exactly. Sweet, solicitous and sexy as he was, Dan never used the word *love* except in the context of making love. Molly told herself it wasn't because he didn't love her, but rather because his shattered confidence had made him reluctant to make any kind of emotional commitment to anyone else.

She'd never considered herself a particularly patient person—patient people didn't climb the ladder of academia as quickly as she had—but in this case she was willing to wait for Dan as long as it took for him to mend.

In the meantime, there was the sheer bliss of being with him. Not *all* of their time was spent in the trailer. They tackled the house with the help of all the do-it-yourself books and magazines they could find in the library. They finished putting up the wallpaper that Buddy Jr. had started in the bedroom.

"That's not half bad, Molly," Dan gloated the evening they finished as he stood in the doorway, sipping a beer while admiring the walls. "If things go south at the Marshals Service, hell, I can just be a paper hanger. What do you think? I could put an ad in the paper. 'Have paper. Will hang.'"

"I don't think so," she said, laughing. "That's how Hitler got started, you know."

"I'm not quite that crazed or ambitious. A little piece of Texas would be plenty of real estate for me. Maybe right here in Moonglow."

She couldn't believe her ears or the way her heart had leapt at the very notion of his settling down. Here! "You're not serious, are you?"

"Maybe." He took another swig from the bottle, then leaned a shoulder against the door frame, cocked one leg and grinned. "Maybe I am. I could retire. Hell, I'm not married to the Marshals Service. It's just a job."

But it wasn't just a job to him and Molly damn well knew it. He was talking about quitting more than merely a job. What he meant was giving up completely, never trying again, refusing to ride the horse that had thrown him. No way was she going to encourage him to do that. As a matter of fact, she was going to do everything in her power to discourage him.

He shifted off the door frame and ambled into the room, still grinning and surveying the wallpaper with obvious pride. "What do you say, Molly? You and me." His green eyes twinkled. "Wallpapers R Us. You Rang, We'll Hang."

"That doesn't even make sense, Dan," she said irritably.

"Okay." He laughed. "How about Dan, Dan, the Wallpaper Man? Does that do anything for you?"

"No. Nothing."

"Okay. Well, how about—"

"Stop it," she shrieked. "Just stop it."

He lowered the beer bottle, looking sincerely surprised, and more than a little defensive. "What's wrong with that? I thought you'd be happy. Isn't that what you *wished* for? You and me. Here. Trapped in my trailer."

"No, Dan, it isn't. I never said anything about being trapped."

"Okay. Sorry." His hand went to cover his heart and the palm trees above it. "Bad choice of words. I should have said living happily ever after in my trailer, just the two of us, away from the big bad world and everyone in it. That's what you wished for."

"Well, maybe I did say that, but it was during the throes of passion. Jeez." She rolled her eyes. "I can't be held responsible for what I say then."

"No," he said firmly. "It was *not* during the throes of passion. I remember. All we were doing was kissing."

"That's right." Molly crossed her arms. "I rest my case."

"What do you mean, you rest your case?"

"I mean, you're the greatest kisser north of the Rio Grande, right? The minute your lips touch mine, my brain turns to tapioca." She tried to make her voice light and carefree when she shrugged and added, "I probably say a lot of things I don't really mean. Most of it. All of it. It's just bull, Dan. Blather. Babbling. Background music. Sort of my own sound track for sex.''

"Jeez, Molly." He set the beer bottle on the dresser, then ripped his fingers through his hair. "What is this? What are you trying to say? I thought you…" His voice faltered. He just stood there, blinking, looking gut-punched.

It was all Molly could do to make herself stand still when every ounce of her being ached to put her arms around him, to tell him she loved him more than life itself, to tell him she'd not only be happy to spend the rest of her life with him in his dented Airstream, but she'd be equally happy in a cardboard box if Dan were in it, too.

But he had to get back on that horse!

"I can't believe you took all those things seriously," she said, trying to look shocked, perhaps even a bit disappointed. "For heaven's sake, Dan, you've had enough experience to know that people get carried away in the heat of the moment. Some more than others, I guess. I probably start babbling poetry and making wishes instead of sighing and moaning. I don't know."

"So this has just been about sex, then? You and me?" he asked.

There was a hard edge to his tone and a flare of anger in his eyes. Good, Molly thought. That was what she'd wanted to provoke.

"Well, not *all* about sex," she said. "Nothing's ever *all* about anything. But in our case I'd say it's probably, oh, ninety-five percent." She grinned, praying her lips wouldn't twitch. "We're great in bed together, Dan. You can't deny that."

"No, I don't deny that."

He was staring at the floor, so Molly couldn't see his eyes as he spoke. Even so, she could detect an odd shift in his posture. His habitually relaxed frame now seemed tense, hot-wired. It felt like an eternity before he finally looked up with a wariness in his eyes that Molly had never seen before.

And it very nearly broke her heart when he put on a cold, calculated killer grin and held out his hand to her and said, "Come on, Mol. Forget the wallpaper. Hell. Let's go out to the trailer and do what we do best. We don't have all that many nights left, you know."

After that night and Molly's revelation, for the next few days Dan got back in the habit of wearing his shades. He was afraid, no matter how good an actor he was, his eyes might betray him.

Sex? He took it up a level, from Molly's ninety-five percent to a hot ninety-nine point nine. He turned all the warmth he felt into fire. And just once, to keep his own heart from shattering, while they made love, he taunted her.

"Sing for me, Molly," he rasped at her ear while he moved inside her, while he brought her higher and higher. "Get your sound track going, baby. Sing me a love song. Tell me you love me."

"No. Please, Dan."

"Go on. Sing it. Say it."

"I don't…"

"Say it, Molly. Now."

"I love you."

"Say it again."

"I love you."

"Bullshit."

He made her cry. Because he couldn't.

* * *

For all she tried to concentrate on the student essay on the screen, Molly couldn't get the sound of Dan's curse out of her head. Violent. Vicious. The sound of a cobra hissing just before it bit.

And as much as it hurt her, she didn't blame him. How could she? She'd driven him to it. She'd been a grand success. Sweet Dan, Dan, the Wallpaper Man, had disappeared. In his place was a hard case, Deputy Marshal Dan Shackelford. She knew he was ready to go back to work, not from anything he'd said, but from the slant of his mouth, the set of his jaw, a certain distance in him even when he was close.

She hadn't lost him, she kept telling herself. She'd saved him.

"Molly?" Dan's voice sounded from the door behind her and her heart kicked an extra beat.

"Yes?" She tried to sound neutral, neither happy nor sad.

She didn't hear him approach, but suddenly she could feel the warmth emanating from his solid body. Just as she began to turn toward him, his hands clamped each arm of her chair and he swiveled her around to face him. His expression was so serious, so intense, it almost frightened her.

"Dan? What…?"

"Don't say anything, all right? Just listen. I was way out of line last night. I'm sorrier than you'll ever know."

"Oh, Dan, sweetheart, you don't—"

"Just listen." He gave the chair a little shake. "I care, Molly." His eyes closed for a second as he drew in a frustrated breath. "No, that's not right. I love you, dammit."

Molly would have laughed if it hadn't been for the intensity in his eyes and the fierce set of all his features. He loved her!

He was about to continue when the phone rang. "Don't move," he ordered her. "I'll be right back."

Move! She could hardly breathe. Her heart was crowding her lungs out of her chest.

She just sat there, smiling like an idiot while she listened to the muted conversation taking place in the living room. Finally, when she heard Dan replace the receiver in its cradle and then his returning footsteps, Molly swung her chair around.

Her heart suddenly shrank a few sizes when she saw his face. All that fire, that fine fury was gone. He looked ten years older. Infinitely sad. Uncertain again.

"My God! What's wrong?" she asked.

"That was Bobby. There's been a change of venue. Ahmad Sharis's trial starts tomorrow in Philadelphia. They want you on the witness stand at four o'clock, Ms. Claiborn."

Chapter 12

While Dan spent the next several hours in a series of conference calls between Houston, Philadelphia and Moonglow, Molly showered and attempted to pack a bag for an indefinite stay in the East.

She reached in the back of her closet for the only suit she'd brought with her from New York. After she'd extracted it from the cleaner's bag, she stared at the navy gabardine skirt and jacket, hardly recognizing them. Then she took down a shoe box from the top shelf, blew the dust from its top and pulled out the navy pumps she hadn't worn in over a year, wondering if they'd still fit. It was as if they belonged to someone else. In a way, they did.

They were Kathryn's clothes—dark, severe and professional. More than ever before, Molly sensed that her former self had disappeared completely.

We'll keep you in WITSEC, naturally, through the trial, but I suspect after that you'll be able to return to

New York and your former employment and everything and everyone else you left behind.

"Not on your life, Chief Deputy Hayes," she said out loud as she tossed the shoes into her suitcase. "Kathryn's dead. Long live Molly." Then she smiled softly as she added, "Long live Molly with Dan."

"Who are you talking to?" Dan was suddenly in the doorway behind her.

"Nobody. Well, Kathryn actually. But that uptight chick is history once this trial is over." She grinned.

"Oh, yeah?" He raised an eyebrow. "All of her?"

She pondered that a moment in all seriousness. "Well, I might go back to my natural hair color. I'm not really a blonde, you know."

Now Dan grinned. "No kidding, Mol? I never noticed."

In the seconds it took for that remark to register, he had crossed the room and wrapped her in his arms. "About last night, Molly," he whispered. "That'll never happen again. I swear."

"I've already forgotten it," she said, holding him tighter. "Oh, Dan, I—"

"Shh." He kissed her to silence her, then said, "We've got a lot to talk about, sweetheart, but not now. This trial deal, Molly, for the next couple of days, I need to focus on that. I can't let anything distract me. Understand?"

She nodded, silently glorying in his determination. He wasn't only back in the saddle, he was galloping. Yee-ha!

"Finish packing," he said, loosening his embrace. "I've got to get a couple things from the trailer, and then we'll hit the road."

He started for the door, then turned back, his gaze

moving slowly around the bedroom. "Nice wallpaper," he said with a little chuckle before he disappeared down the hall.

Dan tossed his garment bag on top of Molly's suitcase, then slammed the trunk. He dragged his sunglasses down his nose and took a last, long look at the house. It looked sorrier than it had when he'd arrived to repair it. Now, not only was the paint peeling, but most of the guttering was gone. Hell. When they got back to Moonglow, he'd—

He shook his head, obliterating thoughts of the future, making himself concentrate on the here and now, doing his damnedest to ignore the cold sweat that kept creeping up on him, the doubts that kept piercing his gut like ground glass.

Molly was already in the car. He slid into the driver's seat, wrenched the key in the ignition, backed down the drive, then hit the gas and laid a good ten feet of rubber on Second Street, for old time's sake, for luck.

"We're outta here," he said.

They reached Bobby's ranch on the outskirts of Houston a little after four. The plan was to spend the night there, then catch the 6:00 a.m. flight for Philadelphia. That would give them just a few hours at the hotel before getting Molly to the courthouse.

"You're early," Bobby said by way of greeting, descending the front steps. "How many speed limits did you blow away, amigo?"

"A few." Dan popped the trunk lid, climbed out and retrieved their bags while Bobby and Molly chatted.

Despite the "happy host" exterior, Dan could sense the tension in his old friend. He'd known Bobby too many years not to read that something was wrong. In his current frame of mind, the only thing Dan could figure was that Bobby was going to pull him off the assignment. Somebody else would be escorting their witness to Philadelphia tomorrow. Like hell.

He was ready to tell Bobby just that when he pulled him aside after they walked into the house.

"Got a little bad news, I'm afraid, compadre."

"Oh, yeah?" Dan asked through clenched teeth. "What's that?"

Bobby leaned a little closer, lowered his voice. "Eileen's put you two in separate rooms. I didn't tell her." He shrugged almost sheepishly. "Well, you know. Sorry about that."

Dan let out his breath. His face was so tense his lips could only twitch. "S'okay, boss. It's going to be a pretty short night, anyway, what with that six o'clock flight. What do we need? About forty minutes to get from here to the airport?"

"I'd make it an hour, just to be on the safe side."

"Right."

As Dan started to move away, Bobby snagged his elbow. Now what? Dan thought.

"You can just kind of tiptoe across the hall, you know, Danny. Later on. Hell, what Eileen doesn't know won't hurt her."

Dan eased into a full-fledged grin. "Thanks, boss. Don't worry about it, okay?"

It was still dark the next morning and there was just a hint of autumn in the air as Molly stood in the driveway with the hostess she'd hardly had time to speak with. As soon as they'd arrived yesterday, Bobby had spirited her into a downstairs office and put her on the phone with the U.S. Attorney in Philadelphia, who proceeded to spend two hours going over her testimony.

"Thank you so much, Eileen," Molly said. "You shouldn't have gotten up so early, though. Why don't you go back to bed? I'm sure Dan will be out in just a minute."

The woman gave her such a weird look in response that Molly wondered if she'd inadvertently said something wrong.

"I'll just wait till Dan comes out," she said again, gesturing toward the front porch where Bobby was deep in conversation with another deputy.

Eileen kept giving her that weird look, only now it was accompanied by a smile. "How much sleep did you get last night, Molly?" she asked.

"I don't know. Five, maybe six hours. Enough. Why?"

The woman's smile widened. She tipped her head toward the porch. "That's Dan."

"Excuse me?"

"I said that's Dan on the porch with Bobby."

Molly looked again. My God, it was. It took her a minute, maybe more, to absorb the serious gray suit, the crisp white shirt, the Repp tie, the tasseled loafers giving off a soft shine in the porch light. And by the time she'd fully absorbed it, he was loping down the porch steps toward her.

"You ready, babe?" he asked.

She opened her mouth, but nothing came out.

"Molly? You okay?" When Eileen started laughing, Dan turned to her. "What's so funny? What did I miss?"

"Nothing," Eileen said, still laughing as she lifted

on tiptoe to kiss his chin. "Take good care, Danny.
Molly, you come back and see us again, you hear?"

Molly found her voice in time to say, "I'd love to.
Thanks again, Eileen," as the woman ascended the
steps on her way back into the house.

"What was that all about?" Dan asked.

"Just girl talk," she said.

He took a step back, giving her an appreciative once-
over, and it suddenly dawned on Molly that Dan had
never seen her in a suit, either.

"Not bad, Professor," he said.

Molly laughed. "Thank you, Deputy. You're no
slouch, yourself."

Then his smile kind of flattened out as he opened the
car door for her. "Okay. Let's get this show on the
road."

Their plane was more or less on time, and, thank
God, the ride more or less uneventful. Molly slept most
of the way with her head on Dan's shoulder.

She woke briefly, long enough to lift her big baby
blues to his face and whisper, "I missed you last
night." Five words that sent him into an immediate,
downhearted funk that he wasn't able to dismiss as
quickly as he wished.

This was a first. He was head over heels in love and
she was just in it for great sex. That was what she'd
said, after all. Well, hell. He told himself he ought to
appreciate her honesty if not her healthy regard for one
of his favorite pastimes. Only it wasn't enough. Not
nearly.

He let his eyes drift closed, tried to blank out his
mind, ease all the knots in his body. When this was
over, he'd make her see they had a lot more going for

them than setting fire to mattresses. She'd have to see that. Wouldn't she?

When this was over. When he got her safely through it. And he was going to get her safely through it. God. Please.

Molly was scrunched on the floor of the back seat of the car that picked them up at the airport. Even though she thought Dan was going a little overboard with the protection bit, she didn't say so. He was wound so tight that she could feel her own muscles aching in empathy.

It was hard not to whine, though. Just a little. "Dan, can't I sit up there just a minute or two?"

If he heard her, then he was doing a dandy job of ignoring her.

"My butt's asleep!"

"We're nearly there," he snapped. "A couple more blocks."

Molly rolled her eyes. Her left foot was asleep, too. She'd be lucky if she could walk. She didn't even want to think about the shape her suit was in. And her hair was a mess from sleeping on the plane. The jury was going to take her for a bag lady.

She swayed against the front seat when the car came to a stop.

"Don't get out until I tell you, Molly," Dan said. "And keep your head down."

"Aye, aye, Captain, sir," she muttered after he jumped out and slammed the door on her. She could hear him barking orders left and right, swearing, shouting. Then the door opened and suddenly he wanted her out of the car...yesterday!

"Come on, Molly. Move it. Let's go."

Once out of the car, she saw the reason for the rush.

A dozen or more men had stopped all foot traffic in front of the small downtown hotel. Another half-dozen guys with serious suits and grim faces and the regulation shades were waiting to surround her on the walk from the sidewalk through the front door of the hotel.

All of a sudden she was scared. To death. Her legs turned to Silly Putty just as Dan's arm went around her and pulled her close against his hip.

"You're okay," he said as if he'd somehow read her mind. "We'll be up in the room in just a minute."

It took way more than a minute, but once they were in the room and Dan turned the lock and fastened the chain on the door, Molly took in a great gulp of air. She thought she'd probably been holding her breath ever since getting out of the car. She was shaking, trying so hard not to wimp out on Dan, trying not to cry.

"S-somebody really d-does want me d-dead." Her tears spilled over. "Oh, God. I want to g-go home. Take me home, Dan. Take me b-back to Moonglow."

"Count on it, Molly," he said as his arms went around her, holding her so tight, so close against him that she could feel every muscle in his body. He held her that way, not saying a word, just silently, almost magically letting his strength seep into her until she was calm, until her tears dried up, until she could lean back a bit and smile up at him and say, "What a wimp, huh?"

He thumbed away the last traces of her tears. "Nope. Never that. I've seen you take on Gil Watson barehanded, remember?"

"Well, Gil's not in quite the same league as the Red Millennium." There was still the suggestion of a tremor in her voice. "I guess I just never took it seriously until

I saw all those men in flak jackets out on the sidewalk. Somebody really does want me dead.''

''Well, somebody's in for a big disappointment then, not to mention life without parole in a maximum security facility.''

She glanced at the clock on the nightstand. It was nearly one o'clock. ''How long before we have to leave for the courthouse?''

''I want to get you there by three,'' he said, checking his watch. ''Just in case Buddy Jr.'s stint on the stand is done early.''

''Buddy's here? In Philadelphia?''

He pointed to the ceiling. ''And Raylene. In the room right above this. She's at the courthouse now.'' He shrugged out of his jacket and tossed it on the bed. ''What do you say we invite them down tonight and send out for a couple pizzas? Would you like that?''

She nodded eagerly. ''That would be almost as good as being home.''

''Consider it done.'' He picked up the phone and as he punched in some numbers, his face hardened again. His gaze might have remained on Molly as he spoke, but he didn't even seem to see her.

''McCarthy? It's Shackelford. Just checking to see that you've got somebody at the elevators on every floor.''

It was nearly three o'clock before Molly was aware of it. She had unpacked, freshened up, lain down to close her eyes for a minute, then Dan was softly shaking her shoulder.

''It's time, Molly.''

She opened her eyes to see Dan's handsome but somber face hovering over hers, to realize that the door to the adjacent room was open now and several grim-faced people were coming and going through it, to witness what struck her as a strange, silent ballet.

Dan sat her up. "Here. Let's get this on." He angled her arms through something heavy and dark.

"What? What are you doing? What is this…this thing?"

"Just a precaution, babe," he said quietly, tugging, zipping, making a few adjustments.

Molly snapped fully awake. He was putting a bullet-proof vest on her. "Is it three o'clock already?"

"Close enough," he said, still fiddling with clasps and catches under her arms, behind her back.

"Wait a minute," Molly said a bit frantically. "Wait just a minute. I need to brush my hair. Where's my lipstick?" Suddenly, irrationally, putting on lipstick became absolutely crucial. A matter of life and death. "I need to put on lipstick," she insisted.

"There's no time," Dan said.

"I need to put on lipstick," she howled, batting at his hands.

He straightened up and stepped back. The look on his face was nearly savage as he stabbed a finger in the direction of the bathroom. "You've got one minute," he snarled.

Molly jumped off the bed, grabbed her handbag and raced for the john. When she looked in the huge mirror over the sink, she hardly recognized herself. Her face was pale as a sheet. Her eyes were enormous. It was the stark face of fear.

But, by God, she was going to put lipstick on it. She thrashed around in her handbag until she found some. Her hands were shaking so badly she dropped the plastic cap on the floor, then she could barely twist the bottom to make the tube of color come up. Tears started stinging her eyes.

There was a sharp knock on the door. "Molly!"

She couldn't even answer. She just stared in the mirror, hardly aware that the door had opened slightly, that Dan had slipped inside and closed it again.

"Molly?" His voice had softened considerably. "Baby, it's time."

She leaned closer to the mirror. "I have to..." She brought the lipstick close to her mouth, but her fingers were trembling so much now that she could hardly hold it. "I have to..."

"It's okay," he said, gently taking the tube from her hand. "Here. Turn around." His warm hands turned her toward him. "Hold still, now."

Slowly, with infinite care, as if he had all the time in the world, he applied the lipstick to her mouth. Somewhere deep in the recesses of her scrambled brain, Molly realized that his hands were absolutely steady. And somewhere deep in her soul she realized she'd never love anyone, ever, as much as she loved Dan this moment.

"There," he said softly. A tiny smile lifted the corners of his mouth. "God, you're pretty, Molly. Did I ever tell you that?"

She shook her head.

"Well, I should have, darlin'. I should have." His warm smile flickered out. "It's time to go now."

The hall looked five miles long to Dan as they walked toward the elevator. He heard himself say, "Molly, this is Deputy Connie Whitman. She's going to ride with us to the courthouse." And the solid sound of his own voice shocked him because even as the words came out, he was thinking this was all wrong. It was too much like the last time. The female partner. The witness. The corridor. The elevator at the end.

But it wasn't like the last time. He'd done everything right. He had men on every floor, at every entrance and exit, at every elevator stop. This time everything was right.

He focused on the pattern in the carpet just ahead of his feet for a second, fighting off the cold sweat that was prickling his chest, the small of his back.

"You better alert the guys downstairs, Dan," Connie said.

"Right." He brought the walkie-talkie close to his mouth. "Two minutes, McCarthy. You read me?"

"Two minutes. Got it," the box squawked back. "We're sending the elevator up, Dan."

"Right."

The edges of his vision blurred for a second and the corridor shrank. Please, God. He was losing it.

Molly was making a concerted effort to breathe deeply as she walked between Dan and the dark-haired female deputy. The heavy vest didn't make that any easier.

As they neared the elevator at the end of the corridor, she could hear the hum of the soda and snack machines in the little alcove off to her left. She glanced in, thinking she'd give anything right now for a cold, wet can of diet cola. Maybe a candy bar, too. Had she eaten lunch? She couldn't remember.

Stupid, thinking about candy at a time like this, she told herself, but perhaps that was the brain's way of grappling with stark terror. Thinking about chocolate and caramel and peanuts and...

Dan shifted in front of her as the brass elevator doors began to slide open.

Dan motioned Connie into the elevator first, then stood aside for Molly to enter. "You're doing fine," he whispered as she passed, wishing he could say the same for himself.

He stepped in.

The Muzak was wafting an old Patsy Cline song. "Crazy." For a split second he thought he probably was, wanting to spend the rest of his life with a woman who cared more about his body than his heart and soul. But what the hell.

"We're in," he said into the handset.

His gaze lodged on the control panel directly ahead of him. Polished aluminum. It reminded him a little of the Airstream. Then his vision honed in on the tiny scratches around all the numbered buttons.

The clean buttons. The pure white buttons. All of them new. Pristine. Untouched.

His arm shot out to stop the closing doors.

"Molly, get out. Run." He shoved her, hard but not hard enough to make her lose her balance. "Go, Connie," he shouted, jamming his shoulder into the door to keep it open. "This elevator's going to blow. Get her away."

"Code Red," he said into the handset. "Code Red. We've got a bomb in the central elevator on five."

The box squawked back. "Roger. Code Red. Dammit. We're on the way."

They were going to be too late. Dan shoved between the big metal doors, saw Molly and Connie thirty feet down the hall and still running, saw the vending ma-

chine alcove a few yards off to his right, saw his life
flash before his eyes as he leapt for it.

The explosion was deafening. Connie had pushed her
down, and thick, acrid smoke was rolling over them
even as Molly struggled to get up.

"Dan!" she screamed.

Connie kept grabbing her hand. "Stay here," she
said. "Stay down."

But Molly pulled away and started down the corridor.
A few lights still flickered from dangling fixtures, but
even so, she could hardly see for the smoke and bits of
ash drifting through the air.

"Dan!" she screamed again.

Ahead of her the elevator doors were twisted sheets
of metal with little tongues of flame licking at their
edges. The interior was a black hole. But he had gotten
out. She was sure she'd seen him in that instant just
before Connie pushed her down.

"Dan!"

She thought she heard something in the room where
she'd seen the vending machines earlier. A crunch of
glass. A groan. She hurried.

He was alive! He was kneeling, leaning against the
shattered front of a soda machine, his fingers gripping
the broken plastic. Through the smoke, she could see
candy and cans and ice cubes everywhere. And blood.
Was that blood?

"Molly." His voice was ragged.

"I'm here, Dan." She slipped her arms around his
waist. "I'm here. Help's coming." She looked frantically over her shoulder. Where were they?

"Molly," he said again. She could hardly hear him.
"You're okay?"

"I'm fine. Just hang on." Oh, where were they? "Connie!" she screamed, and then softly, "Dan, do you want to lie down? Let me help you. What can I do?"

She couldn't hear his reply, so she put her ear close to his mouth. "What, sweetheart?"

"Love me."

"Oh, I do. I love you with all my heart."

"Not just...?"

"Not just what, love?" Behind her, Molly could hear voices in the corridor. Thank God.

Dan turned his head then, just enough for their eyes to meet. "Not...not just for sex?"

Molly couldn't hold back her tears. "No, sweetheart. I love you just for you."

His mouth twitched in a painful, faltering grin. "That's good, Mol, 'cause I don't think I'm going to be able to..." Then his eyes rolled up in his head and he slid to the floor, already slick with bright red blood.

Epilogue

If anyone had told Molly a mere two months ago that coming back to Moonglow would be at the very top of her "Things I Most Want to Do" list, she would have laughed. But not the way she was laughing now, only a few miles outside the town limits. She was laughing for pure joy.

"You better ease up on the gas, Mol." Dan gave her a cautionary look over the rims of his shades. "Unless, of course, you actually like being pulled over by Moonglow's finest."

"Sorry." She lifted her foot, and the needle on the BMW's speedometer dropped from seventy to forty-five. "I'm just so happy we're almost home."

For a while, she hadn't been certain they'd ever get here. By the time help reached him, Dan had lost so much blood that he was in severe shock. From the second an EMT had entered the bloody alcove, taken one look at Dan and yelled "Hurry. He's bleeding out," to the moment he'd opened his eyes three days later, Molly didn't eat or sleep or even take a deep breath. All she did was will Dan to live.

Raylene was with her constantly, even though half the time Molly didn't even know who was holding her hand or offering her a tissue or putting coffee and cookies nearby, just in case. Bobby flew in from Houston, offered her a shoulder to cry on, but she couldn't even do that.

The explosion had sent a fragment of metal slicing into Dan's leg, high inside his left thigh, severing the femoral artery. But he made it through. She glanced to her right, just glimpsing the savage scar near the cuff of his baggy cargo shorts. He made it through only to open his eyes and not know her for the next thirty-six hours, while he refused to believe anybody—her, the doctors, Raylene, Bobby—that he hadn't gotten her killed.

After that, there was the week of profound depression. "It happens," they told her. "It's not unusual after trauma and so many transfusions."

And then one morning she'd walked into his room and he'd smiled. Not one of those blazing grins. Just a fledgling smile. Sweet and warm. And Molly sat down on the cold linoleum floor and sobbed for twenty minutes, she was so damned happy.

She braked at the stop sign on the edge of town, looked over at Dan to find another smile on his lips. This one was fairly Mona Lisa-ish.

"What are you thinking about?" she asked.

"Wallpaper," he said.

"Wallpaper!"

"Yep."

"And that's why you're smiling?"

He looked over his dark glasses again. "It's funny wallpaper, Molly."

She shook her head. "It must be."

"Are we gonna just sit here at the stop sign the rest of the afternoon, or are we going home?"

Home. In Moonglow. Imagine that!

Dan was smiling because, if everything went the way he and Raylene had planned during about two hundred dollars' worth of long-distance phone calls between his hospital room and her beauty shop, Molly was about to be welcomed home in style.

"Just about everybody and their cousins are coming, Danny," Raylene had said. "Oh, and I got the cutest paper lanterns to hang up all over the yard. My Lord. Marly's bringing her chicken salad. Molly likes Chablis, right? Oh, and Herk Stillman, you remember him, is going to bring all his turntables and speakers and what-not to play DJ."

It wasn't that Dan wanted to party. His leg was still bothering him more than he let Molly know. But he'd put her through more than her share of hell these past weeks and now he hoped to put her through as much heaven as he and Raylene could come up with.

He knew Molly was worried about the future. The Red Millennium was no threat to her anymore. Her testimony had put the last of them away for life. And it hadn't taken long for the Marshals Service to find the mole in their ranks who'd rigged the elevator. He'd be on his way to prison soon for a good twenty-five to life. Molly was worried about her future with Dan, Dan, the Wallpaper Man.

She had finally contacted Ethan, her fiancé, to tell

him that she wouldn't be coming back to New York. Good riddance.

They'd spent last night at Bobby and Eileen's, and every time Bobby alluded to Dan eventually coming off disability and getting back to work, Dan could almost see Molly flinch. She knew he couldn't do both—continue with the Marshals Service and live happily ever after with her in Moonglow.

But, thanks to Raylene and a few other notable citizens, he'd worked that all out, too.

"It's awfully quiet," Molly said, guiding the car along Main, a frown playing over her pretty features. "It's practically deserted."

He shrugged. "Must be a football game."

"Dan, it's Thursday."

"Well, then it's probably bingo night at the VFW Hall."

She stepped on the brakes. "It isn't *night*. Besides, bingo's on Mondays." She was surveying the storefronts now, her eyes all slitty and suspicious. "This is very strange."

"Let's just go home, huh?"

"Well..."

"It's been a long ride, Mol." He put just the right little plaintive twist in his voice. Poor ol' Dan. He even angled around and reached in the back seat for his cane. "I really need to get out and stretch my leg. It's been kinda cramping up on me these last couple of miles."

"You should have said something." The look she gave him was so sweet, so loving, Dan felt like an absolute heel for all of about ten seconds.

"Well, I'm saying it now, darlin'. Come on. Let's get home."

* * *

The music was loud even half a block away. The banner—Welcome Home, Molly and Danny—was strung across the front of the house, so huge it nearly hid the little place. Molly's mouth was hanging open wide enough to catch flies, and her eyes were big and misty as she swung into the driveway, almost hitting Raylene.

"Did you do this?" she asked Dan, pulling on the emergency brake and shutting off the engine.

"I had some help," he said just as Raylene yanked open Molly's door.

"My Lord. I thought you'd never get here. Well, come on. Get out. You're not gonna believe it till you see it. Mildred Booth is two-stepping with old Mr. Cooley. Come on. Come on."

Dan got out and leaned on his cane. Much as he wanted to watch all the emotions on Molly's face, he found himself staring at the house.

Raylene came around the front of the car to stand beside him. "Danny, darlin', you didn't think all the surprises were gonna be for Molly, did you? Well? How do you like it?"

"My Lord." He couldn't help it. The words just came out as he gaped at the fresh yellow paint.

"Judge Larsen sentenced Buddy Jr. to two hundred hours of community service, and I told him I thought it'd be doing the community a great service if somebody came and painted this eyesore." She glanced over the BMW's hood. "Well, I'm sorry, Molly, but it was looking a little tacky."

Molly was crying and laughing.

Dan bent to kiss the top of Raylene's pink head. "You're something, friend. Thanks. For everything."

"My pleasure, Danny. Did you ask her yet?"

He put a finger to his lips and shook his head.

"Ask me what?" Molly said, coming around the car.

Raylene coughed. "Lord. I swear a gnat just flew right down my throat." She coughed again. "Be right back. I'm going to get something to wash that little critter down."

"Coward," Dan muttered to her retreating back.

"Ask me what, Dan?"

He cleared his throat and tried to look like an honest, unflappable man. He even leaned a few more pounds on the cane, going for the sympathy vote. "What would you like to drink, Mol? Beer or wine?"

She blinked. "Oh. Well, wine, I guess."

"Okay. Follow me." He grasped her hand and started up the driveway.

It took forty minutes of hugs and good wishes and welcome homes to reach the big galvanized tub in the backyard. Dan stuck his hand into the icy water and pulled out a bottle of Chablis.

"Get a glass over there, will you, Molly?"

She was standing with her arms crossed, looking into every nook and cranny in the backyard. She even looked up into the live oak. "Where's the Airstream?" she finally asked.

"I sold it." Dan reached for a plastic glass since she obviously wasn't going to do it, then he tried to maneuver the bottle, the glass and his damned cane. "Here." He handed her a wet, brimming glass.

"What do you mean you sold it? To who?"

"Don't you mean 'whom,' Professor?" He reached into the tub again and extracted a beer.

Her baby blues narrowed and her pretty mouth

thinned. "I mean who the hell did you sell it to, Dan? I loved that trailer."

"Gil and Linda Watson."

Her jaw dropped and those baby blues popped wide open.

"She'd only take him back on the condition he quit his job. I guess she thought that's what was making him so mean," he said, twisting the cap off the bottle. "So they're going on a second honeymoon of sorts. Just drive around the country for the next year or so. Go wherever the wind takes them." He took a long swig of the cold beer. "Sounds nice, doesn't it, Molly?"

"I guess. Sure, it sounds great." The little crease of irritability deepened between her eyes. "It sounds like something we could have done ourselves if we still had the trailer."

"Well, yeah. I didn't think about that. Still, with my new job and all, I won't have all that much vacation coming. Not the first year, anyway." He tipped the bottle, giving her time to absorb what he'd just said.

"What new job?"

He smiled. "Use your head, Professor."

It took her two or three seconds longer than he thought it would. Then she burst out laughing. "Oh, my God! You're the new sheriff."

"Yes, ma'am," he drawled. "And if I catch you doing seventy again on the old State road like you did today, I'm gonna nail your gorgeous hide."

In all her life—no, in all her lives as Kathryn Claiborn and Molly Hansen, she'd never had a more wonderful time. She'd never felt happier or more loved or more at home than she did that night. People began to slowly drift away after dark.

She poured another glass of wine, went looking for Dan, and found him in the backyard, leaning against the live oak where the Airstream had been.

"You look tired, sweetheart." As soon as she said it, Molly realized he looked more than merely tired. There was a fine sheen of perspiration on his face. His Hawaiian shirt was dark under the arms with sweat. Her heart nearly stopped. "Dan, what's wrong? Are you in pain?"

He took in a long breath. "No, Molly. I'm nervous."

"What?"

"Nervous. You know. Jittery. Anxious."

Her heart rate slowed to normal. "You scared me. Well, what are you nervous, jittery and anxious about, Sheriff?"

"Well, I'm wondering how you'll react when I tell you you're going to have to change your name again."

Molly stepped back. "Oh, no. Oh, God, Dan. I thought the Red Millennium was gone. Dead. I can't go through that again. I just can't."

"Well, do you think you could go through this?" He took his hand out of his pocket. There was a diamond ring jammed on the end of his little finger. "What do you think, Molly?"

Her heart stopped again. The perfect, pear-shaped stone was glittering in the moonlight that filtered through the live oak. "I…uh…I think it's gorgeous."

"Raylene picked it out," he said.

"It's…well, it's beautiful. Very restrained. I mean, for Raylene."

"Yeah." He let out a long sigh. "I was pretty relieved, to tell you the truth." Then he swallowed, audibly. Even so, his voice broke just a little when he said, "I can't get down on my knees, babe."

"You don't have to," she whispered, putting her arms around him, holding him closer than life. "You don't even have to ask, Dan. My answer's always been yes."

* * * * *

Feel like a star with Silhouette.

We will fly you and a guest to New York City for an exciting weekend stay at a glamorous 5-star hotel. Experience a refreshing day at one of New York's trendiest spas and have your photo taken by a professional. Plus, receive $1,000 U.S. spending money!

Flowers...long walks...dinner for two... how does Silhouette Books make romance come alive for you?

Send us a script, with 500 words or less, along with visuals (only drawings, magazine cutouts or photographs or combination thereof). Show us how Silhouette Makes Your Love Come Alive. Be creative and have fun. No purchase necessary. All entries must be clearly marked with your name, address and telephone number. All entries will become property of Silhouette and are not returnable. **Contest closes September 28, 2001.**

Please send your entry to: **Silhouette Makes You a Star!**

In U.S.A.	In Canada
P.O. Box 9069	P.O. Box 637
Buffalo, NY, 14269-9069	Fort Erie, ON, L2A 5X3

Look for contest details on the next page, by visiting www.eHarlequin.com or request a copy by sending a self-addressed envelope to the applicable address above. Contest open to Canadian and U.S. residents who are 18 or over. Void where prohibited.

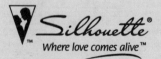

Silhouette®
Where love comes alive™

Our lucky winner's photo will appear in a Silhouette ad. Join the fun!

SRMYAS1

HARLEQUIN "SILHOUETTE MAKES YOU A STAR!" CONTEST 1308
OFFICIAL RULES
NO PURCHASE NECESSARY TO ENTER

1. To enter, follow directions published in the offer to which you are responding. Contest begins June 1, 2001, and ends on September 28, 2001. Entries must be postmarked by September 28, 2001, and received by October 5, 2001. Enter by hand-printing (or typing) on an 8 ½" x 11" piece of paper your name, address (including zip code), contest number/name and attaching a script containing 500 words or less, along with drawings, photographs or magazine cutouts, or combinations thereof (i.e., collage) on no larger than 9" x 12" piece of paper, describing how the Silhouette books make romance come alive for you. Mail via first-class mail to: Harlequin "Silhouette Makes You a Star!" Contest 1308, (in the U.S.) P.O. Box 9069, Buffalo, NY 14269-9069, (in Canada) P.O. Box 637, Fort Erie, Ontario, Canada L2A 5X3. Limit one entry per person, household or organization.

2. Contests will be judged by a panel of members of the Harlequin editorial, marketing and public relations staff. Fifty percent of criteria will be judged against script and fifty percent will be judged against drawing, photographs and/or magazine cutouts. Judging criteria will be based on the following:

   - Sincerity—25%
   - Originality and Creativity—50%
   - Emotionally Compelling—25%

   In the event of a tie, duplicate prizes will be awarded. Decisions of the judges are final.

3. All entries become the property of Torstar Corp. and may be used for future promotional purposes. Entries will not be returned. No responsibility is assumed for lost, late, illegible, incomplete, inaccurate, nondelivered or misdirected mail.

4. Contest open only to residents of the U.S. (except Puerto Rico) and Canada who are 18 years of age or older, and is void wherever prohibited by law; all applicable laws and regulations apply. Any litigation within the Province of Quebec respecting the conduct or organization of a publicity contest may be submitted to the Régie des alcools, des courses et des jeux for a ruling. Any litigation respecting the awarding of a prize may be submitted to the Régie des alcools, des courses et des jeux only for the purpose of helping the parties reach a settlement. Employees and immediate family members of Torstar Corp. and D. L. Blair, Inc., their affiliates, subsidiaries and all other agencies, entities and persons connected with the use, marketing or conduct of this contest are not eligible to enter. Taxes on prizes are the sole responsibility of winners. Acceptance of any prize offered constitutes permission to use winner's name, photograph or other likeness for the purposes of advertising, trade and promotion on behalf of Torstar Corp., its affiliates and subsidiaries without further compensation to the winner, unless prohibited by law.

5. Winner will be determined no later than November 30, 2001, and will be notified by mail. Winner will be required to sign and return an Affidavit of Eligibility/Release of Liability/Publicity Release form within 15 days after winner notification. Noncompliance within that time period may result in disqualification and an alternative winner may be selected. All travelers must execute a Release of Liability prior to ticketing and must possess required travel documents (e.g., passport, photo ID) where applicable. Trip must be booked by December 31, 2001, and completed within one year of notification. No substitution of prize permitted by winner. Torstar Corp. and D. L. Blair, Inc., their parents, affiliates and subsidiaries are not responsible for errors in printing of contest, entries and/or game pieces. In the event of printing or other errors that may result in unintended prize values or duplication of prizes, all affected game pieces or entries shall be null and void. **Purchase or acceptance of a product offer does not improve your chances of winning.**

6. Prizes: (1) Grand Prize—A 2-night/3-day trip for two (2) to New York City, including round-trip coach air transportation nearest winner's home and hotel accommodations (double occupancy) at The Plaza Hotel, a glamorous afternoon makeover at a trendy New York spa, $1,000 in U.S. spending money and an opportunity to have a professional photo taken and appear in a Silhouette advertisement (approximate retail value: $7,000). (10) Ten Runner-Up Prizes of gift packages (retail value $50 ea.). Prizes consist of only those items listed as part of the prize. Limit one prize per person. Prize is valued in U.S. currency.

7. For the name of the winner (available after December 31, 2001) send a self-addressed, stamped envelope to: Harlequin "Silhouette Makes You a Star!" Contest 1197 Winners, P.O. Box 4200 Blair, NE 68009-4200 or you may access the www.eHarlequin.com Web site through February 28, 2002.

Contest sponsored by Torstar Corp., P.O Box 9042, Buffalo, NY 14269-9042.

SRMYAS2

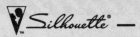

Silhouette®

INTIMATE MOMENTS™

presents a brand-new continuity series:

FIRSTBORN SONS

Bound by the legacy of their fathers, these Firstborn Sons are about to discover the stuff true heroes—and true love—are made of!

The adventure begins in July 2001 with:

BORN A HERO by **Paula Detmer Riggs**

When Dr. Elliot Hunter reports to Montebello Island after a terrorist bombing, he never imagines his rescue mission will include working alongside his gorgeous former flame!

July: **BORN A HERO**
by **Paula Detmer Riggs** (IM #1088)
August: **BORN OF PASSION**
by **Carla Cassidy** (IM #1094)
September: **BORN TO PROTECT**
by **Virginia Kantra** (IM #1100)
October: **BORN BRAVE**
by **Ruth Wind** (IM #1106)
November: **BORN IN SECRET**
by **Kylie Brant** (IM #1112)
December: **BORN ROYAL**
by **Alexandra Sellers** (IM #1118)

*Available only from
Silhouette Intimate Moments
at your favorite retail outlet.*

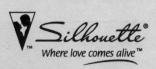

Silhouette®
Where love comes alive™

They're Back!

The men of the Alpha Squad have returned—in Suzanne Brockmann's *Tall, Dark & Dangerous* series.

Don't miss TAYLOR'S TEMPTATION (IM #1087)!

After years of trying to get magnificent Navy SEAL Bobby Taylor to herself, Colleen Skelly had finally succeeded. Bobby was hers, if only for a few days. And she had her work cut out for her. She had to prove that she was a grown woman—and that he was all she would ever need in a man....

TAYLOR'S TEMPTATION

On sale in July 2001,
only from Silhouette Intimate Moments.

And this is only the beginning....

Tall, Dark & Dangerous:
They're who you call to get you
out of a tight spot—or into one!

Available wherever books are sold.

Where love comes alive™

SIMTDD01